Praise for *The Perfect Escape*

'Clever, complex and expertly planned.'
Rachel Abbott, bestselling author of *Right Behind You*

'Full of secrets and twists, *The Perfect Escape* is a fast-paced, edge-of-your-seat thriller about a group of friends who may not know one another as well as they think. With its eerie setting, unsettling plot, and shocking reveals, this book had me completely captivated from the first page to the very last.'
Megan Miranda, author of *Such a Quiet Place*

'Nobody writes twists like Leah Konen – this woman puts Hitchcock to shame . . . A gripping, whip-smart, and unforgettable pulse-pounder that left my head spinning. With its intricate plotting and truly shocking reveals, this thriller is both an addictive page-turner and a brilliant examination of female friendship, shame, and betrayals.'
Andrea Bartz, author of *We Were Never Here*

'When three women embark on a trip to forget their broken lives, they become embroiled in the centre of a murder investigation. *The Perfect Escape* is a clever, locked-room mystery that is compulsively readable and impossible to put down!'
Wendy Walker, author of *Don't Look for Me*

'The type of captivating, masterfully-constructed thriller you'll consume in a breathless rush – and then flip right back to the beginning to figure out how the author pulled it all off. Konen keeps the shocking twists coming while wringing nail-bi̶t̶i̶n̶g̶ allest mome̶

Praise for *One White Lie*

'Intense, unpredictable and completely addictive – *One White Lie*
is everything a great psychological thriller should be'
T. M. Logan, author of *The Holiday*

'Remarkably insidious. Extremely readable.'
Caroline Kepnes, author of *You*

'*One White Lie* reads like the best Hitchcock film never
made . . . An assured and astonishing debut from an author
destined to become a big name in thriller fiction.'
Sarah Pinborough, author of *Behind Her Eyes*

'It's rare that a novel keeps me guessing until the very
last page – but *One White Lie* delivers in a big way.
It's absolutely terrific.'
Sarah Pekkanen, coauthor of *The Wife Between Us*

'Hooked me from the start . . . This book has everything – engaging
characters, a unique story, and an ending that will blow you away.'
Samantha Downing, author of *My Lovely Wife*

'I love Konen's writing style – super pacy and whizzes you
along – I couldn't put it down until I knew how it ended.'
Sandie Jones, author of *The Other Woman*

'Compulsively readable, a gripping page-turner. The tension
builds with every page. Each shocking twist is followed by an
even more shocking twist. This is one of those books you'll want to
read again the moment you finish. A masterful psychological
thriller that will leave you breathless.'
Lisa Regan, bestselling author of *The Drowning Girls*

'Skillfully captures the unnerving tensions that come with building
your chosen family while never knowing quite who to trust.'
Marie Claire

THE
PERFECT
ESCAPE

THE
PERFECT
ESCAPE

LEAH KONEN

PENGUIN BOOKS

PENGUIN BOOKS

UK | USA | Canada | Ireland | Australia
India | New Zealand | South Africa

Penguin Books is part of the Penguin Random House group of companies
whose addresses can be found at global.penguinrandomhouse.com.

Published in USA by G. P. Putnam's Sons 2022
Published in Great Britain by Penguin Books 2022
001

Printed and bound in Great Britain by Clays Ltd, Elcograf S.p.A.

The authorized representative in the EEA is Penguin Random House Ireland,
Morrison Chambers, 32 Nassau Street, Dublin D02 YH68

A CIP catalogue record for this book is available from the British Library

ISBN: 978–1–405–94489–2

www.greenpenguin.co.uk

MIX
Paper from
responsible sources
FSC® C018179
www.fsc.org

Penguin Random House is committed to a
sustainable future for our business, our readers
and our planet. This book is made from Forest
Stewardship Council® certified paper.

For Thomas and Eleanor

PROLOGUE

People think they know what rage is, but they don't.

They know skin-itching annoyance, or perturbation, or your basic garden-variety anger, the sort that sends a flush of heat into your cheeks, that might even make your hands shake. They think, this is rage; it's not.

I know, believe me.

Rage is so much deeper than anger; it's the sort of thing that bursts out of you. It's uncontrollable; that's in its very definition. Rage isn't content to be a feeling, something you jot down in your diary or unpack with a friend over drinks. Rage demands action. It hooks you with its claws, dragging you forward, imbuing you with tunnel vision, turning everything around you bright white, except for that one image, right there in front of you, pulsing along to the blood throbbing in your temples.

I stared at that image now, watching, and I felt it in my belly, in the tips of my fingers and the back of my neck.

Not anger, not frustration, but rage.

Who the fuck *does she think she is?*

They didn't see me – how could they?

They didn't know I was right there the whole damn time.

But that was good. That was how I wanted it.

I took a deep, shaking breath, and then I did what I needed to do.

FRIDAY

1 | SAM

The slice of skin was angry and pale — it looked almost sickly, framed in ridges, the flesh obscenely puffy around it.

My dirty little secret, exposed for all to see.

I'd never taken my rings off, not since Harry put them on my finger.

I loved and hated them in equal measure.

The band was made of clean, unmarked platinum. The guy at the shop had told us it would last forever, while I stared at shiny things on royal-blue velvet and Harry pulled out his Amex. Platinum was as pure as love, and it didn't take a single bit of upkeep, not like silver or white gold.

My finger traced the inside, and I could see the words without even looking. Etched into the interior, etched into my brain: *For my darling, Sam. From your darling, Harry.*

Should his cheesy inscription have been the first sign? Diana had laughed when I told her he always called me 'darling', asked if Harry was some guy out of the 1950s — and I guess I would have to hold back an eye-roll if she or Margaret said that Brandon or Lars almost exclusively referred to them as 'darling'. But to me, it had never sounded like some bad actor playing at Cary Grant. Harry's words were so easy to love, his voice somehow gruff yet smooth, strong as whiskey. *My darling. My Sam.*

The engagement ring was even nicer. It had scrollwork and a bunch of tiny diamonds, a whopping stone in the middle. I'd always thought of myself as the anti-diamond type – they seemed way too traditional – but when push came to shove, the butterfly wings had beat in my stomach just as they had for all those other women. I did draw the line at something absurdly overpriced – no Cartier, thank you very much – and ostentation wasn't Harry's style, either. Still, he'd paid extra for Canadian diamonds because they were supposed to be cruelty-free.

Wanting, and wanting *badly*, was one of Harry's many effects on me. Not just his love but *everything* – meeting him had stretched out my world like taffy. All these things I'd never known I could dream of were suddenly open to me. I was trading my shitty railroad apartment and its sounds of cars whizzing by – urban waves – for the luxury condo with Manhattan views that Harry kept around for crashing in the city. I was getting my first real facial – one gifted to me by Harry shortly after we were engaged. I was honeymooning at the Four Seasons in Anguilla. I'd always been more of a backpacker, a rough-and-tumble traveler, but sitting on an Adirondack chair parked in bright white sand, one hand in Harry's and the other wrapped around a seventeen-dollar piña colada, it was impossible to object. Who would, when it came down to it?

Standing in front of my dresser, I let the rings clank into the ceramic dish, the one my mom had gotten me to hold them especially: *Harry + Sam. May your love bless you forever.*

One year. That's how long it took to change me, our union marking my body like a warning, turning the skin of my finger pale. Three months of engagement. Seven of marriage. Two of being apart.

Diana, a self-branded self-destructive, always the one among the group to suggest a third glass of wine or a side of French fries or one measly cigarette on the patio, had understood why I hesitated to take my rings off. I'd met Diana about a year and a half ago – she was sitting at the bar at the place on Tenth Avenue I used to go after work. She'd introduced herself and suggested we pair up to take full advantage of the two-for-one old-fashioned special. We had, and we'd killed more than one round of strong drinks, and over cigarettes purchased on impulse from the deli next door, I'd told her all about the crush I had on Harry. She'd gotten it then, and she got it now.

Margaret, a semi-neurotic copywriter I'd worked with on and off for years, and by far the most practical of our little trio, had been much pushier. I needed to take off my rings, take a 'step toward acceptance', as she put it. On this trip, at least, we were going to put our pasts behind us, as much as we could.

I turned away from the dresser, the shitty fiberboard model I'd picked up at IKEA that had served me over nearly a decade in New York, one of the few items that had made the trek from my old place to Harry's. On the bed, my suitcase lay open, sundresses, sweaters and underwear spilling out. I must have packed the thing five times. I knew I was probably putting way too much pressure on this trip, nothing more than a long weekend of wine and – let's be honest – more wine, up at a cabin in Saratoga Springs. It was just Diana, Margaret and me – it didn't matter what I wore at all – still, it was my first time leaving the city since Harry had left me.

Well, my first time except for that once.

It was going to be brilliant, so help me.

Like Margaret said, I was going to take the first step toward acceptance and leave my past behind.

I glanced at my watch, snakeskin leather and an oversized gold face – another gift from Harry, for my birthday last year. Diana and Margaret should be arriving any minute. I flipped the lid of the suitcase, and, pressing down hard, zipped it as best I could, then dragged it off the bed.

I pulled the duvet up, covering Harry's imprint in the bed. They didn't tell you that about memory foam – it doesn't forget, never ever ever. It captures bodies, forces you to look at the person you thought you knew, day in and day out.

I rolled the case down the hall and past the nook I'd taken to using as my home office, my desk piled to the brim with unpaid invoices and contact sheets from one of my projects, already two weeks overdue to my client. When I'd taken on the assignment several months ago, art direction for the launch campaign for a new wedding-planning app, Harry had been here. Diana and Margaret didn't even know each other. Everything was different then.

My phone buzzed. It was a text to the group chain, lovingly titled *Sgt. Diana's Lonely Hearts Club* in all our phones.

From Diana:

I made a snap decision and stopped at the shop
for a couple more bottles of vino before going to
Margaret's – running ten late, but you know it's

worth it – I have a feeling we're going to be
getting messy ☺

I laughed. We certainly would, if Diana had anything to do with it, and getting messy with them felt a lot less shameful than doing so on my own.

I shrank into a cardigan, zipped up my boots, and grabbed my handbag. I should make my way downstairs, maybe stop for a coffee at the deli, wait for them outside.

On impulse, like a sharp, quick tug, I turned away, traipsing across the apartment, my boots click-clacking against the un-swept hardwood, back to the bedroom.

The rings still sat in the dish, glimmering.

Like a cat, I snatched them, slipping them into the pocket of my linen dress. Secret rings, tucked away where no one could see.

It can't hurt, I told myself, perhaps a little desperately.

At least it can't hurt anyone but me.

Diana was leaning against the SUV, phone in hand, when I got downstairs. In the pinky late-afternoon light of the city, her silver hair gleamed against the rest of her dark brown strands. She was nearly half-gray, though she wasn't even thirty-five. She was wearing a black dress and black leggings – she almost always wore black, and it had the effect of accentuating her rather abundant curves and making her uncolored hair even more striking.

With creamy skin, a strong nose, hazel eyes, and lips always painted red, Diana looked like a Renaissance woman, someone Botticelli would have painted. She glanced up and beamed like

9

she always did upon seeing me. 'I have good news and bad news,' she said in lieu of a greeting.

'Bad first.'

'Such a masochist,' she said. 'Okay, so I just realized I completely forgot the OJ for mimosas.'

'The good news?'

Diana grinned. 'That means we can have Prosecco for breakfast and not even feel bad about it.'

I laughed, and Margaret hopped out of the driver's seat, walking around to hug me, too.

She cleared her throat: 'I've already told Diana I'm instating a rule for the trip – one glass of water between every drink – we are *not* driving four hours to be hungover every day. I want to go on a hike, damn it.'

Diana pulled Margaret in for a half hug, squeezing her tight. 'Don't you worry – we will have all of the wine, all of the water, and all of the nature. The three aren't mutually exclusive.'

'You know I'll hold you to it – don't think I won't,' Margaret said with a smile. She ran a hand through her shoulder-length hair, cut blunt at the ends, similar to mine (a cut that Diana, a social worker at a therapy practice on the West Side, now referred to as the 'cool-girl agency bob'), though Margaret's was straight and mine was more curly.

In another life, Margaret had been an actress, or had tried to be, at least, in her first several years in New York, but to me, it was hard to imagine her anywhere but at an ad agency. She adjusted her jacket, the red leather one she always wore, shaking the fringe on the sleeves.

Margaret glanced at her phone, then back at us. 'I have it all mapped out,' she said. She was a planner, the type to set a meeting for things that could be a conversation, to walk into a room gracefully and get us right down to business. 'If traffic is manageable, we'll be in the Adirondacks in four hours.'

Diana raised her eyebrows – how far we were driving on this trip had been a point of contention from the beginning – but then quickly forced a smile. 'Just enough time to hit every song in my playlist.'

'You've thought of everything,' Margaret said, and I sensed it, the tiniest bit, the tension.

Diana had first pitched the idea of a trip, but Margaret had suggested we go to her friend's place farther north instead of trying to find a rental. There was a hot tub and a firepit overlooking mountain views, and her friend, who'd just had a baby, wasn't using the place at all. It was free, to boot. Hard to argue with.

Margaret may have done most of the planning, but Diana had a way of taking charge – it was just her style.

After all, Diana was the one who made us a trio.

Only a few days after Harry left, Margaret and I had gone for drinks at that spot on Tenth Avenue – she told me she was in the middle of a messy separation with Lars, and I was absolutely blindsided by Harry leaving. After a couple of hours, Diana walked in. She was a regular there, but I hadn't seen her in at least a year – I'd stopped going out so much once I'd gotten together with Harry. It had felt almost predestined as she told us that she and Brandon, her husband, were separated, too. Apparently, he'd become jealous and obsessive and controlling, and she'd had enough. Diana started the group text, suggested we commiserate together, turned us into a pseudo-support group. Without them, I don't know how I'd have gotten through the last two months.

Now Diana clasped her hands together, the two Cartier Love bracelets she always wore clanging on her wrist. 'What are we waiting for? Let's do this. Come on,' she said. 'I'll help you with your bags.'

As we shut the trunk, Diana's eyes found my hand, taking in the sliver of skin where my rings used to be. 'So you took Margaret's advice?' she asked. 'Embracing acceptance or however she put it?'

I reached for them, grasping the rings like a security blanket. 'Don't tell her, but they're in my pocket. I'm not wearing them, though, and that's a start.'

'It is, indeed.'

We packed into the SUV like the little peg people my sister, Emma, and I used to amass in the Game of Life, and made our way toward the Brooklyn-Queens Expressway, the highway that would take us out of the dirty sunny city and up toward Saratoga Springs, our home for the next four nights.

Ten minutes into our journey, my phone buzzed. It was probably my mom, checking in, or my pushy client, arguing about the extension I'd asked for.

Or maybe, hope against hope, it was Harry. His text from Saturday was so woefully incomplete. Three tiny words, words that had given me more hope than they should have: *I miss you.*

It wasn't him. It was her.

Ten digits, never saved into my phone, but it didn't matter – I knew who it was all the same.

For fuck's sake, please just leave us alone.

12

MARGARET

With every mile on the odometer, I felt it, the past, Lars, and everything that had happened fading into the background. It was poetic almost. The open road. Leaving my problems, quite literally, behind. Every bit of road more space from Lars, who'd been sleeping on our couch for the last six months as we figured out how best to separate, who only Tuesday had come stumbling home with a busted, bleeding lip. From a sidewalk trip or a bar scuffle, I didn't even know anymore. He hadn't been the Lars I fell in love with in a long, long time.

My hands held the wheel at an even ten and two, and the cruise control was set to exactly five miles over the speed limit. A car zipped around me, going near eighty, and my phone vibrated loudly. I ignored it.

Diana turned the music down. She'd been in charge of the playlist the whole time – no ifs, ands or buts about it – but I could hardly argue with her selections. It was good driving music, a virtual course in female virtuosos: Diana Ross and Nina Simone, Fiona Apple and early Britney Spears. 'You sure you don't want a break?' she asked. 'You've been driving for almost two hours. I know I'm an exemplary navigator, but I trust you can handle the position.'

'I already told you,' I said. 'You're not on the rental agreement. It cost an extra fifty dollars a day.'

Diana smirked. 'I won't tell if you won't. We might have to buy off Sam's silence, but I hear she comes cheap.'

'Hey,' Sam said. 'Just because I'm the broke millennial.'

I held back an eye-roll. We were all millennials, technically speaking, even though Sam was thirty to my (very nearly) thirty-six. Besides, Sam was anything but down and out. From how she'd described Harry, they were doing quite well indeed. There was also the fact of his cheating. Unlike me, she would come out great once the divorce was official.

'You're sure?' Diana pressed. 'I love driving, you know, and it would give you some time to relax. I had an easy day at work. My last two clients canceled.'

'I'm sure,' I said, hoping to put it to rest. Though I was certainly more rule-abiding than Diana or even Sam, I wasn't only worried about Enterprise finding out we'd broken our agreement. I'd never told Sam or Diana that I'd been in the passenger seat when Lars had slammed on the brakes, careful not to hit a cyclist who'd pulled in front of us on our way to the beach. The doctors, as well as the internet, had confirmed that the digging in of the lap belt, straight to my uterus the day after we'd found out I was pregnant, had nothing to do with the things that happened to us. Still, that was the first thing that had gone wrong, the first domino among a string of events that had kicked off all the other stuff, causation or not. It was hard to wonder what would have happened if we hadn't gone to the beach that day. It was hard to resign myself to the passenger seat again, put another human in control of my life. I'm sure Diana, if she knew the full story, would call it PTSD, in her social worker way. Only she didn't know the whole of it. I'd told them that I couldn't give Lars children, nothing more. I often wondered if they'd look at me differently if they knew the truth in full.

In the backseat, Sam scratched at her eyebrow, revealing her naked hand. She'd finally taken her rings off. To tell the truth, I'd been surprised to see them when we found ourselves once again working together a couple of months ago. Sam and I had met a few years prior, before I was ever pregnant, and we'd gotten on immediately. She was the rare art director who didn't mind my insistence that the project go by the book, that everything down to the Oxford comma was perfect in layout. I was a copywriter now, but I was trained as an actor, and even though it had never worked out for me, my perfectionism had carried over. I used to read a scene over and over in my mirror, intent on getting every bit of dialogue, every last inflection, right. Now I did the same with punctuation. In those early days at the agency, Sam and I would go out for drinks, and she'd complain about dating apps while I tried not to gush too much about Lars out of respect for the plight of the single girl in the city.

And yet, when our paths had crossed again slightly more than two months ago, there she was, a married woman. And there *I* was, completely lost in the dissolution of my own marriage.

Still, it hadn't taken long to see something deep and torn apart within her, beneath her bouncy curls and heavy eyeliner and trendy Everlane T-shirt. It wouldn't exactly have taken Sherlock Holmes. Her under-eye makeup was caked on heavily, and her trips to the bathroom were incredibly frequent. She either had a UTI, was pregnant or was going in there to cry in private, protected from the fluorescent lights and the virtual acres of space in our open-floor office.

The Friday after we reconnected, I invited her to drinks. Over wine, she'd asked about Lars, and I'd told her as much of the truth as I could stomach sharing. We were living together still, but we were separated for all intents and purposes. He was sleeping on the couch. Her eyes had bulged, she'd practically choked on her wine, and then she'd spit it out: 'Harry left me on Monday. I'm absolutely wrecked.' It had taken her nearly five full seconds to finish the thought. 'Oh, and I'm so sorry about you and Lars.'

Commiserating was easy, even though our stories were so different, her heartache so sudden, mine so awfully prolonged, and then, and this part was always sort of hazy, Diana had walked into the bar, and Sam said she knew her, and we were both tipsy enough to ask her to join us, and another round, and Sam was pouring out her story to Diana, and I was chiming in with my bits, as well, and then Diana stared at us, and this part was not hazy, but oh so clear: 'You're shitting me,' Diana said. 'My soon-to-be-ex-husband and I are separated, too.' Then she was sharing her own tale, of Brandon, who'd morphed from loving and doting to controlling and obsessive, of how she'd had to shut down all her social media accounts to protect herself, while Sam and I tried to say all the right things.

The weekly meetups of Sgt. Diana's Lonely Hearts Club had taken on an almost religious quality. We were our own little support group, helping each other purge the past, move on from our ex-lovers, like Wiccans lighting candles and conducting ceremonies. Or teenagers burning things in a fire they made in the biggest stock pot they could find in their parents' kitchen. Even though I never told Diana and Sam the real cause of the gaping hole in my heart, it was lovely, in its way. So many of my friends were having kids of their own and would audibly wonder why Lars and I couldn't work it out. Diana and Sam were there for me in a way only those who'd lost everything could be.

'Well, *anyway*,' Diana said, interrupting my thoughts. 'Whether you let me drive or no, I found a good place for us to stop for gas. It's an almost exact halfway point, and one review even said there's a good view of the river.'

'We still have nearly half a tank. Do we really need to –'

'I'm the navigator, remember,' Diana said, flipping the visor down and reapplying her red Yves St. Laurent lipstick in the mirror, as if she were off to a date, not a rest stop. 'Trust me, the rest stops get few and far between the farther north you go, and the gas is affordable at this station anyway. You can't have both jobs, Marge.'

I raised an eyebrow. Anyone who wore two Cartier bracelets every day – those things started at four thousand dollars, *each* (I'd looked it up out of morbid curiosity) – could not be trusted to be cognizant of gas prices, but I decided to let her have this one. 'Well, okay, then, *Di*.'

It was something Diana had started, shortening my name, and I'd taken to doing it right back. I'm not quite sure why we did it, and yet I enjoyed it. It reminded me of simpler times, of the way the theater kids in high school all had special names for each other, the way Lars called me Peggy when he was feeling lovey-dovey.

'I have to pee anyway,' Sam said, piping in from the back.

'See!' Diana said. 'There you go. Never doubt the powers of the navigator.'

'Oh, I never will,' I said, resigning myself as usual to Diana's will. It had already been a battle, getting her to agree to go four hours away when there were plenty of beautiful spots to visit closer, but there was no way in hell I could have afforded the cost of a rental. I'd secured that victory, and I had a feeling most every other decision on this trip was going to be within Diana's purview. 'All right, then. When's the stop?'

Diana looked down at her phone and back up at the road. Before us, another cluster of mountains came into view, rolling across the horizon like a blue velvet blanket.

'There!' she said, pointing to a green sign announcing a stop in one mile.

It was only as I pulled onto the ramp that my phone vibrated again. And again and again in quick succession. Lars, I thought, picturing the cut still healing on the bottom of his lip, the way he'd been snoring loudly on the couch, reeking of booze, when I'd left for work this morning, the last day of my contract at my current agency. It had to be Lars.

I ignored it, driving slowly through the parking lot and up to the first open pump.

'Your phone,' Diana said, one hand on the door. 'Didn't you hear that? You've got a bunch of alerts.'

'Thanks,' I said, then grabbed it so she couldn't see. Diana was the sort to want to know what was up. The whole miserable story.

Part of me prayed it wasn't him. That it was some political volunteer asking for donations. Or even one of the creditors, hounding me for money. That part of me wished there was a way for us to magically separate without ever seeing each other again, so he would no longer remind me of all the ways he'd been able to keep on living, loving, when I hadn't.

Of course, it was him. He simply couldn't help himself.

Are you there yet?

Are you guys okay?

Talk to me. Please.

I need you, Pegs.

I need you now more than ever.

3

SAM

I squeezed through a cluster of people waiting to ring up coffees, beef jerky, and Pringles, and headed straight toward the back of the convenience store. In front of a door marked WOMEN, a frazzled-looking mom was handing out gummy worms to two kids under the age of five.

I turned, looking for Diana or Margaret, but they hadn't followed me inside. I imagined the two were arguing about who should pump the gas – it was funny how clearly both of them wanted to control this trip, whereas I was happy to let them do all the planning, so long as I eventually wound up in the hot tub Margaret had promised with a glass of Pinot Noir in my hand.

On my phone, I tapped back to my messages. I'd deleted *her* text, but the missive from my mom, which had come in twenty minutes ago, had been almost as jarring.

Sammy! Been meaning to reach out sooner. Dad and
I finally booked our place for New York. It's just a few

blocks from you two. The link is pasted here. I know
it's a lot for Dad, but his doctor assured him it's okay.
Can't wait to see you in two weeks! Love to Harry!

The door burst open, and the woman and her kids walked in.

I slipped the phone back in my pocket, my stomach tying itself up in knots.

There was no way around it – this was a big giant cluster-fuck. Their plane tickets, their lodging, were all booked. My parents, two of my favorite people in the world, two people whom I'd taken to lying to, would be here in thirteen days. My parents, who, among all the bullshit that had been thrown at them since the diagnosis, thought they at least had my new happiness to cling to, would learn that it was all for nothing. It was going to break their hearts.

When I got the phone call, Harry and I had only been together a couple of months.

My mom and dad, both on the line: 'We have some not so good news,' my mom said. At first, my mind went to my little sister, Emma. I thought maybe she and her girlfriend were breaking up again. Or she'd decided to ditch law school for yoga teacher training or something else wildly unpractical.

'The thing is,' my dad started, and I could feel it then, strong in my stomach – this was worse than one of Emma's impulses. It was there in the gravel, the sluggishness, of his voice. My dad, a sixty-one-year-old man who swam at the Y every morning, sounded suddenly – well – old. 'The thing is,' he repeated. A pause snaked its way from their phone to mine.

'Your dad has cancer,' my mom said, matter-of-fact. 'Stage four.'

Harry was over within the hour. He did everything right, like you'd want a boyfriend to: he rubbed my shoulders, stroked the hairs at the back of my neck, calmed my shaky breaths. Together, we pounded vodka and googled colorectal cancer – 'ass cancer', as my dad had called it.

A few drinks in, it spilled out of me – I told Harry how much I'd failed my dad, how he was such a traditional guy, and he'd imagined walking his daughters down the aisle, showing off his dance moves, 'My Girl' blasting. I was nearing thirty, and I'd fucked around, like nearly all women in the city did, but still.

I hadn't dated seriously, hadn't gotten my ducks in a row in time to give him what he wanted most. Emma was seven years younger than me, and she and Abby didn't have an eye toward marriage at all – *I* was the one who'd been his shot. *My* failures ensured that he might leave this earth, his dream incomplete.

When my headache woke me the next morning, I told Harry I was sorry. I hadn't meant to pressure him, I was talking out my ass – and the vodka didn't help. I knew how difficult things were for him already. I didn't mean to make them more difficult. It was supposed to be easy with us – fun and uncomplicated. It's not like it was a FWB or anything – it was a real-deal relationship – but it was a good one, one that didn't make too many demands. I'd made sure of that.

Harry and I went down to North Carolina a month later to be with my father for his surgery. It was as we were leaving the hospital, bathed in southern sun, the air hot and balmy even though it was only May, that Harry, to my complete surprise, dropped to one knee, right in front of the cancer wing.

My mother screamed. My father began to cry – the nurse pushing his wheelchair did, too – Emma and Abby started straight-up squealing.

And me?

Well, my heart threatened to burst right open.

I was shocked – absolutely *floored* – but I said yes – how? – why? – would I ever say no? After everything, after such a rocky start, Harry had done what had felt so impossible I hadn't even wished for it. He'd given me this moment with my dad.

I know people say love is sacrifice – work – choosing your partner every day, that kind of thing, but that wasn't my experience at all.

For me, for me and Harry, at least, it was magic. Fairy-tale moments you would never have otherwise. Moments when you seem to float right out of your body and look down at yourself and think: This is what happiness is. Me. Him. Right here. The movies are at least a little bit real.

I moved in to Harry's condo immediately, and we pulled the rest together quite fast, because we weren't sure how much time my dad had. There were hiccups, of course, logistics that the timeline made difficult, and a good amount of Harry's close friends and family weren't able to make it to North Carolina on such short notice, but all that mattered when we said 'I do' was that my daddy got his dream. We swayed to 'My Girl', tears in his eyes, under loosely hung string lights that cast shadows in the hollows of his cheeks, half-sunken from the chemo.

'I swear, this has turned your dad around,' my mom said to me that night – and many times since. Dad would never be cured – stage four made sure of that – but his happiness, his

23

delight in seeing his oldest daughter growing up, starting her own family, was sustaining him.

Now I had to tell him it was all a lie. I wasn't just going to break his heart and hers. I feared, sometimes, that I might kill him. That the fact that it had all blown up in my face so quickly would take away whatever life force my good news had provided.

That the cancer would finally win.

In front of me, the bathroom door snapped open, and the woman and kids piled out. I slipped in, locking the door behind me. When I was done, I stared at myself in the mirror. I had never intended to lie – to my parents, to Emma, to all my friends in Brooklyn and North Carolina. And I definitely hadn't intended to lie for this long – two months now.

But Harry's leaving – it was so sudden. I came home one night, and his bags were by the door, and he was telling me he was sorry, that he felt sick about how he was hurting me, but that *she* needed him now, that his feelings for her, he'd tried to deal with them, but they wouldn't go away.

It was the first I'd heard her name spoken in months. I almost wanted to laugh, ask him if this was some sort of early, ill-timed April Fools' joke. And then, when he hadn't cracked a smile, the absolute, horrifying shock of it had kicked in.

Before I had a minute to think, he was walking out the door.

He'd been in touch since. He'd sent me an email, full of clichés and vague words and bullshit explanations about how she'd had such a terrible childhood and he couldn't abandon her now. He'd told me I could stay at his apartment as long as I wanted – oh, how kind, Harry! – but when I'd written back, asking him to meet me, to talk through everything, he'd deflected. He'd said it was still too soon.

And that had been it.

He'd left me for *her*.

Save the text a few days ago: *I miss you*.

As I finished washing my hands, my fingers tingled at the thought of her, her smooth chocolate-brown hair, her pouty, pretty lips. I wanted to load Instagram, check every image in the grid, looking for a hint of him. Of them.

I wanted to text her back. Tell her what I really thought about what she'd done.

Only I couldn't now. She'd made that clear.

For fuck's sake, please just leave us alone.

I had to stop while I still had some semblance of self-respect left.

Back outside, a plastic bag looped around my wrist – Snapple, Gardetto's, and Goldfish, my go-to road-trip snacks – the sight of my friends stopped me in my tracks.

The SUV was parked in front now, but every door was flung open. Margaret was bent over, digging around the passenger seat. Through the windshield, I spotted Diana rummaging around in the back.

'What's going on?' I asked. 'Is everything okay?'

Margaret turned to me, popped a hand on her hip. 'We can't find the car key.'

'What do you mean you can't find it?' I asked with a laugh. 'We drove here, and you moved the car from the pump to this spot. It has to –'

Diana stepped forward. 'It's crazy, right? We can't fucking figure it out. We've been looking for the last five minutes. Margaret turned off the car and went to the trunk to get something out of her suitcase, and now she doesn't have it. It's like, I don't know, it just . . .'

In the distance, I could see the river rushing, slate blue against a sky moving into dusk, and I had that feeling, suddenly, the one in my stomach, that something was deeply wrong here. Like the one I'd had when my parents had gotten on the phone that night. Or when I'd opened the door that evening, seen Harry's bags sitting where they shouldn't be.

Margaret cleared her throat. Her face was pale, and she looked almost sick.

'It's like it disappeared into thin air.'

4

MARGARET

It was a welcome relief when we finally gave up our search.

We'd been meticulous. We'd checked our pockets, our purses, our bags. Inventoried our belongings, laying our devices, our wallets and various ephemera across the backseat so we could turn everything inside out. We'd looked beneath seats, around the vehicle's perimeter, and at the pump. The man behind the counter even turned on an extra set of floodlights so we could pore over the sidewalk outside.

It was quickly darkening, dusk bleeding into night, and I could see the hope dissipating on Sam's face as it hit her fully: the key was not going to be found. We weren't going to get to Saratoga Springs late; we weren't going to get there at all. *Don't look so downtrodden, this was supposed to be* my *trip,* I wanted to say. *This was supposed to be* my *escape.* After all, *I* was the one with the awful anniversary looming, the one who'd pounced on this date at the mere suggestion of a girls' trip. *I* was the one with the hungover husband texting every five minutes to ask me if I was okay. And yet . . .

'So what do we do now?' Sam asked. 'We can't go on looking forever. Do we get a cab or something? Jesus.'

'Saratoga Springs is two hours away,' I said. 'No one's going to drive us that far.'

Sam crossed her arms and huffed. She looked almost petulant. Diana squeezed Sam's arm. 'Don't worry. We'll figure this out. Let me call some other car rental companies,' she said. 'There's better service around on the side.' She walked off.

Sam stared at me. She was trying not to show it, but there was an accusation in her narrowed eyes. *How could you lose the key?*

'Do you have something to say?' I asked.

'No,' she said. 'I just don't get it.'

My phone went off again, and I cleared my throat, a nervous tic. 'Believe me, I don't, either.'

It was another message from Lars.

Where are you again?

I wrote back quickly, eager to get him off my back.

A gas station. Outside the town of Catskill. About
halfway to where we were supposed to be going.

His response came immediately.

And still stuck? Do you want me to come up?

My fingers flew across the phone's keyboard, unable to help myself.

So you can get drunk at the local dive and get into a
fight with some townie? No thanks.

Lars shot back as fast as I had.

Don't say that, Peggy. I tripped on the sidewalk. I
told you.

I clenched and unclenched my fist. I didn't know what to
believe anymore.

I'm sorry. But don't come up. We can figure it out.

'Well, that was a huge bust.'

I looked up to see Diana, one hand on her hip. 'They're all
closed but one, and that one doesn't have cars until tomorrow.
I guess the whole city-that-never-sleeps business doesn't apply
this far north.'

'No, it doesn't,' Sam said, staring at the map on her phone.
'It's a different world up here.'

A woman came out then, dressed in rumpled slacks and a
button-down faded from too many washes. 'I'm the manager
here,' she said. 'I understand you're having car trouble?'

'We lost the key,' Diana said. 'I know it sounds crazy, but
it's gone.'

'Well, I hate to be that person, but you can't leave your car
here overnight. We'll have to tow it if you do.'

'We understand,' Diana said. 'Don't worry.'

The woman walked away.

'So we're fucked?' Sam asked. As she did, I felt the first drop of rain.

'Let's stay calm,' Diana said. 'We are three brilliant women, and we're not *that* far from civilization.' She shoved one hand into her pocket, as if checking for the key once again. Her eyes, wide-set and doe-y, were remarkably calm, and I wondered if Sam noticed. If she did, she most likely attributed it to Diana's job as a social worker, her unflappability in the face of crisis. 'Let's crash here tonight and find a way to Saratoga Springs tomorrow. It sucks, it's a setback, but we'll figure it out, and Margaret's friend's hot tub will still be waiting for us when we do.'

Diana glanced to me, briefly. I nodded, as if on command.

'We need a place to stay, then?' Sam asked. 'The closest hotel is a Howard Johnson twenty miles away.'

'Surely we can do better than that,' Diana said, already tapping buttons on her phone. 'Those places are notorious for bedbugs.'

'Should we go home?' Sam asked.

'We can't abandon the car,' I said. It was in my name, and I couldn't be on the hook for it. Besides, I couldn't go back to Brooklyn – not this weekend, of all weekends. Not with Lars there, waiting and eager for an argument, or at the very least a *discussion*, for something to release the grief we both carried with us every day.

'Aha,' Diana said. 'I think we have a solution. There's a rental a few miles away. We can get the car towed to an auto shop nearby, have them make us a duplicate key in the morning. And in the meantime, we'll be happy and cozy.'

She flipped her phone around, revealing a single photo of a hunter-green clapboard home, with sharp eaves reaching up to a blue sky, covered in shutter-accented windows and flanked by stone chimneys on each side. It looked enormous.

'How much is it?' I asked, the words tumbling out almost involuntarily.

'Two hundred. A steal. I'm booking it,' Diana said.

Sam hesitated, taking a breath, as if to object, but then she turned back to her phone, and that was that.

I texted Lars.

Don't worry about us – we're going to stay the night at a rental here.

And then another text, because I still cared about him, even if I didn't love him like that anymore.

Please take care of yourself.

Diana tapped a few buttons on her phone, then looked up, smiling. 'Done. See? That wasn't so bad. And don't worry,' she said with a grin. 'This is just a little detour. We'll get to Saratoga Springs tomorrow. I promise.'

We hovered around the space like wasps, buzzing on the porch, waiting impatiently as Diana checked her phone and keyed a code into a lockbox, two silver keys falling into her hand. We burst through the front door, a creaky thing painted dark gray, and invaded the home, turning on lights as we went, so eager to be away from the gas station and out of the tow truck, which Diana had paid for. On solid, sheltered ground again.

The house was massive, arranged in perfect symmetry, with a sweeping living room packed with gray linen furniture on one side and a dining room holding a table for eight on the other, the stone chimneys I'd seen in the photo opening up into gape-mouthed fireplaces on each end.

It was old, one of those places likely built a decade or two before Prohibition took hold, and the floors were made of wide planks of wood, the sound of suitcases rolling over them making a pleasant rhythmic sound.

The walls were creamy white, a color that didn't need much decoration, but there were rectangular markings where paintings must have once hung, begging for a fresh coat; the baseboards were sprinkled with a thick layer of dust, and there was a musty smell that hit the back of your nose – damp. Moldings perched on top, extravagantly notched, with an even darker layer of dust in the crevices, making them look like monster teeth. I had an intrusive thought – *They'll eat you alive* – and then immediately felt silly and chalked it up to reading too much Gothic fiction. In the middle, burnished wooden railings flanked a central staircase.

'How the hell was this place only two hundred?' Sam asked, already climbing the stairs. 'It's huge.'

'A steal, right?' Diana said, following Sam.

I left my suitcase near the front door, then headed to the kitchen. I poured myself a glass of water, trying to calm down, and began to look for a book or binder full of instructions that you usually found in these places, the one with the Wi-Fi code and local restaurant recommendations. Nothing on the table or the reclaimed wood island or the granite counters. I admired the cabinets, faced with clear glass, all the dishes on display. They were arranged so neatly. Exactly four of everything. I imagined my kitchen back in Brooklyn, its cheap standard-issue blond-wood cabinets and mismatched glassware, pieces broken or somehow lost over the years. Then I imagined Lars right now, sweat matting down his overgrown curls, his skin flushed, his eyes boyish with excitement as he grabbed a juice glass and filled it with Vinho Verde. Lars seemed to think you couldn't have a drinking problem if wine was your go-to. The whiskey would come later on in the evening, once he was good and sloshed.

I opened a few more drawers, but there was nothing but pristinely arranged flatware and kitchen tools. No welcome book. I supposed it didn't matter. We'd only be here for one night.

Above me, I could hear the creak of floorboards, Sam and Diana divvying up the rooms. I grabbed my suitcase and made for the stairs.

The second story was also symmetrical. Two rooms on the right, two more on the left. Bedrooms, I'd guess. Behind me, at the top of the stairs, an open door revealed black and white hexagonal tiles and a claw-footed tub. There were shut white doors, what looked like storage closets, on either side.

Diana materialized from the first bedroom door on the left. 'Come on,' she said. 'Your room's right here.' She pointed to the door directly across from hers. 'It's got a queen bed, and I figured since you're the tallest.'

'How kind,' I said. It came out harsher than I intended, and Diana shot me a warning look.

My room was lovely and large, and had the circumstances been different, I would have found it in myself to appreciate the wooden four-poster bed, the eyelet-lace duvet cover, and a Queen Anne mahogany dresser, complete with an attached mirror that looked like it was made for a life-sized American Girl doll. Gingerly, I set my suitcase down and tugged it open. My gray tee had been stained through from sweat, and I grabbed a skinny black one instead. I took off my shirt and stared, like I always did. I still couldn't help it.

There, scrawled across the body I'd worked so hard to keep toned and athletic, graceful and capable, were the lines I hated, the marred bits I couldn't control.

Some women called them a road map of their story, an emblem of their strength. I'd been on Instagram and Pinterest. I'd seen all the things we told ourselves to help us accept them, and it's not like I didn't believe it.

Theoretically, there should be nothing wrong with these brown lines, surrounding my belly button like poorly drawn parentheses, shocks of lightning etched across my skin.

I retrieved the oil I always kept with me, shook a little onto my hands, rubbed it in like I did three times a day, hoping and praying they would one day fade away.

If stretch marks were a road map, mine traced a road that led nowhere. I massaged the oil across my abdomen, and as I did, the thought hit me, impossible to push away.

He would have been a year old tomorrow. He would have been named Timothy, after your grandfather. He would have been living, laughing, maybe –

If only you'd made a different choice.

5

SAM

At first, I hadn't even realized it. I'd gone into the gas station, read my mom's text, and hadn't had a clue.

But once the key was gone, once we started to talk about staying the night, once I really gave Google Maps a good look, boy – there it was.

Catskill, New York. It was a quaint little town, not as built up as Woodstock or Kingston. A sweet mountain destination that lost residents and all its businesses sometime in the seventies like so many of these towns did. Only starting to revitalize in the last few years, craft beer tasting rooms and fair-trade coffee shops popping up like flowers breaking through the frost after a long winter.

Population, eleven thousand. Established in the 1770s. The former home of several New York State politicians and artists, a successful baseball player, and, surprisingly, the place where Mike Tyson began his training in the 1980s.

I knew all about Catskill. I'd spent too much time on its

too-short Wikipedia page, devouring every fact I could. Or using Google Maps to walk myself up and down its streets.

Or actually walking up and down those streets, trying to understand – but that was only once. Promise.

Please just leave us alone.

It would all be okay, I'd told myself as we'd chosen our rooms and opened a bottle of wine, as we'd settled on a nearby bar, Eamon's, for a very late dinner – the only one in town that served grub after nine.

As I let Diana do my makeup and run a flat iron over my hair, insistent that we make the most of our night out.

Hell, maybe it would be more than okay.

Maybe this crazy trip would bring us together.

Because Catskill, New York, the setting of our breakdown, wasn't just another upstate New York mountain town.

It was where Harry lived now.

Where Harry lived with Elizabeth.

The woman he left me for.

It was nearly ten by the time we arrived at Eamon's, a brutal, sweeping cinder block building with huge windows on one side – it must have been an old gas station or auto shop before (I'll take a beer and an extra car key, please). It was situated off a small road, a few blocks from the main drag, and surrounded by woods. Half-cool, half-creepy.

Diana led the way, striding confidently, Margaret right behind her. The air was balmy, almost wet, in that early-May way that says summer is coming – stat.

There was no bouncer, no one even checking IDs, but based on the number of cars in the dusty parking lot, the sound of voices bursting from inside, and the cluster of people sharing smokes out front, it was anything but empty. I grabbed the ends of my hair, which felt glossy and blunt when straightened. Between that and Diana's insistence on a cat-eye, I felt overly made-up for this sort of place, like I was trying too hard.

She would never try too hard. She didn't have to.

'So who's going to make out with a townie?' Diana asked, turning to us and grinning mischievously. She ran a finger over the neckline of her slinky black dress. She looked fabulous. 'When in Rome, right? And we're looking fantastic, all things considered.'

'No, thanks,' Margaret said. She wasn't the sort for public make-outs, and if I understood correctly, she hadn't been with anyone but Lars in over a decade.

For my part, I forced a grin – part of me wanted to, *needed* to, I had to shake off my grief – but the other part, the other part couldn't help but imagine . . .

Diana turned away abruptly, tugging open the large wooden door.

If I knew her, and I did, she'd be ordering trios of margaritas or tequila shots in minutes. She was a drink-away-your-sorrows, drink-away-your-stresses sort of woman, and though our hangouts almost always led to headaches the next morning, I didn't mind. There was something about the way her eyes locked on yours as she listened to all your problems, the way she knew how to say just the right thing – never dishing out advice, as Margaret sometimes tended to do, but just *being there*.

'That must be so hard. I'm just mad as fuck that that happened. I hate that for you. Of *course* you would feel that way.'

She was the glue of our group, even if I was the one who'd technically brought us together. She was thirty-three, which put her smack dab in the middle of Margaret and me, age-wise, and her easygoing, up-for-anything spirit was a perfect bridge between my reckless impulsivity and Margaret's careful planning.

Inside, the bar was dark, hazy and cavernous. Large cinder blocks rose high on one side, wood paneling on the other, and doors led off to side rooms, one holding a pool table, another a jukebox, the one in back leading to a hallway that headed who knows where.

The music was loud, homegrown American classic rock, the kind you could never quite place, and a smell of liquor and fried food permeated the air. Diana pounced on a cluster of stools in the corner, then grabbed a drinks list.

I couldn't help it – I found my head swiveling back and forth, looking. Even in the darkness, the blur of bodies and profiles, I struggled to spot a flash of Harry's silver hair or strong nose.

He probably didn't even go out anymore, not with her. They probably made nice steaks at home and split fancy bottles of Cabernet and had sex in the kitchen, that kind of thing. He probably didn't even think of me at all.

'Help you?'

I turned back to see the bartender, face illuminated by the glow of a hanging green glass lamp and a neon Pabst bar sign, his voice almost as scratchy as his beard.

'I didn't see it on the list, but can you do margaritas?' Diana asked. 'Strong ones?'

Ding ding ding! Diana would go on Diana-ing, that was for sure, the bar's typical offerings be damned.

The guy gestured halfway down the bar. The plastic edge of a blender glinted in the hazy light. 'If you can handle 'em, I can do 'em.'

Diana eyed us, as if waiting for one of us to stop her, ask for a very adult glass of red wine. 'My treat,' she said.

'Lord,' Margaret said. 'We still have to drive tomorrow, you know.' She glanced at Diana. 'Right?'

''Course,' Diana said. 'But tomorrow is still a long way away.'

'Fuck it,' I said. 'I'm in.'

When the margaritas arrived, because I couldn't help myself, because the two glasses of wine I'd had back at the rental had loosened me up, because I'd never responded to that text from Harry, and most of all because *she* couldn't tell me what to do or where to go – fuck her – I pulled out my phone and took a quick snap, the light catching the rock salt on the rim just so, the people, the bartender, the oak bar and the cinder block walls, blurring into nothing but darkness behind it.

I opened Instagram and wrote my post quick as I could, before I could stop myself. 'When your girls' trip goes awry and you find yourself stranded, at least there are margaritas!' I tagged it Catskill, NY. I tagged it Eamon's Bar and Grill. I tagged Margaret, and I didn't tag Diana, because she wasn't on social media, wouldn't even allow her face to be on social, not when Brandon could be checking.

As I hit post, my stomach tickled with excitement.

Harry still followed me on there. He was bound to see it.

I lifted my glass and clinked it against theirs, holding back a hopeful smile.

'All right, ladies. Let's drink.'

Two drinks in, and we were all a bit sloppy, our fingers picking over hot chicken wings, bacon cheese fries and a plate of fried pickles – the closest thing we could find to a vegetable on the menu, not that it mattered much either way to me.

'See, this isn't so bad, is it?' Diana asked, licking a bit of hot sauce off her fingers and twisting back and forth in her stool. 'And I'm sure the auto shop can get us going tomorrow.'

'It could be worse,' Margaret said. She finished the last sip of margarita and carefully wiped her mouth with a napkin.

I took a sip, too, then checked my Instagram to see who'd liked my photo.

There was a sudden screech of chair legs, and Diana leapt up. The front of her dress was wet.

'Fuck,' she said.

The guy next to her turned, tossing napkins over the countertop spill as fast as he could.

'I'm so sorry,' he said, wiping furiously. The dim light blurred the lines of his fully tattooed arms. 'Did I do that?' he asked. 'I didn't even –'

'It's okay,' Diana said, forcing a smile.

'Did it get all over – shit, can I do anything?'

'Really, it's fine,' Diana said firmly.

She turned to us, raising her eyebrows. *There goes my outfit*, she mouthed. 'I better get to the bathroom to clean up. Order another round? If I'm already covered in booze, I might as well be consuming it, too. Going to smell like it either way.'

'More margs?' I asked.

'You know me so well.'

'And waters,' Margaret reminded us.

'Yes, waters, too,' she said.

With that, Diana turned and headed across the room, disappearing into the crowd.

A half a margarita later, my phone buzzed with a text from her.

Bumming a cigarette out back. Come join me!

My eyes caught Margaret's. 'Diana's smoking.'

Margaret crinkled her nose, as if she could smell it just talking about it. 'I thought she'd been gone too long. Figures.'

'I know you think it's a nasty habit,' I said.

Margaret cocked her head to the side. 'You want to join her, don't you?'

'Don't judge.'

'I'm not, don't worry. Go on.' Her eyes flitted to her right, where the guy who'd spilled Diana's drink was still sitting.

'You sure?' I asked.

'Yes,' she said, taking a large sip that was very unlike her. She smirked. 'I have my drink to keep me company, at least.'

'I'll just be a minute.'

Winding my way through the crowd toward the back, the smell of stale sweat lifted off everyone's clothes. The tinge of sweet whiskey filled the air.

In the back room, there was another bar, one that stretched halfway down the wall. A girl in a too-tight T-shirt bounced from one end to the other, serving beers. People were packed in, drinks in their hands and coats tossed onto the cushions of junk-shop couches. To the left, another neon sign advertised restrooms, and straight ahead, a door was propped open, leading outside. The scent of cigarettes was pungent.

As I pushed through the crowd, making for the door, my lungs craved the sweet smoke like they always did when I had too much to drink.

Then my eyes locked on the last seat at the bar, stopping me short.

I couldn't believe it. I hadn't seriously thought it would work.

But it *had*.

There, right in front of me, at the end of the bar, nursing a beer.

There, in plain sight.

Wearing the denim shirt we'd picked out together at the shop in Williamsburg. The one he always wore but I thought he might have gotten rid of, in his new life.

There was my love.

My ex.

My heart.

The man who'd put me back together and then torn my world in two.

Harry.

6

MARGARET

'I think you've got one too many margaritas there. Or two.'

The man sitting next to me nodded to our drinks. It was the first thing he'd said that wasn't in the way of an apology.

'My friend went off to clean herself up, but then got distracted by a cigarette. My other friend went to join her.' I paused, sipping on my drink. I sounded like someone in middle school, trying to find my girlfriends at a dance.

'I know,' he said. 'And I can't help but feel that it's all my fault.'

'No,' I said, as I let myself take him in. A bandana was tied absurdly around his shaved head, as if he were off to run a Tough Mudder when this night was over. He looked to be mid-twenties, and his eyes were green, but muted in the soft bar lights. His skin was smooth, but that might be a trick of the lighting, too. He was cute, in a very unusual way. Unlike Lars, whose handsome features were impossible not to notice, this guy could fly under the radar. 'Don't worry about it,' I said finally. 'Seriously.'

I turned back to my drink, thinking the conversation was over. Wishing, in spite of myself, that it wasn't.

'It's nice out there.'

'Huh?' I turned back to him.

'On the patio. They're probably just enjoying it. It's beautiful, on a night like this.'

'Is it?' Heat flushed my cheeks as I found myself imagining it: wandering out onto the patio with a guy easily ten years younger than me, one who wore a bandana around his head, completely unironically. It must be the tequila, combined with my utter lack of action since everything went wrong. A vibrator could only go so far, I supposed.

He gestured to the clock hanging over the bar. 'Right around this time of night, it cools down really nice. The bar backs up to the woods, and they hardly have any light back there. The stars come out, brighter than ever. You can see Jupiter sometimes, it's so clear.'

'Amateur astronomer?' I asked.

He grinned. 'Amateur a lot of things.'

I nodded to the bandana. 'Like X Games competitor?'

'Oh, you mean this?' He ran a finger along the fabric's edge. 'It's stupid, I know. I got this at a music festival last summer. I have this sweating thing. You don't want to see me in a crowded bar without the bandana, trust me.'

I burst out laughing, took another sip of my drink and set it down. 'I should probably go get them, lure them back inside.'

'I can watch your seats if you want. And your drinks, I mean, if that isn't weird or creepy. I know a woman's never supposed to leave her drink behind. I have a little sister.'

The bartender, overhearing us, smiled. 'I can vouch for him,' he said. 'He's good people.'

I hesitated only seconds, then decided it was fine and topped the drinks with napkins. 'Okay. Thanks. I'll be right back.'

I beelined through the crowds, down the hallway, and into the next room, toward a door that opened to the back. I checked for messages from Sam or Diana, but there were none. Lars, on the other hand, had texted back.

I miss you, Peggy

A smell of smoke hit me as soon as I was outside, invading my lungs like a poison, along with a surprisingly cool gust of wind. I coughed quickly, then took in the scene. The patio butted up to darkened woods, trees tall and shadowed. There was only a single lamp, flush against the back wall. It was hardly enough to see well, the only other sources of light a pale silver moon and the glowing ends of cigarettes and vape pens.

The whole area felt eerie, and I thought of Lars before I'd gotten pregnant, how he would have loved a setting like this. He was an actor, too, although it had gone much better for him. He'd gotten a bit part on a cable show right before we started trying, the break he'd been after for so long. He always said a good setting helped him get into a role, that it was half the script. He still had his bit part, and his off-Broadway plays and his job bartending to help pay the bills, but I wondered sometimes if the alcohol would take that from him, too.

My gaze swiveled back as I took in every person and every group. There were probably twenty people out here, but among the myriad patrons dragging on cancer sticks, Sam and Diana were nowhere to be found. Damn it. I checked my phone one more time, then slipped it back in my pocket.

Her face met mine as I turned around.

'Sam!'

'Margaret,' she said. She jumped, like a child caught behaving badly, and then walked through the open door, a man following behind. 'Sorry. I should have texted you.'

I looked from her to him and back again. His hair was gray, and it vaguely called to mind one of her wedding photos from Facebook. I didn't get on social media much. I had all the accounts, unlike Diana, but I tried to steer clear. It was too heartbreaking, all those happy marriages and relationships, all those ultrasound photos and saccharine 'We're pregnant!' announcements and smiling children.

Did the girl simply have a type, or could this guy actually be Harry? She said he'd left her for another woman, outside the city, but she hadn't specified where. Surely Sam would have said something if our unlikely stop had landed her right where Harry lived?

I scanned Sam's face for a hint, waiting for a possible introduction, but she only raised her eyebrows, making the universal sign: *We're good, here. We want to be left alone.*

'I was about to go back inside,' I managed. 'Where's Diana?'

'She's not out here?' Sam asked.

'No,' I said. 'I assumed you were together.'

Sam turned to the man, then back to me. 'I'm sure she's in the bathroom or something – or making new friends – you know her.'

46

'So you're okay, then?' I asked.

She nodded, but as she did, a shiver shook through her, and goose bumps rose on her bare arms.

'Here,' I said, shrugging out of my jacket. 'Take this.'

'Oh, you don't —'

'It's hot as anything in the bar. I don't need it.'

When I was younger, I used to do that with friends, when they were talking to guys they'd just met. Intentionally lend them something — a scarf, a cardigan, my credit card for the tab — give them a reason not to rush home with someone they didn't know from Adam without at least saying goodbye to me first. It was silly, protective, but it usually worked. I was the mother among my group of girlfriends, having skipped the after-hours hookup scene altogether.

I bristled. *Mother*. Something I would never be now.

Whether this guy was a townie or whether the alternate explanation was true, that Sam was making the ill-advised decision to reconnect with her long-lost ex, giving her a reason to check in with me was the only real thing I could do. I pushed the jacket more insistently and after a moment, Sam took it.

'Thanks.'

'I'll see you in there, okay?'

'Yes,' she said. 'Okay.'

I stopped in the bathroom on the way back to the front, waited in line to relieve myself of some of the alcohol.

When I finally got back, our seats were empty, our drinks as I left them, napkins atop each one, except they were sweating, condensation turning the paper coasters beneath them into mush.

I slunk into my seat and slid the napkin off one of the drinks.

'I'm guessing this means your friends didn't turn up?' the man asked.

I shook my head. 'They're . . . preoccupied.'

He smirked. 'I'm Alex, by the way,' he said, extending his hand.

His eyes were kind, the sort old novels would call 'fine.' The sort of eyes that made you smile.

I found myself smiling, in that moment. Smiling without even trying to – unusual for me.

Hell, if my friends were busy talking to guys, I suppose there's no reason I couldn't join in the fun. I took a sip of the drink, the tequila going straight to my head, then balanced it with water. I wondered briefly if this was how Lars felt all the time now, hazy and untethered.

I extended my hand, and his was warm after the cool condensation of the glass.

'Margaret.'

7

SAM

'You always did run cold,' Harry said, squeezing my wrist with his free hand. 'Goose bumps in this weather.'

I pulled Margaret's jacket tight across my chest, hanging on to warmth, then bit my lip, trying to organize my thoughts – wrap my head around exactly what I wanted to say.

When I'd seen Harry at the bar – not even fifteen minutes ago – it was hard not to marvel, to feel like I'd won, just a little bit.

When he'd sent me that ridiculous, cliched 'I miss you' text on Saturday like I was some kind of two a.m. booty call, I'd had enough self-respect to not respond. To push aside the hope that threatened to burst right through.

When there was nothing the next day, or the day after that, or the day after that, I'd been ready to put him entirely behind me – fuck, I'd been *trying*, at least – I did take the rings off, even if I kept them close – but then Margaret had lost our key.

It was goddamn *serendipitous*.

And then, like a fish, Harry had clamped on to the line I'd

thrown out, and when I saw him there, sitting on that barstool like it was the most natural thing in the world, there was anger, there was rage, but there was bliss, too. Relief.

I hadn't even realized it, but one of my biggest fears since Harry left was that I'd never see him again. That he'd disappear – poof. Turn into a ghost, a memory, and float away.

That our time together, my respite from all the shit I'd allowed myself to take from the men I'd met on dating apps, would be like a dream. Nothing more than a collection of memories and photos, an imprint on the mattress that would eventually go away, too. In an apartment that wasn't even mine.

But then there he was, looking exactly the same, his hair thick, wavy and almost completely gray – my silver fox – his eyes, deep set beneath bushy brows that had held on to their brown coloring better than his locks had. His nose, strong and sharp and a tad too large for his face.

And there I was watching him, the south to his north, negative to his positive – would we come together like magnets, like we always did?

I'd slipped my hand into my pocket and the platinum felt cool and strong, a comfort.

I knew Margaret would judge me, would be beyond disappointed in my futile, pathetic lack of willpower.

But I didn't fucking care.

Besides, Diana wouldn't judge. She never had.

The truth was, the moment I saw him sitting at the bar, I knew, beyond a shadow of doubt – *Judge, after careful deliberation, we have a verdict* – that if I didn't take this chance, wrapped up and delivered to me like a Christmas package, I would always wonder . . .

What if?

Before I could lose my nerve, I'd stepped closer, said his name, the sound strong – familiar – as if it was made to spill from my mouth.

As if the past two months hadn't even happened.

He'd turned his head immediately, and in his eyes – pleasure.

'Sam,' he said, my name as natural on his lips as his had been on mine. How many times had we exchanged these syllables? *Harry, just come to bed already. Sam, I thought you said you'd do the dishes before they piled up. Sam – Harry – my darling – I love you.*

'What are – what are you doing here?' he'd stammered.

Lying, obviously. He'd seen my Instagram. He must have.

I muttered something about car trouble, being stuck in town until we could figure out a solution, and then, before I knew it, he was ordering us his favorite bar combo – beer and a shot of whiskey – and I was chasing Jack Daniel's with an ice-cold saison, my beer of choice. Harry had asked if I wanted to talk outside, and of course, I'd said yes.

Why wouldn't I?

And now, here we were.

Alone, or as alone as we could be, packed among smokers, on a night that had so quickly turned chilly.

Harry took a gulp of beer, then cleared his throat, as if he didn't know where to start. His eyes had that glassy look to them, one so subtle only I would notice. I remembered, suddenly, that first night we slept together, the bottle of wine between us, any residual inhibitions dissolved by Pinot Noir. It had felt so natural.

Harry glanced quickly around the patio, then settled on his beer, as if there were answers at the bottom of his glass.

A gust blew past us, and I caught it, the woodsy scent of the all-natural deodorant he always wore – the one I once went to three different Duane Reades to find for him.

Harry looked up, straight at me. 'Your hair,' he said. 'It's straight.'

'Really?' I asked, dumbfounded. 'That's what you're going to say?'

'Sorry,' he said. 'It just looks . . . it looks nice. I mean, it always looks nice, but it looks different nice this time. Sorry,' he said again. 'I'm so happy to see you. *Really*. I know that . . .' His voice trailed off, and anger, hot and raw, invaded my body, tentacling through my chest.

'Let me help you out,' I said. 'You know that you abandoned me? That you left me completely out of the blue? That you gave new meaning to the term *blindsided*.'

Harry grimaced. 'I know.'

'You just *left*,' I said, roiling. 'You hardly even said goodbye.'

'I'm not saying it was right.' His eyes found his beer again.

'Don't do that,' I said. 'Don't look away. That's all you've been doing, all this time. You've been refusing to face me, refusing to even give me a real explanation.'

'Because I *can't* explain,' he said. 'You wouldn't understand. You don't know what it was like for her. You don't know how hard she had it, when she was a kid. She had an impossible childhood, and it wasn't made better by . . .' His voice trailed off again. 'She needed me. I'm the only . . . I'm all she has left.

She was so furious with me, she always had such a temper, and I really thought it was over when we broke up, but I was wrong. I was wrong about so much.'

'What were you wrong about?' I snapped. 'Me? You were wrong about loving me?' People were beginning to look over. Margaret would have been horrified. She hated when Diana or I got a little too loud.

'No,' Harry said. 'No, I wasn't wrong about that. All of that was real. I promise. I swear.'

'Then what changed? I never asked you to propose, you know. I never asked you to do that. *You're* the one who wanted it. You're the one who –'

'You needed me,' Harry said. 'Everything with your dad. I thought it was all over with her. I thought I was doing the right thing.'

'I thought it was over with her, too,' I said, my voice vicious. 'And what do you mean, I needed you? Like I don't need you anymore? Fuck, Harry, that's rich.'

'Please, Sam,' he said. 'Don't do this.'

'Do what?'

'Not here,' he said, his eyes darting around, as if someone might recognize him and report everything back to her.

'Then where?'

'I can't do this with you, not in front of everyone.' Harry pointed to the woods, the trees. The darkness. 'Let's just . . . let's find a place that's not so crowded. To talk.'

Harry never did like to make a scene. He used to say that *she* was quick to cause them, that her anger could burst forth, unexpected. Mine never had. I wasn't like that. Not until now.

53

He took a few quick steps until he was off the patio, nearly swallowed whole by the woods. Then he turned back, his eyes trained on mine.

'Are you coming?'

I had a feeling of standing on a precipice – deciding between one path and the next. There was the right decision, the one you made sober, the one steeped in self-respect and healthy boundaries.

And then there was the wrong decision, the one fueled by whiskey and tequila, by desperation, the one where you didn't care how much you'd hurt afterward because you wanted it to be like it was, just for a moment, however brief.

Because you wanted to feel wanted by the person you loved.

The corner of Harry's mouth turned up like it always did, and I knew it didn't matter.

I lifted my beer to my lips, drank as much as I could in one gulp, and for a moment, I didn't care about anything else. I wanted to dull it all.

And in that moment, I knew it so truly.

All bets were off.

8 | MARGARET

A text made my phone shake against the wooden bar top.

The half-melted margaritas were tasting better as the night wore on, or maybe it was the warmth of Alex's company. I set my drink down and tapped at my screen.

We need ech other Peggy let me come seee you

Lars's spelling was already affected. It would only get worse as the night wore on.

'Everything all right?' Alex asked.

'Yes,' I said, flipping my phone over. 'It's my . . .' I struggled, even now, to find the words. 'My ex-husband. Well, my soon-to-be ex-husband. Nothing's final yet.'

Alex pressed his palm against the bar, taking in this new info. 'But it's over, right?'

My fingers tingled with excitement, but I forced my voice to stay calm. 'Yes,' I said, my eyes averted. 'It's over. Anyway,' I said, grasping at a new subject. 'What do you do? I believe we've already ruled out professional astronomer and X Games competitor.'

Alex laughed and adjusted his bandana, tying it tighter. 'I work at a brewery in town. All local hops and stuff.' He took another sip of beer. 'It's a good daytime spot, the brewery,' he said, raising an eyebrow. 'You guys should come by tomorrow.'

The tingling feeling stretched up through my arms, and I wrapped my fingers around the sweating, ice-cold glass before letting myself glance back his way. He was so easygoing and unassuming, so young and fresh. He couldn't really be interested in me, could he? He probably had girls around the brewery, twentysomethings with tight skin and a notable absence of scars.

Only for a moment, I let myself imagine it. Sunlight streaming through the windows of a brewery, kissing my bare shoulders. Alex going on about ABVs and how they made their hops. His tattooed arms, how they must feel . . .

'We're actually leaving tomorrow morning,' I said, cutting my own fantasy short. 'We're not supposed to be here. We had car trouble, which we have to figure it out in the morning, once the auto shop opens.'

We wouldn't actually need to figure it out, but I couldn't tell him that. He wouldn't understand. I hardly did myself.

'Oh,' Alex said, his smile faltering. And then: 'That's too bad.'

I felt a blush blooming across my cheeks. He *was* flirting with me, wasn't he? Me, deep into my thirties. Wrinkles already firmly set around my mouth. Markings of a life that would never, ever be striating across my stomach.

He didn't say anything more, and I didn't, either. I wondered if this was about to be the end of our conversation. I found I very much did not want it to be.

'So what do you do?' Alex asked, throwing me a line. 'I'm guessing it's cooler than pouring beer and serving warm pretzels.'

'Boring sellout advertising writing these days,' I said. 'But I used to be an actor. Well, I tried to be.'

Alex smirked.

'What?' I asked.

He shrugged. 'It just explains it.'

'Explains what?'

Through the din of voices, of drinks being poured, clinking glass, amid the heat of the bar and the sweat that was, indeed, collecting at the top of Alex's bandana, I wanted it, badly. To be paid a compliment, to be told I was beautiful and worthy.

'I don't want to be a creep or anything, but you've got a kind of, I don't know – presence – something most people don't have. I mean, *I* certainly don't. I saw it from the moment you walked in. I was glad you sat down with your friends. You command the room. That's how my grandmother would put it,' he said. 'I'm sure that sounds stupid –'

'No,' I said. 'No, it's lovely, hearing you say that. Thank you. And especially from someone like . . . from you . . . you're so young. At my age –'

'Stop,' he said. 'What are you, thirty?'

'Good guess,' I said with a laugh. 'Whether you meant it or not. Thirty-six, actually. Well, as of next month.'

'I'm twenty-eight, in any case, even though I know I look about nineteen with my baby face. My last girlfriend, she's thirty-nine now. It makes no difference to me.'

'Oh,' I said. I skipped the water and moved on to Diana's drink. It was strange, but the thought of him with another woman made me jealous somehow, irrational as it was. 'And what happened with her?' It was forward, very unlike me, but the words were out now; they couldn't be taken back.

Alex's eyes found the edge of the bar, briefly. 'She's back in Kentucky, where her family's from. With our kid actually – he's four – he spends the summers with me, the rest of the year with her. Do you want to see a picture?'

My throat felt suddenly thick with emotion and loss, and I swallowed back the sensation. 'Of course.'

Alex took out his phone, cracked on one edge. He didn't have to open it. His kid was there on his lock screen, like most kids were.

A beautiful boy, head sporting a mess of blond curls. A cherub.

'That's Luke,' Alex said. 'My heart and soul.'

'Luke,' I repeated. I didn't know if it was the photo of him or the tequila or the weight of what tomorrow meant, but tears, so rare for me, pricked the corners of my eyes.

'You okay?' Alex asked. 'I didn't mean to upset you.'

I took another sip of Diana's drink, then pushed it away, dropped my hand to the side. All at once, it was too much for me.

'Hey, it's okay.' Alex's hand found mine, linked our fingers together. It felt so nice, I began to properly cry.

'Sorry,' I said. 'I never do this. Really.' It was true. Lars always wanted me to cry more, to get down with him, there in the weeds of his grief. Yet here I was, turning on the waterworks with a stranger. With my free hand, I brushed the moisture from my eyes.

'Do you want to talk about it?' Alex asked. 'Whatever I accidentally drudged up.'

My eyes caught his. 'I don't even really know you.'

'Feels kind of like we do, though, doesn't it?' he asked, squeezing my hand. 'That's not the beer talking, I swear.'

It was a line, a line that many a guy had probably used in many a bar, but a hopeful, long-buried part of me believed it. Or believed it enough to do what I shouldn't: pretend, for a night, that this sweet young man was more to me than simply a guy in a bar.

'I had a son, too,' I said.

Alex's lips parted, and his thumb traced my thumb, and he didn't need it to be explained. He caught the past tense clearly, as anyone with a kid, or anyone who'd ever lost someone they loved, would. He didn't need it to be explained, but I would anyway.

'Timothy, that's what we wanted to call him.' I took a quick breath, steeling myself.

'Tomorrow would have been his first birthday.'

No one ever thinks the world is going to implode, the ground sink right out from under where they're standing, and that the one in however many thousand will ever apply to them. I hadn't, either. If they did, no one would ever try to craft a life, try to build these absurd castles in the sky.

It was shortly after my thirty-fourth birthday that Lars and

I started trying. I'd long given up on acting and had been at the same ad agency for over a year by that point. Lars had recently gotten his SAG card, and we finally had health insurance, thanks to our marriage from a couple of years before. It was the first time the timing actually felt right.

I pushed my birth control into the bottom of a cabinet, and I tracked my ovulation on this pink app that shared all the dates with Lars. To my surprise, it happened, boom, like that, after two months of trying. 'So my swimmers work?' Lars had asked, before leaning in to kiss me. 'Not so fast,' I'd said. 'Don't give yourself all the credit.'

Everything had been fine, had been lovely, in fact, until it hadn't. Yes, there was the time Lars had slammed on the brakes, the seat belt digging into my abdomen, but Dr Google had set our minds at ease on that one. Though we didn't tell anyone the news, we got ahead of ourselves anyway, meandering through the aisles with nursery furniture in IKEA, buying a gender-neutral onesie that declared our baby-to-be was politically active, bandying about names over dinner. Timothy for a boy, after my grandfather. Rose for a girl, after his favorite great-aunt.

Our eight-week appointment had been fantastic. Lars held my hand as the lady shoved the wand into my body, and there was a heartbeat and an impossibly small kidney bean on the ultrasound. I was, indeed, pregnant. They told us about this blood test we could do, raise a flag for any chromosomal conditions or rare inherited illnesses. We had no family history, and I would deliver before I was thirty-five. 'You have nothing to worry about. You're not high-risk,' the OB said, her hair pulled back so tightly it stretched her forehead, made her eyebrows look like she was

60

permanently in shock. 'But many women – many couples – choose to do it for the peace of mind. It's noninvasive.'

We'd gone in at ten weeks for the blood draw, and the nurse told me that they'd only call if there was a problem, that otherwise, we'd go over everything at my next appointment. For another week, I continued on, Lars and I cocooned in our state of bliss. Then we got the call from a 212 number, signaling an office in Manhattan, the call that would only come if something was wrong.

Later, in the genetic counselor's office, the woman, Carolyn, who looked like she was fresh out of college, tried to keep us calm as she passed me a box of tissues. Edwards syndrome, an extra copy of chromosome 18, was bad, yes, very bad, but the blood test was not diagnostic: it could only assess risk. Nearly half of the high-risk results among women my age were false positives. The only way to know was to schedule an amniocentesis, stick a needle through my belly and suck up a vial of my amniotic fluid, see if our baby was as doomed as I feared.

Four weeks later we had the procedure; two weeks after that we got the final results. In the time that passed, I descended into darkness, into hole after hole researching the condition on the internet, despite Lars's entreaties for me to stop before we knew anything for sure.

By the time the waiting was over, the stretch marks had begun to arc across my abdomen. I was starting to show, and I'd purchased a set of expensive tentlike dresses for work.

And then, an answer. Another phone call.

Our baby – our boy, Timothy – he had the condition.

The prognosis was terrible. He had three chromosomes

when there should have been two. Half of infants didn't survive their first week of life. Only ten percent of them lived longer than a year, one percent up to ten years.

To me, the answer was heartbreaking but clear. My body, my baby, was broken. Something in my womb, in that clear fluid they'd sucked out of me with a needle straight from a horror movie, had ruined my son.

Only to Lars it wasn't. To Lars, there was still hope. What if we were one of the one percent whose baby did make it to ten? What if all those years of joy could be ours? Hell, what if the test wasn't even accurate? There was a one in a thousand chance it was wrong. What if, what if, what if?

I didn't tell Alex all of this, of course, but I told him more than Sam or Diana knew. That my baby boy had had a rare condition, that I had elected to terminate for medical reasons, just shy of twenty weeks along. That I often thought about how much I'd deprived my son of, how many little things about this world he'd never get to know. That there is nothing worse than having to deliver a baby into the world knowing full well that there is no world for him at all.

When there was nothing left to say, I stared, waiting for Alex to judge me, like Lars had so many times.

'I'm so sorry,' Alex said, his eyes clear and kind. The relief was so sweet, so wonderful, that in spite of myself, in spite of all my better judgment, I leaned forward.

I kissed Alex on the lips.

9 | SAM

Staring at Harry, tucked in the woods where no one could see us, I half wanted to hit him, I swear to god I did. At the same time, I wanted to grab his face between my hands, kiss him harder than I ever had before.

'Tell me the truth,' I started, the wind kicking up around us, muffling voices like a white noise machine, giving us the illusion of privacy. 'Were you worried one of *her* friends would see you talking to me?'

I steadied myself against a tree trunk, feeling the scratch of bark against my palm. Pulling my hand away, I felt sap, sticky, on my fingers. I had a crazy thought, of reaching my finger to Harry's lips, letting him taste the sweetness.

'No,' he said. 'I couldn't think clearly with everyone around me. I couldn't say what I needed to say with everyone watching us. You know that about me.'

'And now?' I asked, rubbing my finger on the sleeve of Margaret's jacket, trying to get the stickiness off. 'Now do you have the words to fix this?'

Harry seized up, so obviously at a loss, and I took a sip of the beer he'd bought me. It was sudsy and weak; it tasted almost flat, like water from a tap that needed to be cleaned. Quick as I could, I took another sip, anger surging within me. 'Because unless you can rewind time and *not* do what you did, I don't think you can.'

He gulped.

'For chrissakes, say *something*,' I pleaded. 'God knows you've had plenty of time to think.'

'I know,' Harry said, biting at the edge of his lip. 'I'm sorry. God, Sam, I don't know what to say. I should have given you more warning,' he said as if that was the only problem. 'I should have stuck around to talk it out, given you more of an explanation —'

'What explanation could there possibly be? You chose her over me. You made a promise to me, in front of all our friends, in front of my family, in front of my dying father, and then you *still* chose her.' I dug my sandals deeper into the grass, steadying myself. 'I don't even know what to tell them now. They're coming in two weeks. What the fuck am I supposed to say?' I asked, my voice cracking. 'Ask them to help me look for apartments?'

'No,' Harry said. 'No, I said you can stay as long as you want.'

'As I want?' I asked. 'What I *want* is for you to come home. To erase all this. What I want is for everything to go back to the way it was before. Christ. How can you even talk about what I want?'

Harry groaned, and his hand reached for my cheek, the side of his thumb tracing its edge. Just like it had when I'd found out my dad was sick.

64

'Don't,' I said, pulling away.

'I can't stand to see how much I've upset you. And . . . and . . . your dad. Everything. I've made a mess of it all.' His hand found my cheek again. 'I never meant to hurt you, Sam. I swear to god. And I loved you, truly. I did. I do.'

But you love her more. The thought was so terrible, so bitter. So true.

'I still love you,' he went on. 'I never stopped.'

I glared at him, and for a second, I felt so pathetic, so cast aside, so second-rate and cheap.

'Then prove it,' I said.

'What?'

'You heard me. If you still love me, show me.'

Harry's head cocked to the side, contemplating.

I knew it was all wrong, that if I were more sober – or he was – that none of this would be on the table.

But at the same time, I didn't care.

I wanted – *needed* – for him to choose me.

His gaze didn't break from mine, and I gave him that look I'd given him so many times now. The look that says, *I'm yours if you want me, you know.*

I leaned forward, closer to him, and in seconds, he'd dropped his beer to the ground and his other hand was framing my face in that way I'd loved so much. The way that had endeared me, bonded me to him from the start.

Objections rang through my head – *You should have more self-respect than this; he* left *you, for god's sake* – but it didn't matter.

We never even got a proper goodbye.

Maybe this would be it.

Or maybe it would be more.

Harry leaned closer still, and I could nearly taste the whiskey on his breath, and the smell sent me back, to those nights we shared together, early on, before anything had even happened.

The sheer passion, the illicitness of it all.

Now he pressed his body against mine. His eyes were so familiar. Eyes I'd thought I somehow possessed. Eyes I didn't expect to wander. Eyes that still could get my knees buckling, my stomach flip-flopping.

I let myself take a breath, then I lifted my chin, the tiniest bit. I hated him for what he'd done, what he'd turned me into, for forcing me to live a lie these last two months, too broken, too ashamed to tell the truth to anyone other than Diana and Margaret.

Harry sighed, deep and guttural, the sort of sigh of pleasure I'd heard from him many times. Sunday mornings. Tuesday nights. Pleasure and pain, hold and release.

Then his hands found my hair, his fingers diving through the strands, scraping across my scalp. He pulled me to him – jerked, almost – and our mouths came together, hungry and gasping – like coming up for air after holding your breath for so very long, like the first sip of water after a hard workout, the salt on your lips, the rivulets dribbling down your chin.

He felt the same – the space where my lips ended and his began was hard to define – only all of it was more urgent, like time was a thing we were borrowing, tiny bits of sand cascading down to the bottom.

My teeth grasping at his lip, my hand dropping the beer to the ground as I wrapped my arms around him, pulled him closer, as liquid spilled across my sandals, seeping into the earth around us, turning it to squishy mud.

My back pressed hard against the tree trunk, so hard I wondered if I was scratching Margaret's jacket, and his hands lifted the hem of my dress, and out of the corner of my eyes I saw the patrons on the patio, but they weren't even looking, we were in the dark, and I didn't give a fuck anyway as I squeezed out of my underwear, letting them drop to the ground.

And then, as if neither of us had pushed that forbidden button, as if it had somehow just – happened – Harry and I were together again.

It was over in minutes, like bad decisions often were. Like reaching back into the tin of cookies, clamoring for the last crumbs.

'God, I thought about that so many times,' Harry said, breaking the silence with a whisper in my ear. He paused a moment, then leaned in, kissed the edge of my mouth.

'Me too,' I said as I knelt down, shimmied my underwear back up, trying to ignore how dirty they'd gotten in the beer and mud. Questions spun: What next? What now? What does this mean for Harry and me?

I heard a rustle nearby, jolting me out of my thoughts, but when I turned, there was no one. Just the people on the patio.

When I looked back to Harry, my stomach twisted as I saw it, right there in his eyes. Subtle, sure, but there all the same.

A twinge of regret.

'This is it, right? It doesn't change anything, does it? You're going to fuck me and go right home to her.'

'Sam,' he said. 'Don't say that.'

He didn't correct me.

'Fuck you, Harry,' I said.

I walked away, hands shaking with anger, stomach heavy with grief.

Skin still sticky from what we'd done.

Inside, the bar felt somehow even more crowded, or maybe I was drunker, more confused and torn up from what had just happened with Harry.

I stumbled through the back room, down the hallway, past the bathrooms, and into the front.

I needed to see my friends. Even if I was too ashamed, too embarrassed to tell them what happened – Margaret, especially – I needed to be with them. Pull my miserable self together.

But when I got back to our seats, Diana wasn't there. It was just Margaret, and she was leaning in, lips locked with the guy who'd been sitting at the bar, the one with the bandana who'd spilled beer on Diana.

Fucking tequila.

I wanted nothing more than to break them up, beg her to help me find Diana, then call us a car and get us back to the rental, but I couldn't.

Margaret, proper, rule-following, not-one-to-cause-a-scene Margaret. She was making out with a guy. In the middle of a crowded bar.

And she looked so fucking happy. I couldn't ruin her night just because I'd ruined mine.

I headed to the bathroom, stared at myself in the mirror, reapplied my lipstick and stumbled back out, then walked aimlessly until I was once again at the bar in the back.

Sinking into the only free seat, I pulled out my phone. I'd figure out where Diana was, maybe even tell her everything.

I wouldn't have to be alone.

Diana had texted twenty minutes ago.

Having another cigarette. Bbs!

My heart beat mercilessly.

There was a text from Harry. It had come in shortly after hers.

I'm so sorry

What's more, the three little dots were flashing, in and out, beneath the text.

He was typing. He had something more he wanted to say.

The dots disappeared, but I couldn't look away from my phone.

What if he'd changed his mind?

What if he was choosing me after all?

'There you are!'

I looked up to see Diana, her silver hair like a disco ball in the dim light of the bar.

'Diana,' I said. 'Margaret's —'

'Sucking face with some guy. I *know*. Can you believe it? Wait — where were you?'

Harry and I just fucked. We fucked in the woods behind the bar like horny teenagers. I drowned all the self-respect I had in a vat of tequila and whiskey, and he's already regretting it.

'What is it?' she asked. 'Sam, what happened?' Her eyes found mine, narrowing for a moment, as if reading me like she was so good at doing. 'Are you okay?'

'Yes,' I managed. 'Yes, I'm okay. It's just –' Someone jostled me from behind. I steadied myself, feeling the alcohol swimming, sloshing around my brain.

'What is it?' Diana asked, her voice soft now, filled only with concern, no judgment. 'You can tell me.'

I shook my head, hardly knowing where to start. 'Harry. My ex, you know. He's here.'

'Here?' she asked. 'In Catskill?'

'I know,' I said. 'This is where he lives. I was so stupid. I thought it was serendipitous that we landed here. I know I shouldn't have, but I posted a photo, tagged the bar, hoping he'd show up, and then he did and –'

'Whoa whoa whoa?' Diana asked, almost incredulous. 'In this bar?'

I nodded.

Her eyes cased the place, but she wouldn't be able to spot him anyway. My wedding photos were on social, but Diana wasn't. And I'd never gone out of my way to show her a photo. That was the kind of thing you did when you had happy news – *Here, look at my hot partner* – not something you did when someone left you high and dry.

Diana seemed to realize this and turned back to me. 'Like, in this room?'

'No,' I said. 'He's out back. He *was*, at least. We –'

Her gaze stayed fixed on mine. 'You what, Sam?'

The jukebox switched songs, and the sound seemed to pound suddenly, echoing through me. It was all getting so blurry. 'I only wanted to tell him, for him to hear it, how much he hurt me, how terrible what he did was, but then, I don't know – it's like I'm an addict or something – I wanted to know he still had feelings for me. I wanted proof that I still had some power over him. I just, I couldn't help myself.'

'Oh, Sam,' Diana said, pulling me into a hug. I smelled cigarettes in her hair as she tightened her arms around me.

'That's not all,' I said.

'What do you mean?'

'He texted me,' I said, turning my phone around to show her. 'He said he was sorry, and he was typing, but then he stopped. I don't know if there's more he wants to say.'

Diana stared at me a moment, and it was hard to place her look, but when I finally did, it made my insides roil. Her lips formed a firm, thin line and her eyes turned down at the corners.

Pity, that's what it was.

'I'm so sorry,' Diana said, her eyes glancing to the back door.

'What is it?' I asked.

'Nothing,' she said. 'Are you going to talk to him? See what else he had to say?'

The thought of going back out there, trying to put this all into words . . .

'I don't know,' I said. 'I mean I guess I kind of want to, but I don't even know if he's still back there.'

Diana's eyes were still on the door, as if waiting for him to walk in. I turned, following her gaze, but didn't see him.

71

She cleared her throat. 'Do you want me to go scope it out?'

'What?' I asked, taken aback.

'He won't recognize me, right? I can report back. See if he's there, at least. Then you can decide what you want to do.'

I hesitated. I knew I shouldn't. I should put it all behind me. Only it was so tempting. 'Okay,' I said. 'Harry is almost totally gray. Cut short. You really can't miss him.'

Diana nodded. She buttoned her sweater and then squeezed my arm. 'Order me an IPA, okay? I don't think I ever need to see another margarita again. I'll be right back – don't move.'

I nodded. 'Okay. I won't.'

When she was gone, I ordered one IPA and one saison. I knew I shouldn't have any more, but it didn't matter. This was all such a clusterfuck.

The bartender placed two foaming beers in front of me.

I should wait, I told myself. I should order myself a glass of water – one drink, one water, that's what we'd promised Margaret.

I should wait at least until Diana returned to take a sip, until she was back, could tell me whether she'd seen him, could tell me what I should do.

But I couldn't help it – the emotions were too much – the heartache, the excitement, the loss.

And so, without thinking about anything more than this moment, right in front of me, I picked up my beer, and I drank.

SATURDAY

10

MARGARET

I dreamed of grass. I was running, and it was wet beneath my toes. I could smell it so clearly, its verdant tickle in my nostrils. I often had dreams like this now, dreams of the little things in life, all the things my baby would never get to experience, the very things I'd taken away from him. I tripped, falling forward, and suddenly there were rocks, and I knew the ground would break my face right open . . .

Gasping, my eyes shot open, and the first thing I saw was Alex.

One arm covered his eyes, blocking the early-morning sun. At first, the sight shook me. I'd woken in the night to go to the bathroom, and he hadn't been there. I'd assumed he had gone, that it was nothing more than a one-night stand, despite all I'd told him, and though it had hurt, I'd been too drunk to properly process it.

Yet, here he was. He was snoring ever so softly, the kind of snore you could easily grow to love, not one that would ever threaten a marriage but the sort that reminded you that someone was beside you, anchoring you to this world. Lars had slept like a rock, but the subtle rise and fall of his chest had been such a comfort, something I'd missed since he started sleeping on the couch.

Around us, the bed's four mahogany posters rose majestically, and the eyelet-lace duvet was tossed aside; it must have gotten warm in the night. I lifted up one of the silky soft sheets, peeking. There I was, naked as the day I was born. There Alex was, too, his body strong and alert, even at rest. I let the sheet fall back, and as I did, the rest of it pressed at me, cutting through the sweet smell of Alex's sweat, so different from Lars's, preventing me from relishing this moment, this little bit of carnal bliss.

Something had gone wrong.

I'd been so sure that everything was fine. Kissing Alex, holding him tight, my hands on his thighs, steadying; it had been so wonderful. It wasn't the sort of thing the sort of woman like me would do. Not because I was a prude or anything: I'd gone home with Lars the first night I met him. Still, public displays of affection, of *anything*, were decidedly not my thing.

Then, as if a punishment, Sam was there, breaking us up, almost inconsolable: 'I'm sorry to bug you guys, but I can't find Diana,' she'd said, her words slurring awfully. 'I looked everywhere, and I want to get out of here.'

I'd leapt straight to action, ushering Sam onto my stool, ordering her two big glasses of water, telling Alex to make sure she drank them both. Then I'd gone to look for Diana, knowing she was probably off with some guy on the patio, that Sam in her drunkenness had simply missed her.

Diana wasn't in the back room or out on the patio. She wasn't in the women's bathroom or the room with the jukebox or the one with the pool table. I called her and texted her, and I checked each location several more times, in case we'd missed each other somehow. Not a single sign of her.

It was only then that my heart had picked up, replaying what happened between us at the gas station. Wondering if she was in some sort of trouble. Was it Brandon, her ex, and his tendency toward obsession?

Sam could barely keep her eyes open, and we weren't sure what to do. Diana's phone was working. It rang every time we called it. She didn't have a key. Diana had retrieved two keys to the rental from the lockbox on the porch, but they shared one key ring, and Sam had insisted on taking it when we left the house, saying she was the only one who hadn't been outside for the 'Great Car Key Debacle'.

Alex offered to drive us back, suggesting perhaps something had happened and Diana had somehow gotten a ride herself. I texted Diana that we were leaving, and by the time we arrived, Sam was sick, only barely holding it together until we were out of Alex's truck. On the front porch, she threw up, getting puke all over the fringe of the jacket I'd lent her, and I held her hair back while Alex dug in her purse for the rental's keys.

Inside, we put Sam to bed, leaving a glass of water on her nightstand. When her door was closed behind us, Alex turned to me at the top of the staircase, reaching for the bannister.

'You okay?' he asked. 'I should go.'

Hardly knowing what to think, only knowing that things had been going so well between us until Sam broke us up, I'd asked him to stay instead.

Now I got out of bed, digging in my suitcase for the cotton

nightgown I always wore, and as I did, I saw our clothes, strewn about the room, animal-like. It replayed before me, the way he'd lifted my top over my head, his hands on my stretch marks – understanding, not caring – his body strong against mine.

A flush of heat ran over me, all the way to the tips of my fingers. It was matched by anxiety and fear. Quickly, I scoured the nightstand until I found the foil wrapper. Between that and the birth control I'd taken religiously since I'd lost my baby, I was good.

I found the nightgown and tugged it over my head, then checked my phone. It was after eight, but there were no calls or texts from Diana. Nothing more from Lars, either.

I slipped out of the room and made my way across the hallway to where Diana's door was cracked open. *Be here, please please be here.*

Slowly, I opened the door. The bed was perfectly made, Diana's suitcase sitting on the floor, unzipped but largely untouched. She hadn't been home last night at all.

I called her again, but it rang and rang. No answer.

She *must* have gone home with someone, that was the most likely explanation, someone she'd been talking to out on the patio. It couldn't be Brandon, it couldn't have anything to do with what happened at the gas station, could it?

I tiptoed back down the hall and into my room.

Alex sat up in bed, grinning. 'Wondered where you went.'

Carefully, I situated myself on the edge of the bed. It had been so long since I'd done anything like this, and I was entirely out of practice.

Alex started for me: 'Last night was –'

I shook my head. 'You don't have to say anything.'

'Okay,' Alex said, and he leaned forward instead, placed a hand on the back of my shoulder, kissed me softly.

When he pulled black, I had to remind myself to take a breath. 'I'm actually surprised to see you here,' I said finally. 'When I got up to go to the bathroom, you weren't here. I was sure you'd left.'

'Oh,' he said.

'Did you change your mind? Like you wanted to leave but then felt bad about it with Diana gone? You didn't have to stay because of that. It's okay —'

'No,' he said quickly. 'I just . . . I went downstairs to get some water, and I . . . well, I broke a glass. I had to clean it up.' He grinned sheepishly. 'I took the pieces out to my truck because I didn't want you to find out. And look, now you have. Anyway, you okay? You feel all right?'

I had a light headache from the tequila, now that I thought of it, but I smiled anyway. He'd stayed, then. He hadn't left at all. 'I'm good,' I said. 'But Diana isn't in her room, and I haven't heard from her, either.'

'I'm sorry,' Alex said. 'Do you think she maybe — I don't know — maybe she met someone at the bar?'

'That's got to be it,' I said. 'But why wouldn't she at least text us?'

Alex pushed the covers aside, swung his feet onto the floor. He stood, grabbing his boxers, his jeans, and I got a glimpse of his perfect little butt. He slipped his boxers on, the muscles of his back standing out as he did, then turned to face me. 'Is she the responsible type?'

'What do you mean?'

'The sort to text and not do an Irish goodbye.'

'There was one time, actually,' I said. 'We were all out drinking and Diana simply left. But it seems a bit aggressive to do that when you're traveling with people.'

'Totally,' he said. 'But I bet that's it.' He cocked his head to the side. 'Unfortunately, I have to go –'

'I know,' I said. 'Of course you do. Don't worry about –'

'No,' he said. 'I would stay, but I'm due at the brewery by ten, and as chill as they are, I figure I at least need to shower after last night.'

I looked away, my face going hot once again.

'You guys are leaving today?' he asked.

'Yes,' I said. 'Well, we need to go to the auto shop and figure out if they can make us a key. Once Diana is back . . .'

Assuming Diana comes back.

'When she shows up, text me, please,' he said. 'So I don't worry. What's your number?'

I rattled it off, and he sent me a text – a smiley face. Damn, he was young.

'And, er, I was thinking,' Alex said. 'You said you lived in the city, right?'

'Brooklyn.'

'I'd really like to see you again,' he said. 'I'm not just saying that. I haven't really been with anyone since my ex and my son left a year and a half ago. I haven't felt ready, but meeting you . . . all I'm saying is, it's not that far away, you know. Catskill to Brooklyn. A couple hours. Practically nothing for a weekend trip.'

In spite of myself, I smiled.

'So maybe we can see each other again sometime?'

I nodded. 'Maybe we can.'

I walked him downstairs, kissed him one more time, and let him out the front. I watched as his truck pulled away, my stomach flip-flopping, my insides like jelly.

Back upstairs, I cracked the door open, checking on Sam, who was snoring the lawn mower sound of the majorly hungover, and I headed to the bathroom to clean up.

In my bedroom I crouched over my suitcase and grabbed a pair of jeans and a tank. My fingers brushed against the edges of the bills. I pushed my clothes aside and stared at the money.

Crisp, fresh and entirely unexpected.

Fifteen one-hundred-dollar bills.

11

SAM

My head pounded, my mouth tasted like acid and my phone was beyond dead.

I sat up in bed, peeking through the curtains to see if I could tell how early or late it was. Whatever the time, it was too bright, that's for sure.

I swallowed, gagging at the remnants of bile in the back of my throat and had a sudden flash of stumbling onto the porch, of Margaret holding my hair back, of that guy Margaret had been kissing setting a glass of water next to me.

I looked to my right – there it was – I hadn't drunk a drop, but I'm sure they tried their best. I always was an obstinate drunk.

The rest came in flashes. Me and Harry, in the back. Fucking like teenagers under the bleachers. His stupid text. Those three little dots that led straight to nowhere. Searching the bar for Diana.

Margaret's jacket was tossed onto the floor. I knelt, lifting it to my nose, bracing myself. Shit. Leather was easy to clean, right?

My stomach turned. It was hot as hell in here. The windows were shut, even though I remembered opening them when Diana and I were getting ready last night.

That's right. I'd woken, heard a noise, like someone walking around on the porch, and in my still-drunk state, I'd gotten up and shut all the windows. It must have been Diana coming home from wherever she was. Maybe even banging on the front door if Margaret hadn't left it unlocked.

I reopened the windows and stumbled out of the room. I needed about five Advil and a good pep talk from Diana, who would definitely understand.

I made my way down the hallway and twisted at the knob on the door in the middle.

Locked.

'Sorry,' I said quickly, shifting my weight from foot to foot.

When there was no response, I knocked on the door. Knocked again. It took me a full five seconds to realize I was standing in front of the wrong door.

God, was I still drunk?

One door down, I found the *actual* bathroom. I used the toilet, then splashed water on my face. My mascara was smudged, and my hair had started to re-curl and was in complete tangles. I was a vision – if you looked up 'walk of shame' in the dictionary, I was pretty sure I'd be there.

Diana's door was half-open, and I poked my head in. I stopped, frozen solid, my head once again pounding. The bed was neatly made – too neat, really – as if she hadn't slept there at all. She had come home, hadn't she?

I peeked into Margaret's room next – the bed was made, but it was rumpled enough that it was clear she'd at least slept in it. Good. Okay.

In the living room, I found Margaret, legs crossed gracefully, sitting in the middle of the sofa, a cup of steaming coffee in one hand – her phone clutched in the other.

'You okay?' she asked, looking up. 'You look awful.'

'I'm sorry,' I said, in lieu of a greeting. 'I know I was a total mess, and your jacket. I promise, I'm not usually like that. Needing to be taken care of and everything. I should have had more water, I know. You were totally right about that. I'm just, *god*, I'm so embarrassed.'

Margaret shook her head swiftly. 'Don't apologize. You're *here*,' she said. 'That's all that matters.'

It took me a second, in my liquor-handicapped state, to put it together, the emptiness in the room, the lack of sound – of clanking mugs, of laughter and the voice of a friend demanding we debrief her on last night's escapades.

'So she never came home?' I asked. 'I thought it looked like her bed hadn't been slept in.'

'No,' Margaret said. 'I've been calling her, but nothing.'

'Could she have gone home with someone?' I asked.

'Probably,' Margaret said. 'It's only nine-thirty. She could be sleeping off a hangover. But why wouldn't she have at least texted us?'

'Because she's Diana,' I said.

'I know, but even so, while on a trip? It's a lot, even for her.'

It was. 'Maybe she lost her phone? She wouldn't even know

our numbers by heart. I don't know y'all's. Did you check your email?'

'Yes,' Margaret said. 'Only every five minutes. Nothing there, either. And no chance of any messages on Facebook or Instagram. Obviously.'

Brandon popped to mind, but he was in the city, wasn't he? There's no way he could have been here. *We* weren't even supposed to be here.

'Why don't you get some coffee?' Margaret suggested. 'I found some grounds in the freezer and just brewed a pot. No milk in the fridge, unfortunately – well, no good milk in the fridge – the carton that's there expired months ago, but it's better than nothing. We can give Diana another hour. I don't know when checkout is, because there's no damn welcome book and Diana arranged the reservation, but I doubt it's before eleven. She's probably still sleeping. She's got to be.'

So that's what we did. I drank black coffee, or what little of it my weak stomach could take, and Margaret called Diana every ten minutes or so while I used her charger to bring my phone back to life. I didn't ask Margaret about the guy, and she didn't ask me about Harry – if she'd even recognized him from the photos I had on Facebook – and we flicked through our phones, waiting.

Around ten, we headed upstairs. We took turns showering, cleaning ourselves up. Margaret said we should pack our bags, including Diana's, so things would be ready for checkout once she showed back up.

Eleven came and went. And then noon. No Diana.

Margaret's foot tapped nervously. 'We've definitely missed

checkout by now,' she said, eyes glancing to the bags sitting by the door.

'Does it matter?' I asked. 'With Diana gone?'

Over the last couple of hours, we'd tossed out every explanation we could think of. Diana had gone home with a guy, and she was still sleeping. She headed somewhere to try to buy cigarettes, and she lost her phone, and by the time she got back, the bar was closed, and she couldn't remember the address of the rental. She got sick out back, really sick, and someone took her to the ER or called her an ambulance.

'I'm only saying,' Margaret went on. 'The cleaner could walk in any moment, and some other renters could be about to show up, and –' She took a deep breath, composing herself. 'It's another thing to worry about. I'm only pointing it out.'

'Forget about that for now,' I said. 'Just focus on Diana. We have to do something. We can't just sit here.'

'Okay,' Margaret said carefully, eyes flitting to our bags once more. 'Okay,' she said again. 'You're right.'

Organized as always, Margaret made a list on her phone of every possible place we could call, concrete steps we could take instead of sitting here in limbo.

First was the bar. She put it on speaker so I could hear, too. A man answered, told us the place wasn't open yet. Margaret described Diana, asked if the guy had seen her the night before, after we left. He said he wasn't working last night, to call back around four, when the night bartenders were in.

She called the auto shop next. It was a long shot – it made no sense, really – but just in case Diana had gone to check on the car. They hadn't seen her. Obviously they hadn't.

Then we called every hospital in a thirty-mile radius, my heart beats quickening as we did, but nothing there, either.

At that point, the truly terrifying explanations began to pop up in my mind.

'Maybe Brandon found her somehow, and he got mad, and –' I paused, unable to finish the thought. 'Or maybe it wasn't even Brandon. Maybe some creep lured her away. Some *predator* or something. Maybe he has her now. Or maybe she was walking somewhere, and she got hit by a car, and she's lying in a gutter somewhere, *bleeding*.'

'Stop,' Margaret said. 'There's no point saying all this. It will only freak us out, and we have to stay level-headed.' Her eyes darted again to the bags at the door, and then she picked up her phone. 'It's after two.'

'Christ, Margaret, can you forget about the fucking checkout?'

'That's not what I mean,' she said.

I watched in horror as Margaret tapped the buttons on her phone. Three little numbers – 911 – hardly able to wrap my head around the fact that it had come to this.

'Hello,' Margaret said, her voice almost forcefully steady. 'We'd like to report a missing person.'

It was nearly an hour before the officer showed up.

Margaret stood at the sound of gravel. Feeling suddenly sick, I went to the bathroom to splash water on my face. In the mirror, I stared at my reflection as I heard Margaret open the door, heard the sound of footsteps and a walkie beeping officially.

This can't be happening. I let the water run cold across my hands. *This really can't be happening.*

By the time I was back out, the officer was standing in the living room, a piece of plastic in her hand – must be Margaret's ID. The officer was small, short and slim, with black hair tucked beneath her cap. She returned the license, and Margaret slipped it in her pocket.

'Hi,' I said. 'Sorry, I was in the bathroom. I'm Sam. Sam Lochman.'

'Officer Ramos,' she said with a nod, then pulled out a notebook. 'So you think your friend is missing?'

Hearing it out loud, it sounded awful. *Missing.*

'Diana,' Margaret said. 'Like I told you. She didn't come home last night.'

The officer nodded, but she didn't write that down. 'And how do you know she didn't go somewhere else?'

Calmly, slowly, Margaret walked her through the story, detailing the movements of all of us at the bar. Feeling desperate, I explained that the car key had been lost, and we were supposed to be on our way to Saratoga Springs, that it had been a stressful day after all the car trouble. I told her about Brandon, about how Diana wasn't even on social media because of him, about the chance – still small, since we weren't supposed to be here – that he'd followed her.

When we were done, Ramos cleared her throat. 'And who was the last person to see her?'

'Me,' I said. 'Diana was going out to the patio to see if the . . . the guy I was talking to was still there. She was planning on coming back – she asked me to order her a beer – but she never did.'

88

'So you were all drinking, then?' Officer Ramos asked.

I scoffed. 'And *why* does that matter?'

The policewoman sighed, then looked up at us. Her walkie beeped again, but she ignored it. 'Look, I can tell you what my boss is going to say – what any cop would. You were likely intoxicated. It was Friday night. People aren't making great decisions. It's possible your friend went home with someone.' She turned to Margaret. 'You just now told me that a man you didn't know prior drove you all home.' Then she turned to me. 'You say you were talking to a man as well. There's simply no way to rule out that she met someone and left the bar voluntarily.'

'But she would have *called* us,' I said angrily. 'And even if she lost her phone, she would have found a way to email us. *Something*. She wouldn't have just . . . disappeared.'

The officer's shoulders softened, as if she were trying to break it to us gently. 'I know it's scary. I've run into similar situations with friends, but nine times out of ten, instances like these, it *is* something like that. I know you're worried about her ex-husband, but like you said, you weren't even supposed to be in this town, so it seems unlikely. Maybe she met someone – maybe something one of you said pissed her off, and this morning she took the train back to' – she checked her notes – 'Brooklyn.'

I shook my head forcefully. 'She wouldn't do that. And her things are still here, anyway. She didn't leave.'

Ramos cleared her throat. 'All I can do is take her information and check databases. Hospitals. But without a sign of foul play, it's difficult. She's not elderly. She's not a minor. She doesn't have any mental handicaps – correct?'

We nodded.

'Now, do you know if there were any altercations with her

ex-husband? Any time the cops were called? That might help escalate things.'

'I don't know,' Margaret said. 'I don't think so.'

I shook my head. 'No. He wasn't abusive – not physically, I mean. He was obsessive and controlling.'

Ramos sighed. 'That means we're not going to have a lot of resources. In all likelihood, she'll turn up later this afternoon.'

'That's it?' I snapped.

'Sam,' Margaret said, but I didn't care about her rule following, not now of all times.

'Really?' I went on. 'Isn't this your *job*?' I checked my phone again. It was past three already, and every minute made this all feel so much worse. I wanted to grab the officer, shake her, tell her to take us seriously. She was a woman, too. She should fucking know better. Three city women, a town they didn't even know. Diana could have been abducted. She could have been killed, for all we knew. Brandon could have followed our SUV out of Brooklyn, all the way here.

'You have to help us,' I said. '*Please.*'

'I'll do my best,' Ramos said. 'Now, what's your friend's full name?'

'Diana Holbein,' Margaret said.

'Spell that, please.'

'D-I-A-N-A-H-O-L-B-I-E-N,' I said.

Margaret shook her head. 'No, it's E before I.'

'No,' I said. 'You're wrong.'

Officer Ramos raised an eyebrow. 'You don't know your friend's name?'

I swallowed, my throat tight, my heart beginning to race. I

90

checked my phone again, as if willing Diana to magically call. 'Of course we do. It's just that we haven't known each other that long. Trust me, it's I before E.'

'Should you look on Facebook, check?' Ramos asked.

'No,' I said. 'Diana's not on Facebook, like we told you.'

'Right,' Ramos said. 'Her email, then.'

Margaret was already on it. She turned her phone around, showing a glimpse of the chain we'd used for planning this trip. 'It's right here,' she said. 'H-O-L-B-*E*-I-N.'

Sorry, I mouthed to Margaret as Ramos jotted it down.

'Age?'

We glanced between each other briefly.

'Thirty-three,' Margaret said. 'Unless you disagree?'

I shook my head. 'No. I'm pretty sure that's right.'

'Occupation.'

'Social worker,' I said. 'She works at a practice in Manhattan. I don't know the name, though.'

Ramos nodded. 'I'll need a recent photo.'

We exchanged another look.

Ramos scoffed. 'Don't tell me this woman hated to have her picture taken.'

'It was because of Brandon,' I said. 'She was afraid it would end up on social, and he would be able to follow her.'

Ramos stared at us, as if we were making it all up, as if we'd created a woman out of thin air. 'I'll need a physical description, then.'

Margaret gave it.

'And to confirm, she didn't have a car, a license plate we could run?'

'No,' I said. 'We all live in Brooklyn. The car we have is a rental. It's at the shop, like we said.'

Ramos cleared her throat. 'Listen, I'll get a report started, with the info we do have. Hopefully she'll show soon. I have a feeling she will.'

She shook our hands, and like that, she was gone.

We called Diana every five minutes, the phone calls like a metronome, marking her absence, all the things that could have already happened to her.

I practically jumped out of my skin when Margaret's phone finally rang. It was almost five o'clock.

'Is it Diana?' I asked. 'Is she calling you?'

Margaret shook her head.

'Hello,' she answered. Her eyebrows rose. She mouthed, *Ramos*. She put the phone on speaker and set it between us.

'Did you find anything?' I asked. 'Did she turn up?'

'No, I'm sorry. No news on that front,' Ramos said, her voice echoing through the room. 'But I wanted to tell you, I ran her name through all the state databases. I was hoping to pull a photo for the report. The more information we have, the better —'

'And?' I interrupted her. 'What is it?'

'I checked multiple databases,' Ramos went on. 'I even tried multiple spellings. The thing is . . .'

A pause, the air tense between us.

'There's no record of Diana Holbein at all.'

12

MARGARET

Carefully, I ended the call and set my phone on the coffee table, forcing myself to keep my hands steady and my breaths calm. Sam was freaking out enough for the both of us, fidgeting like a three-year-old in time-out.

'This doesn't make any sense,' she said, voice wavering. Translucent blue rings shaded her eyes. She looked like she could be sick any moment.

Officer Ramos, her voice firm and professional, had been more than clear. There was no Diana Holbein. E before I or I before E, it didn't matter. Not in any of the state databases, or even the state licensing board for social workers. The closest match, in fact, Ramos had told us after pressing, was a Diana Holbeck, who was eighty-eight years old and lived in Queens.

'She has to be wrong,' Sam said.

I scratched at the back of my neck. 'Maybe that was her maiden name,' I said. 'Perhaps everything is under her married name, and we don't know it.'

'No,' Sam said. 'Diana told me she never took Brandon's

name, I swear, because I didn't take Harry's, and – and we bonded about it.'

'Then maybe she was using a different name so he couldn't keep track of her? It would make sense, wouldn't it?' Even as I said it, it didn't feel quite right, yesterday's pit stop playing over and over again in my mind.

What happened to you, Diana?

What are you caught up in?

Sam's stomach gurgled, and she rose abruptly, dashing toward the downstairs bathroom and slamming the door behind her.

A clank of porcelain and then a scraping, retching sound, seeping between the crack at the bottom of the door, invading the room like something rancid. I knocked on the door softly, as if I didn't want it, or her, to break. 'Sam.'

'I'm *fine*,' she said.

I took three steps back, waiting, my eyes tracing a crack along the plaster of the high ceiling. The rental felt aged, almost decrepit, like it could crumble any moment, bury us beneath the rubble. A shadow moved slowly across the old hardwood floors, the shape of a tree from outside, the sun crawling closer to the horizon.

The door whipped open, and I tried to be positive, upbeat. 'You look better,' I said. It wasn't a lie. The color was back in her cheeks, as if the monster inside had been expelled.

Sam wiped a bit of water from the bottom of her lip. 'I thought of something while I was in there. I can't believe I didn't mention it before. I was so frazzled by everything.'

'What?' I asked.

Sam blinked slowly. 'I heard someone last night, out on the

porch. I was still drunk, and I assumed it was Diana coming home, and I shut the windows, but if it wasn't her –'

'It was Alex,' I said, interrupting her. 'The guy I was with last night.'

'But why would he –'

'He broke a glass getting water, and he didn't want us to find out, so he took it out to his truck. He told me this morning when I asked him about it.'

Sam raised an eyebrow. 'That's weird, no?'

I shrugged. 'Out of everything that's happened, I'd say it's not that weird, in the grand scheme of things.'

'All right,' Sam said. 'Fine. So what are we going to do, then? The cops aren't doing shit, so it's up to us.'

Pressing my hands to my thighs, I did what I'd gotten good at doing this last year and a half: I disassociated, turning the feelings off as if I were controlling a dial I could turn up and down at will. It was the only way to move forward without getting lost in emotion, a trick I'd found useful in not becoming completely consumed. Get numb, and then get organized. I could do this. It was how I'd managed to focus on my work through everything, how I'd forced myself to stop opening credit cards, to try to get a handle on the damage. It was what I could do that Lars simply couldn't. On the other hand, at least Lars's problems could one day be solved with AA, if he chose to get help. I'd kicked mine, but they still trailed after me, remnants of those darker days. Bills in the mail. Bills in my suitcase now. Fifteen of them, fresh and new.

'Margaret,' Sam said, and her eyes were wide and childlike, scared. They couldn't comprehend tragedy in the same way I could. 'What now?'

'Sorry,' I said. 'Should we try to book another night here?'

Sam sighed, exasperated. 'Clearly no one is coming. A cleaning service would have been here already if someone was. They'll charge us for another night – who cares? I mean, what should we do to try to find Diana?'

'Okay,' I said. 'We should start with the bar, right? The guy who served us last night should be there by now. We can ask him if he saw Diana again after we left, see if we can find out anything to help sort this out.'

'Yes,' Sam said, eyes lighting up as if this could all be solved so easily, far too much hope in her voice.

'Yes, let's do that.'

It took twenty-five minutes to get a car to come to us. Twenty-five minutes spent calling Diana and googling 'Diana Holbein', 'Diana Holbein New York', and 'Diana Holbein social worker', without so much as one promising hit. Eventually, we were tucked in the back of a blue Hyundai, curving away from the place that would be ours for another night.

We wound through thickets of tall trees, ivy-covered stone houses, red weatherworn barns, and meadows of softly rippling grass. Lars and I had imagined coming up here sometimes, especially after we found out I was pregnant. The five-year plan had been to buy something a few hours north of the city, however far we had to go to afford something nice enough to raise our baby. He could take a train down to his auditions – or crash with friends on a longer shooting day – and I could run my copywriting business from home: a project here, a project there.

We could surround our child with fresh air, creeks, streams, places to run and a dog to run around in them. Do the rat race on our terms, not theirs.

Of course, that turned out to be nothing more than a fantasy, one of the many ways Lars and I got ahead of ourselves, far too quickly.

The car pulled into the gravel parking lot of Eamon's bar. It looked different now, moody in the evening's dusk; the woods surrounding the structure deep green and thirsty for summer, the converted-garage windows yawning open.

Sam paid, and we got out, the sounds of the country meeting us at once: rustling grass, a knocking that might be a woodpecker and the distant purr of traffic. There was no sun; instead, it was overcast; there was a distinct chill in the air, and my only jacket was back at the rental, hanging on the staircase's newel post to air out, still reeking of Sam's vomit.

Inside, it was warmer, at least, and smelled lemony and pungent. The floor shone, freshly scrubbed after a night of debauchery.

It wasn't empty, but the people who filled it gave it a different vibe now, eating burgers or wings, talking animatedly, talking *soberly*, their beers and drinks more of an afterthought than an intention. A couple of hours on, and it would look quite different, succumb to the seedy lure of a Saturday night. I checked the time. It was after six o'clock. My stomach grumbled suddenly, intently. We hadn't had a single thing to eat all day. Still, I doubted I could handle much, even if the food was in front of me. I never had been able to eat in a crisis.

The bearded guy who'd served us last night looked up from

behind the bar. 'Aha,' he said, rolling up the sleeves of his Pink Floyd shirt. 'The margarita ladies return. I hope you're not feeling them too hard.'

I cleared my throat. 'They were strong, that's for sure, but that's not why we're here.'

'Left something behind?' he asked, grabbing a rag and wiping down the bar. 'I can get the lost and found for you.' For a moment, I imagined Diana tucked carefully inside a cardboard box, safe and sound.

'No, it's not that. We can't find our friend,' I said, my voice wavering only slightly. 'We couldn't find her last night, either, and we were hoping she would find her way back to our rental, but she didn't. She still hasn't turned up, and we were wondering if you saw her. I think we left around one a.m. Perhaps you saw her after that?'

The bartender's eyebrows scrunched up with concern. 'Did you call the police?'

Sam scoffed, but I pressed on. 'Yes,' I said. 'They say there's nothing they can do at this point.'

'Useless,' he said, dropping his rag, his gaze ping-ponging between Sam and me. 'The woman with silver hair, right? Wide-set eyes?'

'Yes,' I said. 'Her name's Diana.'

Is it, though?

The man crossed his arms, resting them on his belly. He got a faraway look in his eyes, as if cataloguing last night's events. 'No,' he said finally. 'I don't think I saw her. Only when she was with you.'

The flash of hope dissipated instantly. Damn it. 'Then can we go out back? That's the last place we saw her.'

'Sure,' the guy said. 'Have at it.'

I turned to follow Sam, who was already beelining toward the back.

'Oh, and miss?'

'Yes?'

'I hope you find her,' he said. 'I'm sorry that happened.'

I blinked slowly. 'Thanks. We are, too.'

The back patio was overcast and dim, and it looked even smaller now that it wasn't packed with smokers, the space shadowed by the clouds, the woods already dark.

Sam walked the edge of the property, then returned to me. 'Obviously she's not here,' she said.

I nodded. 'Obviously.'

'Should we check out front?' Sam asked. 'In case she . . . in case, I don't know, a car?'

My spine tingled with fear. 'I suppose we should.'

Together, we walked around the side of the bar and then back and forth in every haphazard row of the gravel parking lot, then up and down the road, a couple of blocks each way. No Diana, which was a relief.

I was about to call us a car when Sam grabbed my arm. 'Wait,' she said. 'Maybe we should check the lost and found? What if she lost her wallet or her phone? If we had her ID, we could make sure to get her name exactly right.'

'Good idea,' I said.

Back inside, the bartender retrieved the box quickly, and together, in almost the exact same spot where Diana had ordered us all margaritas, we picked through nubby sweaters and stale T-shirts.

'Hang on, I remember something,' he said.

Sam's head snapped up eagerly, dropping a threadbare scarf back into the box. 'You do?'

'There was a guy here, asking after you.'

'Alex?' I asked. 'The guy I was with?'

'No,' he said. 'I know him. It was someone from out of town, I think, someone I hadn't seen before.'

'What did he look like?'

The bartender sighed. 'I'm terrible at these things. Medium height, medium build. Brownish hair. Brown eyes, I think. White guy.'

'Any tattoos?' Sam asked. 'Glasses? A hat? Anything identifying?'

'Not really,' he said. 'Just an average guy.'

'Beard? Clean-shaven?'

'No beard,' he said. 'Maybe a little stubble? It's hard to say. I see a million people a night.'

'What time was it?' I asked.

'Late,' he said. 'Close to two, or maybe a little after. We make a fuss about last call at one-thirty, but we don't really clear everyone out until closer to two-fifteen.'

'What did he say?' Sam asked. 'How did you know he was asking about us?'

'That's the only reason I remember it,' the bartender said. 'He said, "What happened to the ladies who were ordering margaritas?" I told him I hadn't seen you in a while. I assumed he was trying to pick one of you up. It was that time of night.'

My pulse sped, a persistent pounding, and Sam and I exchanged a look.

'You don't remember anything else?' I asked.

'No,' he said. 'I'm really sorry.'

We were quiet as we walked out of the bar, back into the parking lot.

I ordered a car, preparing myself for the interminable twenty-minute wait, and Sam stared straight ahead, face pale.

'Brandon,' she said finally, turning to me. 'Christ. It had to be Brandon.'

13

SAM

Dutifully, I picked up a slice of pepperoni-mushroom pizza and took a bite. It was dry and bland, like cardboard, but I ate it anyway.

Margaret had gone into full mom mode since we'd gotten home from the bar, insisting we have something to eat and finding a place that would deliver us pizza and a salad – *don't forget to eat your greens!* While we waited for the food, she called the police station and left a message for Officer Ramos, detailing what the bartender had told us. I went upstairs and returned our suitcases to our rooms, then riffled through Diana's while texting Harry, hoping to find anything that could act as a lead. When I was back downstairs, empty-handed, Margaret was working on a new list of to-dos: Check in with the auto shop about replicating the car key. Try to figure out the owners of the rental to book another night. Etc.

With the fork Margaret had laid out for me, I ate some more salad, but the dressing was well on its way to congealing, and my stomach roiled. 'What if we could have helped her,' I said miserably. 'We just *left* her.'

Margaret pressed her palms firmly against the table. 'We've been through this,' she said. 'We looked and looked. We didn't have another choice. Don't take on guilt that isn't yours. Trust me.'

'Maybe if we'd looked harder, stayed longer. Maybe if I hadn't been so drunk.'

Margaret ran a finger along the rim of her plate. She was the one who'd wanted us to eat, and yet her portion was largely untouched. 'I don't think that would have made a difference. I promise you I looked everywhere.'

I took another bite, finishing my slice. Eating had always been a comfort when the world got too hard for me – my Grub-Hub history since Harry left was proof enough of that. 'But if it was Brandon, maybe we could have done something? If he asked about us that close to closing, that means when we left, she wasn't with him. Right?'

Margaret stiffened, sitting up straighter against her chair. 'Maybe,' she said. 'But even if it was Brandon, we don't know anything about him. Not so much as a hint of where he could be – or where *she* could be. And we don't know it's him, after all. All we know is that someone asked about us. It could have been a guy who wanted to hit on one of us, like the bartender thought.'

I stood, picking up my clean plate. 'You done?'

She nodded, handing me hers. I tossed her food in the trash and set the dishes in the sink, rinsing them clean. I would have just left them, if it was my place, but I had a feeling it would drive Margaret nuts if I did. Then I reread my texts to Harry.

I need to talk to you

It's important

Can you call me please?

He hadn't written back. Fucker.

'I'm going to make a phone call,' I said. 'My cell service is shit downstairs. I'm going outside.'

'Sure,' Margaret said carefully. 'You okay?'

'I mean, I'm not, but whatever,' I said.

Her face fell.

'I'm sorry,' I said. 'I just –'

'No,' she said, rising from her chair. '*I'm* sorry. It was a stupid question.'

I managed a half smile, then walked out of the kitchen and through the hallway onto the porch. It was cool out, like it had been last night, but there was a dampness in the air, too, like it might rain soon. A pair of lights illuminated the remnants of my puke still caked onto the slats from the night before. It was dark, dreary and sullen, even the stars obscured by cloud cover.

A chill ran up my spine as I wondered where Diana was, how cold it would get in the dead of night, if she was outside or somewhere safe.

I dialed her again. When I got the generic message for what felt like the millionth time, I did what I knew I had to do.

I called Harry.

It rang five times before going to voicemail.

'Hey, it's Harry. Leave me a message. Or don't. Your call.'

I hung up, anger surging within me, and sent him a text.

My friend is fucking missing. Can you call me?

Back inside, Margaret was loading the dishwasher. I checked the app for available cars. There was one, twenty minutes away. I called it, telling myself I could always cancel if Harry called in the meantime. Then I went up to my room, carefully put on makeup – concealer, eyeliner, mascara, blush. On my phone, I watched as the car slowly made its way toward me. I waited for Harry to call. He didn't.

The car was two minutes away. Was I really doing this? Yes, I was doing this. I had to.

Downstairs, Margaret was still in the kitchen, wiping down countertops and arranging the salt and pepper just so.

'I'm going out,' I said.

She jumped, flipping around. 'What?'

'I can't sit here, doing nothing,' I said. 'I'll lose my mind.'

'But where are you going?'

'The guy I was talking to last night . . .' I started.

Margaret's eyebrows knitted up. 'Wait. Wasn't that Harry?'

So she did know. Shame burned my cheeks, and my body thrummed, remembering. 'I didn't know if you knew.'

'I didn't for sure,' Margaret said. 'But I thought it looked like him.'

'Well, it was him,' I said. 'We broke down in his town. What are the odds?'

Margaret pursed her lips. 'What happened with him?'

'I really don't want to talk about all the details right now.'

She nodded. 'Okay.'

I scratched at a piece of peeling paint on the wall until it came right off. 'Anyway, he was out back, and Diana went out there to see if he was still there. He might have seen her.'

'Did you try calling him?'

'Yeah,' I said, without elaborating.

Margaret walked over, pulled my fingers from the peeling paint. 'Do you want me to come with you?'

'No,' I said.

'For moral support?' she added. 'We should stick together, right?'

I turned and walked back into the hallway, grabbing my purse from where it was hooked over one bannister of the staircase, Margaret's jacket still airing out on the other. As if on cue, I heard the purr of a car's engine out front and an alert popped up on my phone, announcing the driver's arrival.

'Sorry,' I said. 'I need to do this on my own.'

From the cab, I gazed at the array of windows, a veritable shadow box. Above them, the roof ran parallel to the ground – a sandwich house, in the style of Frank Lloyd Wright – a dream home, one any of us would kill for. The house was perfect for a creative director like Harry. Every line so precise, so perpendicular, so planned, like a rendering meticulously crafted in InDesign.

In a flash, I saw us, Harry and me, pressed against that tree in the back. Saw myself, too inebriated, too desperate, to have any goddamn self-respect.

'Here good?' the driver, a jovial kid from one of the colleges nearby, asked.

'A little farther,' I said, pointing to a grove of what looked like maples on the edge of the property. 'That's perfect,' I said. 'Thank you. And, err, you don't have to wait for me to get inside. I'm good.'

'Whatever you say, miss.'

Beneath the cover of foliage, I steadied one hand on the tree trunk as I adjusted the strap of one of my sandals, decided it was too tight and then adjusted it again, trying to breathe slowly but failing completely.

I'm not a stalker.

I'm not one of those people who can't let go, who follow their ex around, delude themselves into thinking that it's all going to be okay when it's not.

Yes, I failed to tell my parents, my sister and my friends about Harry leaving me.

Yes, I called him a lot right after he left me, as anyone would have done.

Please just leave us alone.

Yes, I came here before. But only once.

Again, I checked my calls and texts. Nothing.

I closed my eyes for a moment, remembering Harry in that way, before we were us, when he was the executive creative director filling in at the agency where I worked.

I'd heard about Harry before I met him. He was the person you called when shit was hitting the fan on a project, when the agency was about to lose a client. He'd made a business of swooping in to save the day. It was his *thing*.

I hadn't even looked twice when he'd walked in that morning. I mainly went for guys my age, the ones with thick glasses and unkempt hair. But I did notice that he was prompt that morning, whereas most ECDs rolled in somewhere between eleven and noon. *And* that he repeated my name when I shook his hand, as if he wanted to make sure he got it right. Which is nothing, I know, but in the advertising world, you can't swing a cat without hitting at least five douchebag creative directors, and instantly I could tell Harry wasn't like the others.

Everything changed a week later, after the other art director on the project walked off abruptly and the copywriter assigned (Margaret was at a different agency then) had an emergency and had to leave early, and suddenly it was just Harry and me, papers spread out across two wooden tables in the sprawling loft space in SoHo, trying to figure out how to inject 'meaning and purpose' (a client directive) into a multimillion-dollar campaign for discount sneakers. We'd been through three rounds already before Harry came on, and none of them had been 'purposeful' enough. He was a ringer, and this was our last chance to get it right.

We ordered sushi to the office, and we dug into the stash of wine HR kept tucked away for special occasions, and over sashimi and paper cups of thirty-dollar Bordeaux, we stopped talking about sneakers altogether. Harry told me how he'd originally wanted to be an architect, but he'd never been good enough at math, and I confessed that I'd wanted to be a painter, but it had seemed like an absurd thing to go after if you weren't independently wealthy, and so I'd studied graphic arts instead. And then, suddenly, we were talking about art – and my semester abroad in Florence, one I'd put on a private Sallie Mae loan I was still paying off – and sunlit afternoons in the piazzas, and the way the olive oil was so rich there, so much better, how it tasted as green as it looked. Harry was telling me how he dreamed of spending a year in Italy, getting a villa and working remotely, buying bread from shops and pouring Chianti from jugs. Rolling his own pasta and getting at least a little bit fat.

As Harry cleaned up our molded plastic containers, our eyes caught, and for a second, I could see it, our future unspooling, long and stretchy as a piece of handmade fettuccine. And I felt it, somewhere deep. Harry and I. *We have something. Already, we have something that most people don't.*

Nothing happened, of course. We were professional. We finished our wine and slapped together a 'meaningful' sneaker campaign, which the client ate up the next morning, but in the cab that night, bundled up in scarves and heading east over the Queensboro Bridge, the lights of the city sparkling like diamonds, the old Silvercup sign from the '20s mammoth and tall, watching over me, it began to lightly snow. And in that moment, I felt warmth pulsing through me, a warmth I hadn't felt in so very long, from my heart to the tips of my fingers. I felt promise – of what, I wasn't sure – but of something, that much I knew.

That was a year and a half ago now. So much had happened in such a short time, and I had been so very naive.

Slowly, I walked along the edge of Harry and Elizabeth's property. Through the overcast sky, the moonlight tossed terrible shadows into the road, every tree like a giant. Prowling.

I picked up my pace.

It was so dark on their street, not so much as a streetlight. There was one house across the road, but like theirs, it was set far back.

The path up to their perfect house was winding, nothing

rigid or geometric about it. Bluestone, uneven and natural. Pieces jutting out, each on a different plane.

One of them caught my toe, and I tripped, my hands landing on the stone, stopping myself before my knees hit the ground. I stood, catching my breath, and brushed my shaking hands against the sides of my jeans. I counted to five, trying to stay calm.

I took another step forward, and that's when I spotted her, sitting in the living room, her back to me. Houses like this never have curtains – it would disturb the perfection of it all. Instead they're lit-up dioramas, everyone on display.

Even from this angle, it was easy to see: Elizabeth was more beautiful than I had ever been – and would ever be. Her hair hung down over the midcentury sofa, glossy and thick and deepest brown. Even the way she sat was graceful. Relaxed but stunning, like those Degas drawings I'd fallen in love with in Paris. A woman, reclined.

My eyes cased the room, but among the minimal furniture and the sculptural chandelier, I didn't see Harry. It was no surprise – he often retreated into the bedroom at night, reading a book, or tinkering with one of his side projects on his Mac-Book Pro.

There was no way around it. I would have to go through her to talk to Harry. But if he *had* seen Diana, even for a moment, it would be worth all the humiliation, every ounce of her wrath. I didn't know a single other soul at the bar last night, and the police had made it clear that they weren't going to do a thing – Harry was all I had.

I swallowed, my chest tight, and walked the rest of the path, up to the sheltered patio. The door was painted a bold char-treuse that I never would have chosen but seemed somehow to fit. I raised my finger to the bell and pressed.

It was instant – the jolt of her shoulders, the quick rise from the sofa.

I stepped into the shadows before she turned around, nervously shifting my weight from foot to foot, afraid if she saw me she wouldn't come to the door.

My cheeks burned. I couldn't believe it, that soon I'd be face-to-face with her, the woman he'd left me for. The woman he'd blown up our union to be with.

I wanted to melt away – fucking disappear – turn to nothing and seep between the cracks of the bluestone sidewalk.

The door opened slowly, and I stepped forward, into the light.

Elizabeth's reaction was immediate, her eyes widening, her perfect cheekbones almost protruding. 'What are –' she stammered. 'What are you doing here?'

I reached for the doorjamb, in case she wanted to slam the door in my face.

'I need to talk to Harry,' I said. 'It's not about – it has nothing to do with us.'

'Haven't you already done enough?' she asked.

I felt a thickness in my throat as I pictured us back against those trees – he hadn't told her, had he?

'Can you ask him to come down? My friend is missing, and I need to know if he saw her.'

Her eyes narrowed. 'Are you serious? Do you honestly expect me to believe that? I know you've been here before. I'm not stupid.'

'I know,' I said. 'But it's true. I wish it wasn't, but it is. Please.' I stepped forward, raising my voice. 'Harry?'

Elizabeth was too quick for me. She forced me back and pulled the door shut behind her.

'What the hell do you think you're doing?'

'*Please.*'

'Just leave,' Elizabeth said. 'Harry's not even here.'

'What?' I asked. 'Where is he?'

'Leave,' she said again. 'Don't make me call the cops. Don't make me tell them what you did before.'

'Will you just – when he comes home, will you tell him to call me? It's important.'

'You think I, of all people, would do *you* a favor?' she asked. 'You must be out of your damn mind.'

'Please,' I said. 'I need to ask him if he saw her.'

'Stay away from my house and away from my family,' she said. 'I already told you – I don't ever want to see you again.'

'I know,' I said. 'But this is different. This is . . .' My voice trailed off, my words lodging, sticking – peanut butter in my throat.

Elizabeth's tone was suddenly desperate. 'Just leave us alone,' she said. 'You've already proven your point. You've already won.'

112

14 | MARGARET

I wasn't used to being alone; I'd never properly gotten accustomed to it. Lars and I had met so young, and before him there had been roommates, Chloe and Jessica, fellow would-be actors, standing in the kitchen of our cramped fifth-floor walk-up apartment to vent about auditions and service-industry jobs.

Lars and I, we'd been *that* couple, the ones who never seem to be on their own, who share not only a bed, but friends, hobbies, and in our case, a profession. If we weren't working, we were together, and in the early days, there were times when we even shared that, when I'd pick up shifts at his place of employment or he at mine.

The credit cards were the first secret I ever kept from him. One might think it would have been hard to open them without him knowing, but it was surprisingly easy to apply: a couple of clicks, and the world was yours. The companies even give you a temporary number so you don't have to wait for the hard copy to arrive.

It's not like I was out there buying Gucci handbags. It was a 'personal development course' that Chloe had recommended when I opened up to her about everything that had happened with the pregnancy and how hard it had become to move past it, despite the sliding-scale therapy Lars and I had carefully budgeted for. The course was nearly a thousand dollars for one weekend, two days in a conference room in midtown Manhattan, where you could learn to 'redefine what's possible' and 'create a fundamental shift in your perceptions'. It sounded a little cult-y, but Chloe was a fairly level-headed person, and she said it had helped her let go of her childhood trauma. Lars and I were barely scraping by between medical bills and decade-old student loans. I didn't want to ask him to take a big chunk from our joint account, or for the charge to show up on the credit card we shared.

With Chloe's encouragement ('This is for you, you know, not Lars; *he* didn't have to carry a baby he never got to meet'), I opened a new credit card in my name only.

I told Lars I had to work that weekend on a last-minute client project, and I went.

The course helped, in its way, all those exercises, all those promises to let go of what was 'blocking me', preventing me from realizing my full potential. Of course, it hadn't been enough. There was another course: longer this time, more advanced. And there were dinners with friends I'd met there, drinks after, and it was easy not to care quite so much about budgeting when it was all going on a card Lars didn't know about.

To get me through the time between courses, there were therapeutic massages designed to target the places where the body holds grief, and there were pink and purple healing crystals from the shop Chloe recommended, faceted with hope. There was a Reiki healer, there were yoga classes, there was acupuncture and a guy who promised to realign my chakras. In Brooklyn, there were a million ways to spend money in the pursuit of 'self-care'. Chichi, woo-woo and vaguely culturally appropriative, but it didn't really matter, did it? For a length of time, anywhere from a few moments to a few hours, I felt something again. The emotions came back.

Now I stared at my phone, wondering if I should call Lars. Today was the day, after all, and I hadn't heard from him since last night, which was surprising.

I began typing.

I'm sorry to leave you on your own. I know this is hard for both of us.

Slowly, I deleted each letter. I needed to set boundaries with him. I needed, at least, to try. I placed the phone facedown on the coffee table and surveyed the room. There was a stereo in the corner beneath the TV we hadn't bothered to figure out. I briefly considered turning on the TV, but scouring Netflix for something to watch felt like an enormous amount of work. Needing something to fill the space left behind by Sam's departure, I turned to the stereo instead. In moments, Madonna's voice filled the room: the opening beats of 'Like a Prayer', pop-y and heretical.

The phone vibrated against the table, and I braced for something from Lars, prayed for something from Diana, but when I turned it over, there was excitement instead. That flip-flopping, roller-coaster feeling I'd been told that women felt in their third trimester. A flip-flop I hadn't experienced since my early days with Lars.

Hey there, it's Alex

My lips parted as I stared at his message, a tingling feeling creeping into the tips of my fingers. They hovered there, not knowing what to type.

Another text.

You guys find your friend? I didn't hear from you. I hope your silence means everything's okay and you're on your way to Saratoga Springs?

The tingling in my fingers halted, and guilt, heavy and oily, coated my stomach. How could I be sitting here, pining over Alex? Happy and excited, when Diana could be . . . who even knew? I tried to figure out how to put it: *No, actually, my friend never came back, and now Sam, the one ally I have in all of this, has gone off to see her ex on her own. How's your night?*

I forced myself to type.

Diana never came home, so we're staying another night. We reported everything to the police, but they don't seem to know what to do . . .

The phone rang almost immediately, vibrating urgently in my hands. I was so startled I dropped the damn thing. It clanked against the hardwood but thankfully didn't break. I couldn't spare a hundred dollars to fix the screen right now.

There are fifteen hundred-dollar bills sitting in your suitcase upstairs.

'Hello,' I said, attempting to keep my voice calm as I got up and turned down Madonna. 'I didn't think your generation liked the actual phone.'

'And here I thought yours knew better than to obsess about a silly little age gap,' Alex said, his voice warm.

'Touché.'

The line was silent, a sensation I'd come to hate, after one too many phone calls delivering bad news. Finally: 'I didn't want to bother you or anything,' Alex said. 'But I thought you might need someone to talk to. God, what happened?'

'Nothing happened,' I said, because that was the truth of it. 'You left, and I kept calling Diana. Sam eventually woke up, and she called her, too, and we kept expecting her to show up, but she never did. So we called the police.'

'Shit,' he said. 'And what are the police doing?'

'There's not much they can do,' I said. 'This officer came shortly after we called, and –' My voice caught.

'What, Margaret?' I liked the way he said my name, the way he enunciated the end. Marga*rette*.

'We didn't have any photos of Diana. She didn't like having them taken because she kept a low profile. She has an obsessive ex. This guy, Brandon.'

'Okay. Does that mess up the report?'

'Kind of,' I said. 'The officer called us after she left. She was trying to get started, but she couldn't find any record of Diana at all, not with the name she'd given us.'

'Well, that's fucking creepy,' Alex said, refreshingly matter-of-fact. 'That's like true-crime Netflix-special creepy.'

'It gets worse. We went back to the bar to ask the bartender from last night if he saw Diana, and he says some guy was asking about the "ladies who were ordering margaritas." We're worried it was Brandon.'

'Damn,' Alex said. 'That's also creepy.' He paused, as if collecting his thoughts. 'So what are you two doing now? Just sitting in the rental?'

'No,' I said. 'Sam left, actually.'

'What? Why?'

'Apparently her ex was at the bar last night, too,' I said. 'She went to try to talk to him to see if he saw Diana.'

'Damn,' Alex said. 'That's a lot of exes.'

'I know.'

'So you're alone, then?' he asked.

'Yes,' I said, my eyes casing the home. Old and spacious, a place that had held so many lives, so many hopes and heart-breaks. The kind of place that made you feel lonelier than ever.

'Do you want company? I just got home from my shift.'

I hesitated, and as I did, there was a creak upstairs, right above my head. Nothing more than an old house settling. I'd grown up in one, so I knew this, but still, I hated that Sam wasn't here with me to fill the space with chatter, noise.

'Yes,' I said, trying not to sound so eager. 'Yes, I do.'

Alex drove me to his place, apologizing on the way for his dog, who had separation anxiety and shouldn't be left again tonight.

He promised to get me home by midnight, like a polite prom date, so Sam wouldn't have to be on her own.

I texted Sam as we pulled up to a tiny bungalow with an oak tree in front.

Alex asked me to come over, and I didn't want to be
alone. I'll be back by midnight. Hope you're okay.

'It's not much,' Alex said, as we got out of the car. 'And I didn't have a ton of time to clean. But it's better than leaving Rosie.'

'Rosie? That's your dog?' I asked, following him up to a slatted front porch that looked like it had been freshly stained.

He nodded, digging in his pocket for the house keys. 'Yes, after Eleanor Roosevelt. She's always been my favorite first lady.'

I smiled.

He opened the door, and I followed him inside. The smell hit me first: a light hint of sweat, stale coffee and a twist of weed. It wasn't a dorm-room scent by any means, but it was musky, salty, not covered up by soy candles or lavender cleaning products, the scent of a man.

Rosie bounded up to me, sniffing and licking my hand. She was the size and coloring of a golden retriever, only her snout was shorter and her ears were, too. I sank my hands into her fur, soft and a touch curly, and she nuzzled me as I knelt down to greet her. I had wanted a dog so badly with Lars. I had wanted so many things. I stood, composing myself.

'She'll calm down after five minutes or so,' Alex said,

taking my bag and hanging it on a set of hand-carved hooks. 'If you grab a seat on the couch, she'll come up and put her head in your lap. It's the sweetest thing.'

I did, sinking into a beat-up leather sofa that sat, off-center, against the opposite wall, taking in the room as Rosie placed her head gently on top of my legs.

The living room, if you could call it that, was tiny, holding the sofa, one chair and a coffee table strewn with coasters, junk mail and paraphernalia. It bled into the kitchen, which wasn't much more than a butcher's block – about three feet worth of counter space – an oven and a fridge. A table that looked like it had been sawed in half sat propped against the front windows, two mismatched chairs nestled into it.

'I'm going to heat up something frozen,' Alex said. 'I haven't had a chance to eat. You want anything?'

'No, thanks,' I said. 'I already ate.'

'A beer, then?' he asked. 'I brought home a growler of our just-released summer ale.'

I nodded, eager to take the edge off.

Alex tossed a tray into the oven, set the timer, then popped open the growler and poured two glasses tall, head foaming above the rim. He set them on the coffee table, then turned to me. Rosie, for her part, didn't move from her new favorite spot. I scratched behind her ears, her presence a balm.

We grabbed our pint glasses, printed with neon-green logos. 'I feel weird cheers-ing,' Alex said. 'After everything that's happened.'

'Then let's just drink,' I said.

He nodded. 'Okay.'

We did, and the beer tasted good, flowery, citrusy, something you should drink in the sunshine in the summer.

Alex set his glass down, but I held mine tight. 'I'm so sorry about your friend,' he said. 'It's crazy. Do you think –'

'I don't know what to think,' I interrupted him, quickly taking another sip. 'Sam thinks Diana's ex did something, she seems so sure of it.'

'But you?' Alex prompted. He sat only a couple of inches from me, and it's like I could feel his warmth, emanating from beneath a well-worn T-shirt. 'You're not so sure?'

I twisted one of the earrings I always wore. 'What the bartender told us, it could have meant anything and nothing.'

'And what about the name business?' Alex asked. 'Do you think it was just some misunderstanding? Or do you think she, I don't know, lied to you?'

I know she was comfortable lying about some things, at least.

'I don't know,' I said. 'I told Sam it was probably a misunderstanding, but it's hard to be sure. I've only known Diana a couple of months, and it seems strange that nothing would turn up in any databases. Sam said she never took Brandon's last name, and that would have been the most reasonable explanation.'

Alex took a sip of his beer. 'I hope she turns up,' he said. 'God, she's got to turn up. People get drunk at Eamon's, sure, but nothing like this has ever happened. People don't just . . . they don't . . . disappear.'

His eyes locked on mine then, and he swallowed.

'What?' I asked.

He blinked twice, then gazed into his beer.

'What is it?'

Alex patted his lap, and Rosie leapt off the couch, then walked around our knees, nestling against his legs. He rested his hand below her collar.

'It's so weird, you know. I mean —' He offered a half smile. 'Meeting you was so nice. And then this happened. I'm glad you're here, but I hate that it's for this reason.'

Heat crept into my cheeks, a flush of pleasure, in spite of everything. Still, it was too much, too soon. I stood. 'Can I use your bathroom, actually?'

Alex nodded. 'Second door on the left.'

I padded down the hallway, relishing the thrill of being in a new man's home, but before I got to the bathroom, I was paralyzed by the sight through the first door. It was wide open, a dim lamp illuminating the space, and I couldn't help but look.

On one side was a bed in the shape of a race car, blue and red, with a comforter speckled with shooting stars. On the floor, a rug covered in city streets, perfect for pushing Matchbox cars around. The walls were yellow, and a pint-sized bookshelf held story after story. The dresser was small, too, short enough for a four-year-old to pick out his clothes with only a little bit of help.

And in the opposite corner, perhaps the most heartwrenching thing of all. Stacks of presents, all shapes and sizes, wrapped in baseball paper, topped with sticky bows. A Christmas morning waiting to be graced with a kid's presence. At the bar, Alex had told me that he couldn't help it, that he sent stuff in the mail, too, but that all year, he would buy things, little things and big things for Luke to unwrap the moment he arrived.

There was a sense of waiting here, of something's-about-to-happen, a wire pulled so taut you could almost feel its vibrations. A physical embodiment of how much Alex loved his kid, how much he missed him all year.

My stomach clenched up. I'd never had a bedroom or a nursery for my child, or even so much as a corner set aside, but I'd imagined it all, of course I had. I found out he was a boy right before I found out the pregnancy was high-risk. 'You're having a boy,' they'd said to me on the phone, when I'd answered that number with the Manhattan area code. And in that moment, I forgot, however briefly, that they'd said they'd only call if something was wrong. In that moment, he became Timothy. In that moment, he went from a clump of cells, a kidney bean on the ultrasound, to a little person. A little man just waiting to be.

But that moment was so short.

'A risk factor has come up on the test. We recommend meeting with a genetic counselor. We can help you set up the appointment.'

I felt shame sometimes, at how much all of this affected me. We weren't even twenty weeks along, by the end. Some people gave birth to stillborn babies. Some had babies who died at a year old. *They* were able to move on with their lives. *They* didn't wade into seemingly insurmountable credit card debt while their husband drank away their sorrows. *Their* marriages didn't implode.

I forced myself to turn away. I didn't want Alex to find me staring like this outside his son's room. In the bathroom, I tried to pull myself together. Diana was gone, and I had to stay focused. I could not think about my son right now, even on this, the anniversary of my due date. I could not think about Lars.

My phone vibrated, urgent and loud against the counter.

When I looked at it, my heart clenched up.

The text was from Lars, but it was the last thing in the world I'd expected.

I know you fucked that guy. I saw you last night, youuu fucking slut.

SUNDAY

15

SAM

For the second morning in a row, I woke with a headache.

Shoving the covers aside, I sat up, averting my eyes from the mess of last night, a half-eaten slice of pizza and glass of wine that had seemed like a bang-up idea at one in the morning.

It wasn't.

I grabbed my phone, praying for word from Margaret. I couldn't lose someone else, too.

She'd texted – thank god – and I read it over three times.

Proof in my hands that we weren't all disappearing, slowly dissolving into dust while stuck in this stupid town.

Tapping out of my messages, I dialed Diana again.

It didn't ring this time, just went straight to her generic voicemail.

Fuck. It hadn't been like that last night, had it? I'd called her about a million times. I shivered at the thought of what it might mean, where she might be . . .

I slipped on shorts and a T-shirt, then headed downstairs.

There was still no sign of Margaret, but it wasn't even eight o' clock.

I made myself some more milkless coffee, then returned to my room, taking in the drunken, hungover mess of things. I took a sip, but the coffee was still too hot, scalding my tongue.

Setting the cup down, I tried to make things look at least a little better. I tossed the leftover pizza in the trash, pulled up the comforter so it covered the tangles of sheets, and opened the curtains.

The view was beautiful, and I'd hardly taken it in. Grass edging up around the long winding driveway, nothing ahead of us for miles but trees and woods and mountains, off in the distance. I wondered, for a split second, what it would be like to live in a place like this with Harry. To stretch out. Have acres upon acres to get lost in.

Would he still have left me if I'd been here instead of Brooklyn?

Would he still have chosen her?

You've already won.

Had he told Elizabeth what happened between us? It didn't seem like Harry. Unless it truly had been no more than a drunken mistake, and he'd gone home that night, repentant.

My bones felt heavy – the idea hit me for the first time that maybe I was just a player in their fights, a woman to return to in arguments. That this was their story, and I was an outsider, a catalyst, not the other way around.

I tested my coffee again and turned to the mess of my clothes. They were strewn around the room as if I'd been here a week, not two days. I stuffed the dirty underwear in the zippered pouch of my bag, then folded up the vintage cardigan that had been tossed aside carelessly. My stomach churned, acid rising, as I fingered the dress I'd been wearing the night Diana disappeared. Clean blue and white stripes. A six-inch slit at the hem. It had been all wrong, of course, not nearly warm enough when it got right down to it, but it had looked fantastic, even with Margaret's fringed red jacket tossed over it. It had been too expensive, too, nearly a hundred dollars, but I'd been won over by its two oversized patch pockets, one on each side.

My heart thumped wildly. How the hell could I have forgotten?

Of course there'd been the haze of alcohol, of misguided sex with Harry, of Diana disappearing – poof – of the news that we might not know who she was at all, but still.

Still.

I shoved my hand into the left pocket, grasping for each corner.

Nothing. I checked the other pocket.

I returned to the left. Then back to the right.

My rings. My very last tie to Harry. Proof I hadn't dreamed it all up, that our union was real.

I turned the dress over, shaking it as hard as I could, and I flipped my suitcase over, too, undoing all the work I'd done, pawing through every T-shirt, every layer, frantic.

For my darling, Sam. From your darling, Harry.

My rings, my precious rings. The embodiment of our love. The platinum that was supposed to never, ever wear, to last for fucking ever.

The diamond we'd picked out together, the setting Harry had designed himself.

I checked my purse. My bed. Beneath the cushions of the sofa downstairs.

Every nook and cranny I could think of.

It was no use. The rings were gone.

Eamon's was empty this early in the morning, not a single car or truck in the parking lot, which was good. I didn't like the idea of being watched.

I walked through the dew-kissed grass and around the side, past littered cigarette butts, an overflowing trash can, and a side entrance that must be for employees.

When I got to the back, I took the scene in properly.

In the bright morning light, I could hardly believe that we'd hooked up back here. The woods behind the bar were way too close – not nearly private enough for what Harry and I did.

I saw us again in a flash: Harry's mouth to my neck, my fingers digging into his shoulders. Frenzied limbs, tugging at clothing. At buttons and zippers and anything that stood in our way.

God, we'd been crazy. All of it right there behind the bar, not twenty feet from other people. Between the darkness and the wind and the haze of alcohol, it had somehow seemed okay.

Or maybe it had been desperation on my part. Drunken hormones on his.

It was a mistake, I knew that, but I couldn't manage to blame myself for making it. Having Harry to myself for a few moments had felt triumphant then, even if it was pathetic now.

They have to be here, I told myself. It had all happened so

quickly – beers tossed aside, underwear pulled down – of *course* the rings would have fallen out as Harry pushed me against the tree, as I lifted my legs, wrapping them around him.

I mentally cursed Harry as I walked over to the patio. He'd still never responded, the prick.

Fuck him. And fuck Elizabeth, too. Fuck their perfect fucking house.

And yet . . .

I'm so sorry

Those three tiny dots.

What had he been wanting to say before he chose her once again?

I paused at the edge of the patio, attempting to orient myself. I was after a pair of rings, and I had to be precise. I had to know exactly where we'd stood. Otherwise, I was looking for a needle in a haystack.

Harry had led me straight back, right down the middle, stopping only when we couldn't be seen.

I steeled myself, then walked forward.

At the edge of the woods, I turned back, but I could see the bar too clearly. I hadn't gone far enough.

I walked a few more steps to where the grass thinned, edged with dirt and moss and rocks, toward a big oak tree, surrounded by others.

I turned again, and the scene looked familiar. The curve of the branches from the trees in front of me. The way the view of the bar was framed just so.

And then, it was like I could feel Harry on me – inside me – and I wanted to be sick.

I pivoted around, and a glint of sunlight caught the rim of two pint glasses – *our* pint glasses. This was the spot then. My stomach twisted again.

I took another step forward and knelt, pawing through the dirt, but I didn't see my rings anywhere.

I couldn't stop. I *wouldn't* stop. I turned over rocks, pushed the broken glasses aside, dug into the brush, hoping there was no poison ivy.

Furious at myself for keeping them in my pocket, furious at myself for falling back into Harry's arms, I brushed aside more leaves, more moss. I widened my circle, moving a couple of feet in either direction, and then farther still.

Eventually, I had to admit it to myself: my rings were lost.

There was something awful, something horribly final about it.

Until now, it had always felt like we could go back, if he decided to repent and I decided to forgive him.

No one but Diana and Margaret knew what had happened. If Harry did come back, I could pretend to the rest of them – my family included – that he'd never left me. Not now. Now I would need a story, an explanation.

I began to push myself up, off my knees, dirt caking my hands.

Then I stopped.

A few feet to my left, I saw it.

Something wrong – something off – something strange about the grass.

Crawling forward, I got a closer look.

I gasped as the color burned itself into the edges of my brain, the bright morning light betraying the difference between this and the dirt around it.

With two fingers, I reached out.

I pressed down, then examined the pads of my fingers.

Nothing there. Was I imagining it?

Reaching out, I scratched at the ground, then lifted my fingers to my face again.

I couldn't help it – I screamed.

There beneath my nails, it was unmistakable.

It wasn't brown, sepia hued like the rest of the dirt.

It was dark red.

Breath caught in my throat as I struggled to wrap my mind around what I was looking at.

Blood.

16

MARGARET

'There's one more slice of bacon,' Alex said, pushing a greasy plate my way. 'Pretty sure it's got your name on it.'

'All yours,' I said.

'If you insist.' He grabbed it eagerly, eating it in two quick bites.

We were sitting at Alex's makeshift table, a cast-iron pan askance on a burner, jam dripping down the side of a glass jar, and butter slowly melting in a dish. Alex's bandana was tied around his head again, and he was still in the T-shirt he'd had on last night.

I'd always wondered if people *actually* did this, like they always did on TV. A night of sex and then a morning of eggs and bacon and buttered toast. Coffee and OJ and strawberry jam.

Lars and I had never. In the early days, we'd wake up hungover, drag ourselves out of the apartment no earlier than noon, and order bagels the size of my head. But even that tradition had been lost, years go. Lars had jumped on the anti-carb wagon when he started to put on a few pounds, craft beer one of his only exceptions. Lars had been all about his health . . . until he hadn't.

Lars. His text had been horrifying – *fucking slut* – and I'd gone straight into Alex's arms, trying to numb it all with another night of good sex. *You think I'm a slut, Lars? Well, I'll show you.*

Afterward, we'd put a movie on, and at some point, I'd fallen asleep.

When I'd woken an hour ago to a gurgling sound and a warm, roasting smell, I was on Alex's couch, half-naked, a blanket draped over me, Rosie curled up at my feet. I'd reached for my phone immediately to find a string of texts from Sam (nothing more from Lars, thankfully). I'd assured her I was okay and apologized for worrying her.

Now I picked at a bit of eggs, my belly heavy as a brick.

'You okay?' Alex asked. It was amazing how in tune he was to my emotions, much more than your typical twentysomething guy, but he was a dad. I supposed that changed things.

'Yes,' I said. 'I can't eat anymore. It was delicious, though,' I added. 'You know your way around a cast iron.'

Alex's look of concern faded, replaced easily by a grin. 'And you haven't even had my famous T-bones yet.'

He stood, grabbing my plate and his.

As soon as his back was to me, I flipped my phone over. It had been there, all last night and this morning, the undercurrent of horror. More than his awful words. The truth that was impossible to ignore now.

Lars followed you. He spied on you. He watched you.

He wouldn't, I kept telling myself. Not Lars. Not the man I'd loved for so long, the one I still loved, in my way. He wouldn't stalk me, not like that. But the Lars I knew had been lost sometime in the last year and a half. That man only showed up in fits and starts.

I was holding on to hope that it was somehow a misunderstanding, that it had been something drunken and rambling, that Lars was in Brooklyn still and he was making things up.

Only how could it be? His words were so . . . specific. And it explained things, too, why he hadn't said anything to me yesterday, even after he'd begged us to spend this anniversary together.

While Alex was still hunched over the sink, I opened the finder app on my phone, needing official confirmation. Our accounts were linked so we could easily locate each other. Before everything happened, I'd mainly used it to help Lars pinpoint the exact location of his phone. He was notoriously bad about losing things, nervously leaving his device behind at an audition or plugged in to charge where he was bartending. His phone would appear as a little dot on a map so he could easily retrieve it. That had changed these past six months, when I had occasionally used it to check in on him if he was out late drinking. To make sure he was safe, that he wasn't lying in a gutter somewhere after a wasted walk home. I'd never really considered the fact that the mirror, of course, went both ways, that Lars could keep tabs on me in the way I did him.

I tapped 'Lars's iPhone,' then watched as the dot appeared on the map. Sure enough, there it was, in a motel not ten miles away.

Lars had come, even after I'd asked him not to. He'd used

this app to find out exactly where I was staying, and he'd watched Alex and me that night.

When Sam heard someone on the porch, it could have been him. It was a sickening thought, and I took a sip of coffee, as if to clear a bad taste at the back of my throat.

My phone rang then: Sam.

'Hey,' I said as soon as I answered. 'I'm so sorry I didn't text you last night. I should have let you know.'

'No,' she said. 'It's not that.'

It was impossible to miss, the wavering of her voice, the confusion and uncertainty and pure unadulterated fear.

'You need to come to Eamon's,' she said. 'You need to come right now.'

By the time we reached her on the back patio behind the bar, my breaths were short. Sam was standing, statuesque, in the shade of a large oak tree. Her eyes were wide but glazed, as if focused on a point far off in the distance, and her skin was sickly pale. Her palm was turned upward, an offering.

'Oh my god, Sam, are you okay?'

She shook her head, and as she did, I caught the glisten of tears on her cheeks.

'What happened?'

She twisted her torso, pointed. She was sullen, somber, like the Ghost of Christmas Future, gesturing toward Scrooge's would-be grave.

I took a small step forward, trained my eyes on the spot.

Behind me, Alex's voice: 'You guys okay?'

I didn't turn around, and neither did she. It was like I couldn't, even if I wanted to, like when you're trapped in a dream, your legs too frozen to run. Or when I'd occasionally get that petrifying bout of fright before a big audition or client meeting.

This was more than a dream, though, or even a career-crucial performance; this was life and death.

Upon first look, you almost couldn't see it, but once your eyes adjusted, once the too-bright sun put it into focus and you could pick out the difference in the pale dirt and crimson red, it was impossible *not* to see it.

The stain was large, maybe two feet by three feet, with irregular edges, the kind the dermatologist told you to look out for on moles. Beyond the stain was another, an offshoot, a satellite. And beyond that, perhaps the worst of it: spatters. Above and to the side. Against the rocks. All across the grass and moss.

Blood. It had to be blood. More blood than any human could possibly lose and survive.

Diana.

I keeled over, turning away from the stain, not wanting to compromise it, and retched three times. A hand on my shoulder – warm, rough, Alex's. I stood, shaking him off as I did. I spat the excess from my mouth, wiped it with the back of my hand, then retrieved my phone.

'Have you called the police?'

Sam shook her head solemnly. 'I just called you.'

We waited nearly an hour for anyone to arrive. Sam and I, wordless and glued to the spot, both of us afraid of disturbing a thing. Alex, shifting from foot to foot in front of us, not a clue in the world what to do. I'd told him he could go, but he insisted on staying.

'There she is,' Sam said, the first words she'd said in at least twenty minutes. I looked up to see Officer Ramos, the one who'd taken our missing person's report, cutting across the grass, a man in uniform by her side. Her hair was wet, as if she'd freshly showered, her cap smashing against her curls.

'Sorry it took me so long,' she said. 'I wanted to answer this one, since I worked with you on the report.' She nodded to the man standing next to her. 'This is our liaison with the detective unit.'

Detective unit. Damn.

'Can you tell me what happened?' Officer Ramos asked, turning to Sam. 'My colleague mentioned you spotted some blood.'

'Not just *some* blood,' Sam said. She pointed, as she had with me. 'Look at it. Right there. Right behind the bar. Right where Diana disappeared. I saw her go out to the patio. That was the last I ever saw of her. And now, now this . . .'

They stepped forward, but neither officer betrayed a single emotion.

Ramos retrieved a notepad. 'Did you touch it?'

Sam nodded. 'It's under my nails. I didn't know,' she said. 'I wasn't sure what it was. I was in shock. I still am. I've hardly moved since then. I called Margaret with my other hand, and –'

'Alex drove me over to see what was wrong,' I interrupted her. 'We haven't moved since,' I said, trying to pull it together. 'We haven't touched anything else.'

Ramos nodded, jotting something else in her notepad. Her writing was surprisingly neat. The officers exchanged glances, then Ramos gave a nod. The other officer pushed a button on his walkie: 'We're going to need forensics on this. And see if Detective Conway can get over here.'

Ramos tapped at her notepad, then turned to Sam. 'I want to stress to you that this doesn't mean anything. It could be from an animal. Someone could have been hunting.'

'By the bar?' Sam said, the pitch of her voice rising.

'Yes,' Ramos said. 'But since this is the last place you saw Ms Holbein, we are going to take it seriously. Now, then,' she said. 'Can you explain to me what you were doing here this morning?'

Sam's eyes widened, deer in headlights – why *was* she here? We'd been to the bar the day before, gotten all we could out of the bartender. Amid the chaos, I hadn't even taken a moment to wonder.

'The other night, the night Diana disappeared, I lost some jewelry.' Sam's voice quaked. 'With everything that happened, I didn't even realize it, but this morning, I did, so I came out here to look.'

'On a Sunday, the bar won't be open until four,' Ramos said, matter-of-fact, as if everyone around here should know this. 'Wouldn't it have made more sense to check the lost and found?'

'We checked the lost and found last night,' Sam said. 'My jewelry wasn't there.'

'I thought you said you didn't notice the jewelry missing until this morning.'

'I didn't,' Sam said. 'But if they'd been in the lost and found, I would have seen them.' She paused, collecting herself. 'The jewelry has sentimental value. I didn't want to wait.'

140

Ramos tapped her pen against her notebook. 'And why in the woods?'

Sam swallowed. 'Well, I'd walked back here.'

'With Ms Holbein?' Ramos asked.

Sam shook her head, and her eyes met mine for a moment. 'With a guy, okay?'

Ramos nodded, catching the implication. She didn't push it any further, simply tucked her notebook into her chest pocket and crossed her arms.

'Well, hang tight. Forensics will likely want to look at the blood on your fingers and what's on the ground.' She turned to Alex and me. 'You both should stay as well. The detective might want your statements.'

'Of course,' I said.

'Anything to help,' Alex added.

My eyes caught his for a moment, and I wondered if he was regretting getting caught up in all of this. He broke my gaze, looking down at his feet, and I trained my eyes on Sam instead. She was watching the officers intently, as if daring them to mess up.

A cloud passed by overhead, the sun breaking through, beating hot on my shoulders. I could feel them beginning to burn. I stepped a few feet to the right, away from the blood. Alex and Sam stayed where they were, as if rooted to the spot.

I looked down at my feet and took a few deep breaths, like I'd learned to do in acting class, and tried to make sense of this.

Could Diana really be dead? The thought was horrifying. No, I told myself. It couldn't be. It probably was from an animal, a coincidence. Diana wasn't honest about a lot of things. She must have simply left. My brain repeated it so strongly it was almost like I could believe it.

That's when I spotted something: lying there, nestled into the grass. A glint of shiny metal.

On instinct, I knelt down, picked it up. Here it was, and in the last place I'd expected to see it. *What in the world?*

I stared at the black fob, the Enterprise key chain. Our lost key.

My heart began to race. I should tell Sam. No, I should tell Officer Ramos.

'Ma'am.'

I jumped, turning to the other officer whose eyes were fixed on me. My hand clasped the key so he couldn't see it, and I could feel my pulse beating against it.

'Ma'am, can you wait over there, by your friends? We want to keep this area clear.'

Do it. Show him the key. Do it now.

The key was already in my hand. Would he even believe it had been here, on the ground? He might think I'd planted it. Or that I was tampering with evidence. And even so, how would I explain to him or Ramos how Diana had gotten it? I was the one driving, I was the one who'd supposedly lost it, Sam had said as much in our first report to Ramos.

What if I got caught up in this, and I couldn't find a way out? I could barely keep myself above water as it was, much less afford an attorney.

'Ma'am?'

'Yes,' I said. 'Of course.'

I turned, began walking toward Sam, and as soon as my back was to him, I slipped the key in my pocket.

17

SAM

I wanted the blood off me – every last bit of it.

A man in a blue scrubs-like uniform used a small metal object to scrape beneath my nails, transferring the remnants into a tiny bag.

But it wasn't enough. She was on me now, under my own nails.

Jesus.

Finally, the man finished, handing me a wipe that smelled of disinfectant. I rubbed it across my fingers quickly, trying to get everything off, but there was something too mundane about it, as if I were wiping away barbecue sauce at a ribs joint.

Margaret stood near me, but it was like she was an island, like she couldn't be further away. She'd mentioned once or twice that Lars had wanted her to connect more emotionally. Margaret wasn't one to do that. One time she and I had presented a new concept to a monster of a client. He'd been patronizing and verbally abusive. I'd walked out of the room practically shaking, that heat in my face that signified oncoming tears if I didn't pull myself together. Margaret had walked out stoic. 'Well, let's get started on these edits' is all she'd said.

Margaret turned toward me. Her hair was rumpled, ends pointing in every direction, and black flecks of mascara clung beneath her eyelids. Her T-shirt was half tucked into her high-waisted jeans.

If the situation were different, I'd be grilling her on her hookup with Alex, who was still standing, awkwardly, a few feet behind us. It was her first tryst since Lars, and I wished we could just be friends like we'd intended to be. The sort of friends who help each other get through life-altering breakups. I wished Diana could burst onto the scene right now. I could practically see her, smile bright, eyes mischievous, shaking a bottle of Advil like a maraca – *Here, take two, have some coffee, and then tell me* everything *that happened last night. Did your one-night stand became a proper two-nighter?*

Margaret glanced to Alex, then back to me. She cleared her throat. She looked . . . *nervous*.

'What's going on?' I asked.

'What do you mean?'

'Something's on your mind,' I said. 'What is it?'

Her shoulders jolted, and for a moment, she looked caught out, but then she straightened her posture. 'I wanted to ask you something.'

'What?'

She nodded toward the patio, just a few feet away, then turned and walked to it. I followed.

The sun was blistering now, even more so away from the partial shadows cast by the trees of the woods, and I felt exposed. Like the person who hurt Diana could be out there now, watching us.

Margaret put her hand in her pocket and just as quickly pulled it out. 'What were you doing out here, Sam? And why this morning?'

I turned to see if anyone was watching, but Ramos and the other officer were chatting away, as if none of this mattered, and the forensics guy was fully wrapped up in his work.

'The jewelry I lost was my rings,' I said. 'I realized I didn't have them this morning.'

Margaret tilted her head. 'I thought you weren't wearing them. I *know* you weren't wearing them, I saw, myself.'

'I wasn't wearing them,' I said. 'But I had them in my pocket that night.'

Her eyes narrowed. 'Why?'

'Because I wanted them with me, okay?' I said. 'Does it really matter?'

'I'm sorry,' Margaret said impulsively. 'I didn't mean —'

'Do you really have to judge me?' I asked. 'Now of all times? Because you have no idea.'

'I wasn't judging,' she started, but there was no time for her to elaborate.

'Look,' I said.

There was a new woman on the scene, walking confidently across the grass, long legs taking quick, purposeful strides.

She stopped before us, right on the edge of the patio, and I took in her ensemble, a black blazer and pencil skirt over a cream-colored blouse that looked like it was made of silk. Clumps of sod from the dewy grass clung to the heels of her pumps.

'I'm Detective Conway,' she said, extending her hand.

I checked my hand once more for blood, then took hers in mine. Her nails were buffed to a matte sheen, and her hair was a deep brownish black that fell just past her shoulders in the sort of waves I'd imagine it took an hour to perfect. Nothing on earth like you'd expect a small-town detective to look.

She introduced herself to Margaret, glanced at Alex, whose hands were shoved deep in his pockets, then pulled out a brown Moleskine notebook. She didn't open it, only ran one manicured finger beneath the elastic holding it shut. 'Local law enforcement has briefed me on the situation here, as well as the missing person's report on Diana Holbein.' She paused, dropping one hand to her side, as if remembering a cue she'd forgotten in the school play. 'I am very sorry to hear about your friend, but I also want to be clear about the facts as they stand. What we have is a missing person's report that's woefully incomplete and a scene that we can't say is connected.' She gestured to the bloodstain, where the guy was still working, then set her lips into a firm line. 'We have to be careful not to jump to conclusions.'

'Jump to conclusions?' I asked, unable to help myself. 'This was the last place we saw Diana, and you're saying it's a huge coincidence that a massive amount of blood is there on the ground? She could be, she could be . . .'

Dead.

The detective cleared her throat and tucked the notebook back into her blazer, never having opened it at all. 'We're going to do everything we can. Now to start, we'll need to take statements from all of you down at the station. Completely voluntary, of course, but we figure you'll want to do everything you can, as well.'

I nodded, and Margaret did, too.

'Me too?' Alex asked, reminding us of his presence like a kid who didn't want to be forgotten.

'Yes,' she said quickly. 'All of you. I'm going to take a closer look at the scene, but I'll meet you back at the station.'

Like that, she walked off, toward the blood.

Blood we all knew could be – *must be* – Diana's.

I honestly couldn't believe it.

Not as Officer Ramos drove Margaret and me across the river toward the station in Hudson, Alex following behind in his truck.

Not as she turned down a two-lane road. Not as we got out of the cop car, traversed a blacktop parking lot, entered a brick facade to the sound of bells, whistles and general bustle. Not as another officer separated me from Margaret and Alex, leading me down the hall to an interview room that held a white table and two molded plastic chairs, shutting the door behind him, leaving me alone.

Not as I picked at the beds of my nails and gagged at the thought of Diana's blood beneath them.

I couldn't believe Diana could really be dead.

There was a knock at the door, and Detective Conway walked in without waiting for a response, her heels clicking smartly across the hard floor.

She pulled out a chair and sat on it gracefully, as if it were an Eames chair in a chic SoHo office and not a banged-up thing that couldn't have cost more than twenty bucks, then laid her hands flat on the table. She reminded me, suddenly, of those obsessive detectives you always saw on TV, getting into the killer's head at the expense of their own relationships. I glanced at her hand – there was no ring.

'Ms . . .' A pause.

'Lochman,' I volunteered.

'Thank you,' Conway said. 'We'll be recording this interview. Is that all right?'

I swallowed. Nodded.

She paused, and I realized she was waiting for me to vocalize my answer.

'Of course,' I said. 'Whatever I can do for Diana.'

It's too late to do anything, I thought shamefully. Way too fucking late.

The hairs on the back of my neck stood up as it fully hit me that *I* had been the one to send her out there, searching for Harry. I imagined Brandon, stalking her obsessively, the two of them arguing . . . Then I imagined some horrifying attacker, some stranger, grabbing her, arms jutting out from the darkness of the woods, pulling her in, a real-life bogeyman . . .

The detective leaned down and pulled a file from a structured leather bag, then took out her Moleskine and a pen.

'Like I said, we don't want to get ahead of ourselves. But when there is a missing woman and blood on the scene, that's when someone like me gets called in. We want to avoid an officer who's not as trained as I am in handling these initial first steps, if it does turn out to be connected. But please remember, there is always the possibility that it is entirely *unconnected*. Understood?'

'Yes,' I said. 'Understood.'

'So first things first, I'd like to fill in some holes in the missing person's report. Can you help me make sure we've got all the info?'

'Yes, of course,' I said, releasing a breath, happy to do something. Anything.

'So as I understand, you and' – she checked her notes – 'Margaret Cahill. You don't have any photos of Ms Holbein?'

'No,' I said, shaking my head. 'I've known her loosely for about a year and a half, but we've only been proper friends for a couple of months, and we didn't really take any.'

'Three girlfriends don't take *any* photos? That's hard to believe, in this day and age. Even my seventy-year-old mother knows her way around a selfie.'

'I wanted to take them, and at first, I tried, but it made Diana nervous,' I said. 'She was going through a divorce with her ex, Brandon, and he was stalking her. That's why she wasn't on social media. We said this in the first report. And Margaret left a message with Ramos last night. The bartender who was working on Friday said that a guy was at the bar near closing, asking about the three of us. We think it was Brandon.'

'Yes, I'm aware of that. We'll follow up with the bartender.'

I wondered if she would.

Conway flipped another paper in the file. 'And you don't have this Brandon's last name, correct? You say it wasn't Holbein?'

'Right,' I said. 'Diana didn't take his name. She told me.'

Conway tapped her pen on the table. 'It seems like there's a lot you don't know about a friend you were close enough to travel with.'

I knew that Diana always asked for a couple of ice cubes with her sauvignon blanc. That she'd tried dyeing her grays in her mid-twenties and they'd turned an awful shade of orange, and she'd vowed to go natural after that. That she knew exactly the right thing to say to make you feel supported, never judged. That she treasured each and every one of her therapy clients, that she spent two hours going over her notes each night so she wouldn't forget anything the next session – even if she always drank a glass of wine when she did it.

I knew Diana was a little loud and had a propensity for booze and greasy takeout, and that her very presence could add life to any situation. She was the sort of woman you met and instantly thought: that's it, I've made a new friend, someone who gets me, someone who will be around for a while . . .

I blinked, holding back tears, but didn't say anything else.

Conway stared at me a moment before moving on. 'You have her phone number and email.' She read them off to me. 'That correct?'

I double-checked, then nodded again. 'Yes, but now her phone isn't ringing. Just straight through to the voicemail. Starting this morning.'

'We're waiting to hear from the service provider about the registration behind that number. Hope to clear up this name business since it's not turning up in our databases.' Conway shifted in her seat, then leaned forward. Her face was firm. Unreadable. 'I'd love for you to walk me through the night

Ms Holbein went missing. Cover any details you may have overlooked.'

Carefully, I went over everything: The planned trip, the lost car key, the rental that was only supposed to be for one night, the way we'd all gotten separated at the bar, how Diana had gone out back and that was the last time I'd seen her. The discovery that Diana was still gone the next morning. And then, *this* morning. A quiet Sunday morning.

Looking for something else entirely and finding blood.

Conway pressed one palm against the table. 'It would be helpful to know why you were out there this morning. Behind the bar, I mean.'

'I told Officer Ramos. I'd lost some jewelry on Friday night, and it was very important to me.'

Conway glanced over her notes. 'Something sentimental, yes? May I ask what?'

I swallowed. 'A platinum band and a diamond ring.'

Conway blinked. 'A bridal set?'

I nodded.

'Are you married, Ms Lochman?'

I paused.

'That's usually a pretty straightforward question.'

'It's complicated,' I said. 'We're separated right now, but nothing is official. It's only been two months since he left.'

'Okay,' she said. 'And you took your rings off?'

The room suddenly felt hot. 'Yes, but I'd left them in my pocket. It was an oversight,' I lied. Telling her that I'd wanted them near me, like a pathetic security blanket, seemed too much.

'And you believe you lost them when you were out back with a man from the bar? This was a man you'd just met?'

151

'No,' I said. 'My, uhh . . . Harry. Harry Brant. It was the first time I'd seen him since the separation.'

Conway raised her eyebrows. 'You just happen to break down where your ex is?'

'Yes,' I said. 'It was a coincidence.'

'And have you spoken with Mr Brant since that night? Perhaps he saw your friend?'

'No,' I said, shaking my head. 'I've tried, but . . . like I said, its complicated with us.'

'I see.' She leaned closer, as if we were girls in a locker room, exchanging secrets, but when I didn't say anything more, she closed her notebook. 'Thank you. That's all for now. We'll let you know if it turns out this is at all connected to Ms Holbein's disappearance. And we'll follow up with Mr Brant.' She stood and led me out of the room and down the hall. 'An officer up front will take a copy of your ID and all your contact information.'

'Okay,' I said cautiously.

'I'll be talking to Ms Cahill now,' she said. 'When we're done, someone can drive you back together.'

At the front, at a faux-wood laminate desk that looked like it could use a cleaning, a woman click-clacked behind a dinosaur of a computer. 'I'll need to see your ID,' she said.

I nodded, reaching into my bag and grabbing my leather wallet.

'Just one second,' I said.

My license wasn't in the front, where I usually kept it. I flicked through old receipts, my personal credit card, my business credit card, a library card.

'I know it's in here somewhere,' I said.

I pulled the wad of bills and papers out, picking through. Then I took out every card, fingering each one.

'I'm sorry,' I said, as the woman looked at me, impatient. 'I don't have it.'

'You don't have it,' the woman repeated.

No! I wanted to scream. *No. Somehow, I don't*.

It was gone. Missing.

Like the car key.

Like Diana.

Like everything else in this godforsaken town.

18 | MARGARET

My interview went quickly, no more than a rehash of what I'd said in the initial statement, the car key burning a hole in my pocket the entire time.

I hated lying, but I felt I had no choice. Perhaps it all *was* a strange coincidence — a dead animal, or a particularly vicious bar fight — and the car key had been dropped by Diana while she was out there smoking?

If I told Conway anything more, she'd surely want to know *how* Diana had gotten the key. *Why* she'd gotten it.

Sam practically pounced at me as soon as I was back up front. 'It's gone,' she said. My muscles tensed, and for a second, I thought she was talking about the car key. 'My fucking license.' She waved around her wallet, as if the sight of it proved the absence in some way. 'It's not here.'

'Okay,' I said. 'Does that create problems with the report?'

Sam huffed. 'I'm not talking about the report. Don't you

think that's weird? First we lose the car key and then my license is gone, too?'

My heart beat fast, and it almost felt like the key in my pocket did, too. If she was this upset about a lost license, what on earth would she say if I told her what I'd done? She'd blame me, that much was clear.

I struggled to keep my voice calm. 'Are you sure you brought it with you? Maybe it's back in Brooklyn, in another bag?'

'Yes, I'm sure. I always check when I pack my bags for a trip. Always.'

'Could you have lost it at the bar?'

'I didn't even take it out. There wasn't anyone checking IDs to get in. Remember?'

'Okay,' I said. 'Calm down —'

'Don't tell me to calm down,' Sam said. 'Everything is falling apart. Everything is —'

Behind us, Ramos cleared her throat, announcing her presence. 'I'm ready if you are.'

'Thanks,' I said. I glanced at Sam, who looked borderline distraught about something that didn't seem to matter much at all. Still, it was easy to sympathize. Minutiae were exactly the things we focused on when our worlds were falling apart. I'd nearly lost my mind tearing our apartment apart when I couldn't find a check to an invoice I was sure had been paid, shortly after the bad news came about our baby. It wasn't even about the money. At that point, things were tight, like they always were, but I was still floating easily down the river of financial stability; I wasn't treading water yet, and I definitely wasn't drowning. It was more that with my body, my baby, my marriage and all the plans Lars and I had made entirely out of my control, I wanted, so badly, to control this one thing.

'Shall we?' Ramos said, the slightest hint of impatience in her voice.

'Yes,' I said, turning to face her. 'One moment.' I shoved a hand in my pocket, making sure the key hadn't fallen out, then retrieved my phone, checking Google quickly to make sure the place was open on a Sunday. When I saw that it was, I put on my sweetest, most innocent voice, so she wouldn't suspect a thing. 'Actually, if you don't mind, could you take us into town?'

Sam sighed as we got out of the car, as she'd been doing for the last five minutes, but she waited until Ramos had driven off to speak. 'My license is not going to be here.'

'I doubt it is,' I said, slipping easily back into my role as a planner, a checklist maker. 'But we can see what name Diana used to pay the tow bill.'

'Fuck,' Sam said, and I could almost see the lightbulb flickering on in her head. 'We should have done that yesterday.'

'We were in reaction mode,' I said. 'Not to mention we were both completely hungover. When we're back at the house, we can try to figure out what name she used for the rental as well.'

'Right,' Sam said. 'Exactly. Thank you. I'm not thinking straight.'

'We haven't had time to think straight,' I said. 'It's all been happening so fast.'

Sam nodded, and we approached the auto shop, a cinder block building coated in a sickening shade of what I believe would be called puce. Sam, emboldened by the chance to find something out about Diana, moved with purpose, the same way she did when she walked into a meeting in the conference room, ready to pitch the idea we'd come up with the night before with all her heart, no matter how shallow the work might be. I was the organized one, the one who ticked off every box, but she was the one who could really sell it.

She spotted a guy in a blue jumpsuit, a shadow of stubble across his face and cuffs rolled up to the elbows, grease smears and callused creases spidering across his hands. His name tag read GEORGE.

'Help you?' he asked, with one of those thick old-school Brooklyn accents that were getting rarer by the day, even in Brooklyn.

Sam straightened up. 'We had our car towed here the day before yesterday,' she said. 'To this shop. We were wondering –'

'The black CR-V?'

'Yes,' she said. 'It's just –'

'I tried to call you earlier a bunch of times but didn't get an answer. These new cars, they don't make it easy to dupe keys – *yuge* hassle. You gotta call the rental company and see if they have a backup. Then we can make a copy. Or else we gotta call Honda and –'

'That's not why we're here,' Sam said with a quick shake of her head. 'Our friend – Diana Holbein – we can't find her, and she may be –' Sam stopped short of saying it out loud. 'We're trying to help the investigation, but her name isn't coming up in the police databases. We were hoping to see what name she left you – I mean, what spelling.'

George raised an eyebrow. 'So you don't wanna know about your car?'

'No,' Sam said. 'We need to find any information we can about our friend. But we need to check the car, too. To see if she left anything in there. And, this is a long shot, but you never saw her, did you? After the day we got the tow? We called yesterday, but I'm not sure if the person we spoke to asked everyone. She's about my height, with silver and brown hair. Mid-thirties. Curvy.'

'Haven't,' George said, shaking his head. In the sunlight, I spotted another smear of grease at the bottom of his chin. 'But you can ask the other guys. And the manager, Sue – she's the first one here in the morning. She'll have the paperwork, too, if you want to give it a look.'

He motioned to the other side of the shop, where a few people gathered around stacks of spare tires and a makeshift desk.

'And the car?' I asked.

George pointed with a greasy finger to our SUV, parked in the front right corner. Within eyesight of the desk, still, but comfortably far away. 'It's open,' he said.

'You good?' I asked Sam. 'I'll get started looking while you check the paperwork.'

In truth, I was *telling* her she was good, telling her not to follow me, not yet, but she didn't know that. All she knew was I was in charge, I was the one with the idea to come here, I was the person giving her hope that there would be answers.

'Yeah,' Sam said, turning back to George. 'Yes, I'll follow you.'

They walked away, and I turned toward the car, trying to keep my breaths calm.

When I'd seen that glint of metal in the grass, I'd acted on impulse, not reason. It was a mistake I now had to fix.

At the car, I made a show of opening every door and sliding back the front seats. I did give it a cursory glance, but truth be told, I wasn't looking that closely. I doubted very much that Sam's ID was here. I figured she lost it in her drunken state on Friday, simple as that. We'd all been a mess that night, myself included. Besides, I didn't know how long Sam would be up there, looking through papers, and I didn't want to screw this up worse than it already was. My phone rang as I shut the driver-side door: Lars. He was probably only just waking up and definitely hungover. I ignored it. I knew what it would hold in any case. Apologies, surely. Lars was always apologizing the morning after a particularly drunken night, but this time was different. This time he really had crossed a line.

Shoulders rigid, I walked around to the back, then undid the hatchback.

The door opened smoothly, easily, like new cars always did. I surveyed the back, where our suitcases had been loaded less than forty-eight hours ago.

I glanced to the front. Sam was at a desk with the manager, bent over a clipboard.

Without hesitation, I lifted up the fuzzy fabric floor of the trunk, exposing the spare tire. I pulled the fabric panel out, and I gave it a dramatic shake.

At the same time, I slid the car key from my pocket, and I let it go.

It clanked against the cement, jingle-jangle.

'Oh my god,' I said, my voice unnaturally loud. 'Sam!'

Up ahead, my friend turned. 'What?'

I hated to lie to her, but I had no choice.

'Come over here,' I said, pointing to the key on the ground. 'You are not going to believe this.'

19

SAM

Margaret drove us home in our rental car as if this were normal, as if the last two days hadn't even happened.

When we were back inside, she hung the pair of house keys on a hook near the door and tucked the car key inside her bag.

I sank into the cushions of the plush sofa, exhausted by this mindfuckery. 'So you're telling me the key was just there? But *how*?'

Margaret jolted. 'It must have fallen beneath the floor of the trunk when I got something out of my suitcase. That's the only explanation.'

'So that's it,' I said. 'It just turns up, fresh out of whatever wormhole it fell into?'

Margaret shrugged, and I didn't know what else to say.

The key thing was nuts, but so was all of this. The paperwork for the tow had been under the name Diana Holbein, but she'd paid with cash. No leads there.

I glanced around the room. Though the space around us was still foreign and strange, the ivory walls, the old wooden floors – they were becoming less so now. The place where everything had gone to shit. Taking on the familiarity of a bad boyfriend.

A question stretched before us, taut and tense, like the quiet moment in a movie before the killer jumps out of the shadows. *What now?*

It was Sunday. We were meant to be at Saratoga Springs, enjoying Margaret's friend's hot tub, drinking wine and eating cheese and *relaxing*, until Tuesday morning.

I wasn't supposed to have seen Harry. Diana was never supposed to have gone out to that patio. A man we didn't even know was never supposed to drive us home from the bar . . .

Margaret began tapping on her phone intently.

'What are you doing?' I asked.

'Trying to find the rental on Airbnb. If we can get the owner's info, maybe they'll have a different name.'

'Or it will be her name again, and we'll be just as confused as ever.'

'It doesn't matter either way,' Margaret said. 'I don't see it.'

'Try VRBO, then.'

'I am.'

I took out my phone, began to do the same. There was nothing on either service. *What the fuck?* 'How did Diana even find this place?'

Margaret stood. 'Maybe there's a book. Some welcome info. Anything. I looked when we first got here, but I didn't look very hard.'

We checked all the typical places: Kitchen drawers. A lone bookshelf in the living room. Cabinet drawers beneath end tables. Nothing.

'I don't get it,' I said. 'I don't get how she found this place and why someone hasn't shown up to kick us out. It's May in the Hudson Valley. You'd think it would be booked. And I don't get what the fuck happened to my ID or why she paid the tow in cash or why we had to break down exactly where Harry lives or any of this.'

Margaret's eyes scrunched up, almost as if she wanted to cry. But she would never cry, never break down as I did, it wasn't her style.

'What is it?' I asked.

She shook her head. 'I wanted to say I'm sorry.'

'This isn't your fault.'

She grimaced. 'No, I'm sorry you thought I would judge you for wearing your wedding rings. I'm sorry I pushed you to take them off.'

'Oh,' I said, and her face was genuine, and it made me feel better, a teensy bit, to know that Diana wasn't the only one who didn't care that people made dumb decisions, even if she was the *only* one in my life who knew the truth, or at least part of it. 'I guess I should tell you all of it, then. Harry and I slept together. Out in the back.'

Margaret's eyes widened.

'I know,' I said. 'Diana found me after, and I told her about it. She was going to go out there to scope him out for me.'

Margaret laughed. 'Sounds like Diana.'

I couldn't bring myself to laugh along with her. 'That's the last I saw of her. If something *did* happen to her, if the blood is hers, it's my fault. I should never have let her go out there.'

'No,' Margaret said. She stood, closing the space separating us in two quick strides, and sat next to me on the sofa. 'No,' she said again. 'It's not your fault at all. None of this is your fault.'

Her arms around me, I lived up to my Sam ways. The tears started, and as she held me tight, I spit it all out: how pitiful I felt, how Harry wasn't even answering my calls now, even after I'd told him Diana was missing.

Margaret listened, and she held me, rocking me back and forth, until my breaths finally calmed, until the storm of emotion passed.

'Sam,' she said, looking at me earnestly, her hand falling back to her lap. 'Please believe me that I don't judge you at all. If you knew about me and Lars, how messed up we are. You wouldn't even believe it. Lars is up here. I think . . . I think he even came to the house that night. It wasn't Alex you heard going out to the car. It was Lars, watching us. I got this text, this text that he saw me sleeping with someone. He must have seen Alex take us home.'

'Lars?' I asked, shock rippling through me like an earthquake. 'Really? Jesus. He's *here*?'

'Yeah,' she said. 'In a motel. I haven't spoken with him. I don't even know what to say. He's never done anything like this before.'

'Christ,' I said. 'Did we fall into some kind of *Twilight Zone* of exes?'

'I know,' Margaret said. 'We were supposed to be getting away from them, and we smashed into them instead.'

I imagined, for a second, Diana's ex, smashing her – literally. Killing her.

'Lars was worried about me being on my own,' Margaret went on. 'It's . . .' She hesitated. 'It's a big weekend for me.'

I cocked my head to the side. 'What do you mean?'

'I haven't been fully honest with you,' she said. 'With you or Diana.'

There was a quick uptick in my heartbeat, and for a moment, I felt that tautness, the tension of fearing what someone was going to say. 'What do you mean?' I asked again, tentatively.

Margaret looked down at her hands, folded carefully in her lap, then back up at me. 'I told you Lars and I split because I couldn't give him children.'

I nodded, urging her along.

'In a way that's technically true, but I'm not —' She paused. 'I don't have fertility issues.'

'You don't?' When Margaret had told me, I'd imagined visits to clinics, sperm counts and ovulation trackers, IUIs and IVFs and an alphabet soup of conception attempts.

Margaret's fingers found the bottom of her shirt. Slowly, she lifted it up.

'What are you —?'

Colored striations arced around the sides of her stomach. My mouth fell into an O.

'Margaret,' I said. 'I'm so sorry.'

She let out a mirthless laugh. 'I'm one of the rare women who got them early, first week of the second trimester. I moisturize them three times a day but the damn things still won't go away.'

'Oh god,' I said. 'You had a miscarriage?'

Her laugh was even more bitter this time. 'It sounds awful, but I wish it had gone that way, instead of how it did. He was a boy,' she said, her voice cracking at the last word. 'We would have called him Timothy. We did this genetic testing, and he was diagnosed with Edwards syndrome. It's a chromosomal disorder. It's really bad. Most-babies-don't-make-it-past-a-year kind of bad.'

'Oh my god,' I said.

She nodded. 'Lars wanted to go forward with the pregnancy. He found these super rare stories where the kids would live until ten, maybe even longer. He thought we would at least get to know him, you know, that every day would be a blessing.'

'I'm guessing you didn't,' I said, my voice soft.

'It wasn't only for me, I swear,' she said. 'It wasn't that I didn't want to carry a baby and raise him and go through all those sleepless nights for him to die on me.' She shook her head. 'To be honest, I don't know, maybe it was all for me, maybe I was too damn selfish, but how could I condemn my son to that kind of life? How *could* I?' She pressed her lips together, composing herself. 'You worry about me judging you, but me, I've caused more pain than you ever have.'

'No,' I said earnestly. 'Don't do that to yourself, Margaret. Anyone would have made the same decision.'

She jerked back, almost viciously. 'Not anyone,' she said. 'Lars wouldn't. He wanted to get right back to it, to start trying again, but I was wrecked. At first, it was the recovery from the termination. Then it was the depression. But months went by, and it didn't change. We went from having this awesome sex life to . . . roommates with this shared heartbreaking past. Somewhere in the midst of all that he started drinking, really drinking, and it's like the man I knew was completely lost.'

I reached out to hug her, but she stiffened, making it clear she didn't want that, so I let my hand drop to my side. Aimless.

'He wanted to be with me this weekend, because yesterday was the anniversary of our due date. Our son would have been a year old. It's why I homed in on this weekend in the first place when Diana threw out the idea of a trip – I had to get away from Lars – but I never thought he would take it so far. I never thought he'd actually follow me.'

'I'm so sorry,' I said finally, not knowing what else to say.

Margaret's eyes caught mine. 'I'm sorry, too. I'm sorry we haven't been able to be there for each other in the ways we should. I'm sorry all of this happened. I'm sorry Diana isn't here right now, cracking jokes and pouring wine and telling us exactly how to solve all our problems.'

I let out a laugh. 'God, me too.'

Margaret took charge, like she did. While I showered and cleaned myself up, she called the police, updating them on what we'd found – or hadn't found – regarding the rental and the auto shop. She went to the grocery store after, returning an hour later with healthy things – broccoli and cauliflower, organic skinless chicken breasts and instant-cook quinoa, Greek yogurt and berries.

I poured us wine, and we sat in the living room next to each other, googling Diana some more, looking up the address of the rental on Trulia and Zillow, but all we could find in the way of an owner was a holdings company called Over the River Properties. Margaret called the police to let them know that as well, but neither of us thought it would do much good.

Just after seven, Margaret began chopping, laying out vegetables on a foil-covered pan, each one of them cut into perfect one-inch pieces, coated evenly with oil. As she boiled water for the quinoa, I went to work on the chicken, seasoning it with garlic and paprika, tossing it into a cast iron pan and watching it sizzle, waiting until it got a good sear, then flipping each breast. There was something rhythmic and relieving about doing this little thing, and I wanted to do it right.

The chicken was near done when my phone rang. A local number. Fingers slippery from oil, I had to swipe it three times to answer.

'Hello?'

'Is this Ms Lochman?'

'Yes,' I said. The chicken sputtered – it was definitely done now.

'This is Detective Conway.'

'Okay,' I said. I glanced at the clock on the stove. It was after eight, a strange time to call, unless . . .

'I'm sorry to disturb you,' the detective went on.

I had a terrifying sense of standing on a knife's edge and not wanting to fall off. A sense that what she was about to say was going to change everything. And this large part of me wanted to sit on this knife's edge, make myself a home there, uncomfortable as it was, say, *Actually, Detective, we were about to sit down to dinner, can you give me a ring tomorrow?*, and go back to the chicken in the pan, sit down to a nice meal with Margaret, pour us a couple of glasses of wine, and . . . relax. Forget the blood. Forget Harry and what happened. Forget Brandon and the questions about where the 'margarita ladies' had gone.

Go back to believing that Diana had just met a guy while smoking on the patio, gone home with him, forgotten our address, that she could walk in any second now . . .

'Ms Lochman.'

'Sorry,' I managed. A dark, bitter smell. The chicken would burn soon.

'What is it?' I asked, jumping off the knife's edge with my eyes wide open. 'What happened?'

Conway cleared her throat, giving me one more tiny moment of reprieve, however small.

'We've found a body, in the woods, not far from where you spotted the blood. It was hidden in bushes, covered over with brush, but we found it all right. Didn't take long. We need you to come in tomorrow for identification.'

I found I suddenly couldn't breathe, like my own body was shutting down.

Margaret was in front of me, asking what was wrong, what had happened, but I could hardly hear her. She started flipping off burners, waving away smoke that I hadn't even noticed coming from the pan.

A shrill scream then. High and piercing. Diana's scream?

It was only as I saw Margaret, waving an oven mitt frantically at a contraption on the ceiling, that I realized what had happened. The smoke alarm.

'Ms Lochman?' Conway asked. 'Did you hear me?'

I stared at the chicken, blackened.

'Yes, I heard you,' I said, robotic.

'So we'll see you then? Nine o'clock tomorrow morning?'

'Okay,' I said, hanging up the phone on autopilot.

Margaret's eyes were wide. At some point, and I hadn't even realized it, the shrieking of the smoke alarm had stopped.

'What is it?' Margaret asked. 'What happened?'

'They've found her,' I managed, my voice preternaturally smooth, calm with shock.

'They've found Diana.'

MONDAY

20 | MARGARET

Bright and early Monday morning, I backed meticulously out of the long, winding driveway, my eyes locked on the rearview window. Frankly, I didn't know how we got through the past twelve hours, I really didn't.

The news had sent Sam into a near-catatonic shock. I'd poured her a glass of water, led her upstairs, and spent the evening alone, ruminating on all the things I didn't want to think about: A body, *Diana's* body. Two arms, two legs, ten fingers, ten toes. Eyes that lit up when you walked into the room, like Diana had been waiting all week to catch up, like *you* were the highlight of her whole social calendar. I tried not to go there, but I couldn't help it: I thought of Timothy's miniature body, growing in my womb, how he'd had ten fingers and ten toes, too.

Lars's texts had come around ten. He'd been calling all day Sunday, and I'd ignored every last call.

I'm sorry I said that, Peggy.

I never meant it.

I was just so shocked.

I know we can still work it out.

It's you and me. It's always been you and me.

I'd been putting off answering, but alone downstairs, alone with such horrible news about Diana, it seemed like none of it really mattered anymore. I retyped it three times before I landed on what I wanted to say. Simple and short:

You crossed a line, coming up here. Please leave.

Before I went to bed, I texted Alex, telling him the news. He'd asked to come over, but I'd told him no. I had to be there for Sam, in case she needed me.

She did need me, that much was clear now.

I drove onto the bridge that crossed the Hudson River, that would lead us across, to the station, my hands clutching the wheel. Sam was quiet, cocooned in her grief, leaving me to process it all on my own.

Diana's blood all over the ground. The key I'd taken a potential clue, one I'd obscured from the police. Money, still stashed in my suitcase, money that was supposed to help me get out from under the mess I'd made of my life, might be blood money now.

A chalky, minty taste lingered in my mouth, and I ran my tongue over my teeth, trying to get rid of it. The GPS voice called out instructions, and I made a final turn. I eyed Sam, contemplated asking if she was okay, then thought better of it. Of course she wasn't okay. I had to stop asking her if she was.

'We're almost there,' I said instead. My voice was too calm, and Lars would have given me hell for it, more proof that I was cold and unfeeling. Sam had cried so much this morning, exactly like she was supposed to, but my tears never came. Except for when they shouldn't have, like at the bar with Alex.

I parked the car, then turned to Sam. 'You ready?'

'No,' she said. 'But we might as well go in.'

We traipsed across the parking lot. My phone rang – Alex – but I ignored it. I held the door open for Sam as we walked into the station, the influx of noise making my head pound. I approached the desk, but the man behind it didn't look up, only shuffled through what seemed like reams of papers.

All at once, I imagined Diana standing next to me, one hand on her hip, the other tugging impatiently on a hair's split end. *Can we get on with it already? We're supposed to be in a hot tub! We're supposed to be eating six-year aged cheddar and doing sheet masks!*

It was so strange to think that she would never speak again, that she wouldn't burst into a wine bar and say, as she did one Friday, only a few weeks ago: 'Okay, on a scale of one to ten, how much do our exes suck? I'll start with mine: Eleven!'

Could Brandon really have found her that night, killed her? Was he out there somewhere now?

'Can I help you?' the man said after a minute or so.

'Yes,' I said. 'We're here to see Detective Conway.'

'Take a seat.' He motioned to two hard chairs by the window. 'I'll let her know.'

I led Sam by the elbow, and we did. My eyes bounced

175

around the walls of the station, covered in notices printed on colored paper, all of it feeling far too ordinary for what it entailed.

I retrieved my phone, eager to do something other than stare at the walls of the station. There it was, yet another text from Lars.

I have to see you. I'm not going to leave until I do.

I didn't have time to process it: the now-familiar click of heels rang across the linoleum. Conway.

I stood, Sam following my lead, then slipped my hand in hers and squeezed before letting it go. 'I'm here,' I said, mothering her, as was my way. 'Right here with you the whole time.'

'Where do you need us to . . .' My pause was only brief. 'To do the identification?'

Conway blinked but didn't answer, her face entirely unreadable. She was wearing a crisp black button-down and slacks, accented with a string of the tiniest pearls, her hair swept back away from her face into a low bun, like a ballet dancer.

'Thank you for coming in,' she said, but her gaze was trained only on Sam. 'If you could follow me, Ms Lochman.'

'What about me?' I asked, my mouth going dry. 'We were both with Diana the night she disappeared.'

Conway's head cocked to the side, and the officer behind the front desk finally lost interest in his paperwork. 'Just Ms Lochman for now. This . . .' She let her hands fall to her sides, then folded them carefully together so they rested below her small waist. 'This might take some time.'

'But I thought you wanted me to . . .' Sam's voice wavered. 'To identify her.'

'We'd like to ask you a few questions first,' Conway said. She turned to me: 'Perhaps Ms Lochman can call you when we're done. Or an officer can drive her back to where you're staying.'

'I can't – I can't do it on my own,' Sam stammered.

'She's right,' I said. 'And she shouldn't have to.'

Conway cleared her throat. 'I'm afraid I have to insist in this instance. Follow me, Ms Lochman.' It wasn't a question this time, more like a command. Conway was already walking down the hall.

'What the fuck?' Sam's eyes were wide with panic. 'What the fuck is this?'

'I don't know,' I said. 'I don't –'

'Please, Ms Lochman,' Conway said, turning on her heel to face us. '*Now.*'

Sam bit her lip, then, evidently unsure of what else she could do, she turned, following Conway.

I wanted to stop them, insist that we do this together, ask Conway what this was all about. I wanted to tell Sam that it would be okay, that I would be here for her. That I would protect her, somehow. But in moments, they were gone, around the hallway, where I couldn't see them anymore.

It was only then that it occurred to me: Was there a reason for all of this? Was there something Sam hadn't told me?

Did Sam have secrets of her own?

21

SAM

Conway deposited me in a room that was nicer than the one I'd been in yesterday and went to get us coffees. A sofa sat in the corner, hunter green and faded on the sides. The walls were a creamy pale yellow. You wouldn't call the color homey, but it was better than the bright antiseptic white of the rest of the station.

I adjusted myself in the chair. Was this the room they used to break terrible news? It must be. Only the news had already been broken. The worst had already been said.

We've found a body.

Shouldn't Conway have told me in person? Shouldn't there have been more formality than a phone call? Didn't Diana deserve as much? And shouldn't Margaret be part of this, too? None of it made any fucking sense.

Trying to calm my breaths, I stretched my fingers against the table, turning my hands to fleshy starfish. I examined beneath my nails. From looking, you'd never know that Diana's blood had been beneath them only yesterday.

Conway walked in holding two mugs, ones that looked like they'd been left here over the years by one officer or another. Hers proclaimed that Mark Johnson supported the Humane Society. Mine had a photo of someone's cat, a black-and-white thing stretching languorously toward the camera. The coffees were milky and tan, with a bit of froth on top.

Conway took a sip. 'I keep an espresso machine in my office. I prefer it immensely to the mud that sits burning round the clock in a pot in the kitchen.'

I forced myself to taste it. It was warm and rich, but heavy in my stomach.

'We all have our indulgences, I suppose,' Conway went on, taking another sip. 'This one's far less dangerous to my career than booze.'

I looked down, then back up at her. She was being nice, going out of her way to make me feel welcome, like she and I were colleagues, equals – whatever. For a strange instant, I imagined her coming to one of our Friday night hangs, detailing the ins and outs of her breakups, too. Diana would ask when she'd had a sense that things had begun to go wrong, if she'd at all seen it coming. Then she'd joke that we were all blind when it came to love, tell us that even when Brandon had begun following her, she'd still found ways to excuse it in her head.

Jesus. It was hard, even now, even sitting in this room, not to imagine her walking in. Picking up where we left off.

I forced myself to look up at Conway, to remind myself why I was here. I pushed the drink forward. 'Is it because I found the blood?'

Conway raised an eyebrow.

'Why you want to talk to me and not Margaret. Why I have to do the identification alone.'

'Yes, you could say that's part of it.' She took out her notebook and a pen. 'Let me remind you, Ms Lochman, that this conversation is being videotaped and is completely voluntary on your part.'

'I want to do whatever I can to help figure out what . . . what happened to Diana.'

Conway glanced to me, then looked back to her notebook, flipped to a blank page. 'Ms Lochman, I want to thank you for being so cooperative thus far, but I'd like to use this meeting to go over some things that we haven't had a chance to discuss yet.'

'Okay.'

Conway set her pen down. 'Tell me about your relationship with Harold Brant.'

I jolted, thrown by the question. 'What? Why?'

'We're trying to get a fuller picture.'

My head spun. How would she even – why would she be asking about Harry? Had Diana managed to find him that night out on the patio? Had they exchanged words? God, did the police think that Harry had something to do with it? It wasn't possible. He wouldn't.

Conway adjusted herself in her chair. 'Ms Lochman.'

'Sorry,' I said. 'Harry and I are separated.'

She flattened her palm against the table. She was wearing new nail polish: a chic pale gray. I imagined her heading to a salon, refreshing her phone with one hand while a lady clipped cuticles on the other. 'Can you walk me through the timeline?'

'Of Diana going missing?'

Conway shook her head. 'Of your separation.'

What was she on about?

'If you don't mind,' she added.

'And what if I do?'

Conway tapped lightly with her pen on the table. 'Ms Lochman, you've been nothing but forthcoming so far, and it's been a huge help, believe me. I know that it can be intrusive, the way we have to poke and prod, but truly, we wouldn't if we didn't think it was necessary.'

She was smooth, I'd give her that.

'What do you want to know?' I asked.

'The date you separated, what your relationship has been like since then. The basics. What you'd tell a friend, an acquaintance.'

She couldn't possibly know the meaning, the irony, in her words. I hadn't told any of my old friends or acquaintances a goddamn thing.

Conway leaned forward. 'I've been through it myself, you know. My husband thought I was too dedicated to my job,' she said with a scoff. 'And it's funny because he was the first guy to call himself a feminist but deep down I suppose he really wanted a 1950s wife to cook him dinner.'

My eyebrows scrunched up; I was surprised more than anything at her candor. 'I don't know what your marriage – or Harry, for that matter – has to do with any of this.'

Conway stared, as if waiting me out.

'Harry had nothing to do with Diana's disappearance,' I said. 'He wouldn't hurt a fly.' Not physically, at least, I thought bitterly. He wasn't a fighter. He didn't get angry. He loved to save the day, even if it had made him wishy-washy, leaving me because Elizabeth *needed* him, whatever that meant.

But he would never. He didn't have it in him . . .

'I didn't say that, Ms Lochman. I only said I wanted to better understand the timeline.'

'Okay,' I said, trying to pull myself together. 'Harry left on March sixth.'

'You're sure about that date?' she asked.

'Yes. You don't forget a date like that.'

She nodded me along.

'When I came home from work that night, his bags were packed. He told me he loved someone else and that she needed him.'

Conway paused for a moment. 'Ouch,' she said finally. 'Had to hurt.'

'It did,' I said. 'It does.'

'And what has your contact been since then?' she asked.

In a flash, I saw him, pressing me against the tree outside of Eamon's, only a handful of feet from where I discovered Diana's blood.

Conway cleared her throat.

'We didn't really talk much after that. A couple of times on the phone, that was it. Some texts.'

I miss you.

'Not to make arrangements, anything like that?' Conway asked.

'No,' I said. 'And I don't understand . . . I don't understand what *any* of this has to do with Diana. You said you found her body. God, her blood was on my hands. How does this help her? Unless he's a suspect, which I promise you, he had nothing to do with it – he didn't even know her – I don't get what you're after.'

My palms had begun to sweat, and I wiped them against my thighs. I could feel Conway circling, a vulture above a picked-over corpse.

'Why are you wasting time on Harry when her ex, Brandon, is out there? When . . . when Diana is *dead*?'

The word, finally uttered, brought tears to my eyes, and I wiped them away with the back of my hand, spent.

'Ms Lochman,' Conway said carefully. Her eyes widened with sympathy, understanding. *Tell me everything* eyes she probably used on everyone she ever interviewed.

She glanced at the camera briefly, then turned back to me.

'I told you we found a body, but I never said it was hers.'

22

MARGARET

I agreed to meet Lars, knowing he wouldn't leave until I did. He picked a place on Main Street, a coffee shop sandwiched between an art gallery and a Mexican restaurant, both of which were closed at this hour.

I parked and turned off the car, my mind still twisting around what had happened at the station, the thought I couldn't seem to shake, that maybe we all had secrets. Diana, Sam and me.

This strip had its share of small-town charm, with bluestone sidewalks and historical buildings in a rainbow of colors and facades, but even so, it was empty. Perhaps it was different over the weekend, but looking at it now, on a Monday morning, it felt less like the quaint upstate towns Lars and I had longed for and more like an abandoned ghost town. Fitting, because we were surrounded by ghosts. Our lost loves, our lost dreams, my son, and now, Diana.

I spotted him through the glass, my own ghost. Lars.

He was at a table in the corner, the *New York Times* open to the Arts section in front of him, his long wavy hair tousled, a tiny bit greasy and pulled back into a small ponytail. He was wearing a simple gray T-shirt and black jeans. The crazy thing was, if I saw him now, a stranger in a coffee shop, I'd be attracted, I wouldn't be able to help myself. I'd restart our history, all over again.

I opened the front door, the bell jingling cheerfully behind me, and took a deep breath, steeling myself.

'Peggy,' he said. 'You came. Here.' He motioned to the chair next to him as if this were run-of-the-mill, as if we'd planned to meet, as if we were exploring a cute little Hudson Valley town, adding it to a list of places we wanted to live one day.

'You didn't give me much choice, Lars.'

He forced a smile. 'Do you want to get something? The espresso is really good.'

I sank into the chair, suddenly exhausted. Beneath the aroma of Puerto Rican beans and the dusty scent of newsprint, I smelled that tang of alcohol, leaching from his pores.

You fucking slut.

'I don't want anything,' I said.

'Oh, please,' Lars said, rising from his seat. 'I'll get you something.' He made his way to the counter, and I didn't have the energy to stop him. The barista smiled, charmed by him, unsurprisingly, as he ordered an almond-milk latte and a plain croissant, my coffee shop go-to. Once, when we were first dating, Lars had flipped the script and ordered me a regular latte and an almond croissant. He'd never forgotten again.

After a moment, he returned with my fare, the latte's foam shaped like a heart.

Lars took a careful sip of his drink, and it left a print of milk on his upper lip, and in spite of myself, this old long-dead part of me, part of us, wanted to lean forward and kiss it off before the smell of alcohol quickly reminded me of all that had come between us. 'Aren't you going to try it?' he asked with a nod to my drink.

Dutifully, I did. It was good, delicious, actually, and my body probably needed the sustenance. I ate nothing last night – neither did Sam. I flaked off a piece of the croissant, let the butter layers melt on my tongue.

'See?' Lars said. 'Isn't this nice?' He smiled. 'Like it used to be . . . before.'

I hated that word now, *before*, hated how our loss had cleaved our timeline in two.

'We've both changed a lot, Lars. It's never going to be like it was before.'

His hand clenched around his mug, rattling it against the minuscule silver spoon that sat, foam covered, on the saucer. His frustration, his quickness to anger, that was a part of our *after*, too. Something he mostly kept at bay during the day and only really came out when he was well into the drink. He wasn't pushing me around or anything, it wasn't like that, but his mood was so different, like he was always trying, very hard, not to explode.

Out at the bars, away from me, he did explode sometimes, he must. I looked at the cut beneath his lip from last week. At the scuffed-up skin around his hands. He must.

Lars took another sip and set the mug down carefully. 'It could be, though. There's no reason why we can't go back. I get it. I pushed you too quickly to try again, I know that.'

'And the drinking?'

'Yes,' he said. 'The drinking. I'm working on it. I'm cutting back.'

'I think you're past the point of *cutting back*, Lars.'

Even as I said it, the guilt and shame washed through me. Who was I to judge him when I was in as much of a mess myself? Worse, even. I couldn't quit cold turkey. I had, actually, but the ramifications were still there: the phone calls, the bills I hid from him. The numbers, mounting, interest compounding faster than I'd ever thought it could.

Lars stirred his latte, and I took another bite of my croissant, the accusation hanging between us.

'So we've had a rough year,' he said finally. 'Can you blame us? Things like this, they test marriages. It doesn't mean —'

'But it does, though. We don't work anymore. Can't you see that?'

'I know what I said was unforgivable. I know I should never have used those words. I was just so shocked, to see you, to see you like that.'

I pushed my chair back. 'Because you never should have seen me. You shouldn't have followed us. You crossed a line, Lars.'

'I know,' he said. 'I know that. But I'm sorry. We can do therapy. We can work it out. Shit happens. People cross lines. It doesn't mean it's all up in smoke.' He reached out, taking my hand in his, but his palm was clammy; it always was, now that he was drinking. I realized, with a tinge of disgust, that his latte most definitely had booze in it. 'I can forgive you for that,' he said. 'I know it meant nothing.'

'Forgive *me*?' I asked, whipping my hand away.

'Yes,' he said. 'For . . . for sleeping with that guy. It was just a one-night thing. I know that. Right, Peggy?'

I stared at him, my heart beating with pain and loss and resentment and disillusionment.

'Peggy?'

I found I couldn't do it. I couldn't sit there and say that I actually kind of liked the guy. That I'd told him about Timothy and he'd understood. That we'd lost Diana — that Diana was dead — and in a strange way it had bonded me to this place, to this man I'd only known a couple days.

'Yes,' I said. 'It was a one-night thing.' I stood. 'But it doesn't change this between us. You and I are through. You need to accept that.'

'No,' he said. 'I won't. I can't. We can get past this, if you'll only work on it with me. I'll stop drinking. I swear. It can't just be *over*. After everything we've been through. You're my family, Peggy.'

Lars looked at me, so incredibly hurt that it had come to this.

'I have to go. Please, Lars,' I said, my eyes begging. 'Please, if you ever cared about me, please do me this favor. Go home. Let me, let *us*, go.'

I broke my own rule; I sped. Nine miles over to start. Then ten, eleven, twelve. There was something wild about it, no cop in my rearview, no one to tell me I was doing anything wrong. Freedom, in its way.

I wanted to be away from Lars, from the horrors waiting back at the police station. I wanted to put this whole weekend, what was meant to be our escape from the city and had turned into something more awful than I could have ever imagined, behind us.

Back at the rental, I ate ravenously, the little bit of croissant only cueing up my appetite as my mind spun, worried that Sam still hadn't called. Why her and not me? What was really going on?

I took a shower, scrubbing myself nearly raw. In front of the mirror, I rubbed the steam away and carefully, slowly, applied makeup, trying to control something in a world of things that were heartbreakingly uncontrollable.

My phone buzzed, and there was a text from Alex.

Are you still at the police station? I have to go open up at work. I tried to call you. I'm so sorry about everything. I don't even know what to say. Come by the brewery anytime if you want to see me: Two Friends Brewery. It's on Main Street in town.

I started to text him back but found I didn't know what to say. So I got dressed instead, rubbing oil into my stretch marks, pulling on worn-in jeans and an oversized tank.

It was noon, and Sam still hadn't called.

I walked down the hall, past the room Diana had been using, the door opened wide, her clothes splayed out. Sam had riffled through them on Saturday night, looking for answers. Had she missed something?

The house was quiet, pin-drop still, and I walked in, knelt down, and carefully began to go through Diana's things.

A long-sleeve black dress that looked fantastic on her – size

189

12, made in Italy, lay flat to dry – a soft knit cardigan made of virgin wool and cashmere, a lacey nude bra with satin straps, 36D, a size someone like me could only dream of, whose third fastening prong was bent, as if about to come undone.

All these remnants left behind – things she'd bought at stores I could never afford, or ordered online, things she'd dry-cleaned or sent out for wash and fold, things she'd worn through good times and bad, through the beginnings of a terrible separation with Brandon and the rebuilding of her life.

There is no record of Diana Holbein at all.

Maybe she hadn't been who she told us she was, but not all of her was a lie. The way she tossed her head back in laughter. The way she could wrap you in a hug that made you feel like you were twelve again, being comforted by a best friend. The way her push-up bra sent a hint of tasteful cleavage out the top of her necklines. These things were real, if nothing else was.

I found myself digging into pockets, praying for a note, a clue, anything that could explain why she'd brought us here.

I picked up a pair of designer jeans, bright white with intentional holes at the knees, one of Diana's only non-black items. I dug my hands into each pocket, even the tiny little pocket on the front right side. Then, flipping the jeans around, I checked the back.

My pulse ticked up as my fingers landed on the edge of something.

Carefully, I pulled it out, stared at a matchbook in my fingers, flipped open, the matches exposed, all but three of them torn off.

Of course, I thought. Diana was only an occasional smoker, only really a drunken one. A regular smoker carried a lighter on them always, but a casual one, like Diana, one who only reached for cigarettes after a couple of drinks, often relied on matchbooks. That's how Lars was, at least, in those early days. Matchbooks were always coming out of his pockets, turning up in the wash or at the foot of the bed, after a big night out. You decided you wanted a cigarette, grabbed free matches from the bar, and went out to try to bum one.

I carefully undid its flap, knowing it was unlikely to offer any sort of answers. It's not like she'd have her real name printed on the thing. It was probably from a bar in Brooklyn, anyway.

I flipped over the flap, then froze. There, printed on flimsy cardboard, was something I hadn't expected at all.

My pulse began to race, and I grabbed my phone, reading over his message multiple times, checking it against the name on the matches.

Two Friends Brewery.

The place where Alex worked.

23

SAM

Conway's words seemed to ripple through me:

I told you we found a body, but I never said it was hers.

'What do you mean?' I asked, hopeful. 'You mean it's *not* Diana? She's okay?'

'I don't know where your friend is or if she's okay. I don't even know *who* she is,' Conway said. 'All we have to go on is what you've told us.'

I blinked, trying to make sense of it. 'So it was someone random? Then why . . . why do you want to talk to me?'

Conway glanced at her hands, then back up at me. Pausing. Assessing.

Just before it hit me, I wished I hadn't asked the question, hadn't opened Pandora's box. I wished I'd pushed my chair back, stood, turned around and run. Called Margaret and demanded she take us both home – not to the rental but back to Brooklyn and out of this terrible town.

Conway continued to stare, as if trying to understand whether I was bluffing or not.

That's when it properly connected.

The unreturned phone calls.

The fact that he hadn't been at Elizabeth's house, either.

That the blood had been right there, right where he and I had been standing.

No.

It couldn't be.

No. No. No.

'Ms Lochman, we found the remains of who we believe to be Harold Brant in the woods behind Eamon's yesterday evening.'

Harry.

My love. My darling. My Harry.

My *everything*.

'No,' I said, shaking my head as if I could ward off the truth if I only shook hard enough. 'No,' I said. 'It can't be. *He* can't be.'

All this time, every moment since I'd woken up Saturday morning, walked downstairs to see Margaret clutching her phone, hoping Diana would call, I'd been thinking of her, focusing on her.

Diana. Diana. Diana.

But what if . . . what if . . .

Had I gotten it all wrong?

Had he not been ignoring me? Had he wanted to say more?

Those three little dots, the unsent text message, shot a chill through my spine.

'No,' I said again, more forcefully this time. 'How could it, how could he –'

Harry.

Conway pressed her lips together, the silence uneasy. Terrifying.

Even after he'd left, even after he'd gone back to her, I hadn't actually thought . . .

I'd never thought it was over. I'd thought, maybe naively, that we'd find our way back to each other some way, somehow. Part of it was the shame of having to tell my parents, my friends, that our union had been so short-lived, but a bigger, deeper part wasn't that at all.

It was the feel of Harry's hips behind mine as I washed the dishes, the way he tucked his body against me when he slept, almost like a child, the texts I'd get every morning without fail, telling me he loved me, asking how I was. It was all the tiny little LEGO blocks that make up a life together. Each touch, each word, each look a different colorful piece, stacked on top of each other, staggered and interlocked so the building doesn't fall. Harry had stopped adding to our tower – stopped abruptly, and that wasn't fair – but I never stopped believing he would return to it one day, that I would forgive him and we would find a way to stack up more blocks – together.

And Christ, maybe I hadn't even been wrong. Maybe Friday night really *had* meant something to him. Would I really never know what else he'd meant to say?

Was this it?

I glanced up. A box of tissues had appeared on the table, seemingly from nowhere, but my eyes were bone-dry.

A flutter of hope burst forth in my chest.

'Are you sure it's him?' I asked. 'Are you absolutely positive?'

'We are fairly certain,' Conway said. 'And it's not yet possible to say conclusively, but this is likely a homicide investigation. That's why it's so very important that you continue to cooperate with us.'

Without another word, she procured a folder from the black leather bag that was sitting by her feet. It was pale yellow, manila, and I had a sharp, awful feeling, a stabbing in my stomach. Once I looked inside, things would never, ever be the same.

Slowly, the detective's manicured hands pushed the folder toward me. She left them there, unmoving, as if I were a child, and she, an elementary school teacher, not wanting me to look in the day's activity packet until she'd properly detailed the lesson.

She pushed the folder another inch farther, and it hit me then:

I was here to identify Harry.

Oh god, oh god, oh god.

'We'd like you to confirm Mr Brant's identity. Do you think you can help us with that?'

I swallowed, my throat suddenly dry, as I imagined what was in there. Photos of Harry, of my love, the life sucked out of him. *Oh god, oh god, oh god.*

My tongue felt like sandpaper. 'Can I get some water?'

Conway nodded and slid the folder back to her side of the table, then walked out of the room.

I hardly knew if it was a minute or ten, but I stared at the folder, right there in front of me. I had to do it, I knew that. I had to know for sure whether I would ever see Harry again.

I was the important one now, after all. Fuck Elizabeth.

It was me they were turning to. Me. Not her.

It was me who'd said those vows in front of my friends and family.

Conway returned, a sweating bottle of Poland Spring in her hand. 'Are you up to this?'

I took it from her, fumbled with the cap and finally got it off, my fingers like fat sausages, anything but nimble, then drank half the bottle in one gulp.

Conway didn't sit. She didn't wait for my answer, either. She walked around to the other side of the table, grabbed the folder, and returned to me.

Gingerly, she set it in front of me and placed one hand on my shoulder. 'I'll give you a few minutes,' she said. 'Take your time.'

Then she left me again, alone, the folder sitting, tempting, in front of me.

I drank the rest of the water, sip by sip by sip. Stalling. Knowing somewhere, deep down, that these were the last seconds of me being me, of us being us. In these moments, it didn't matter that he'd left me, that he'd hurt me and betrayed me and turned my world inside out.

It only mattered that I'd promised to love him always.

Till death do us part.

I set the empty bottle down, and it wobbled back and forth, then fell, like the king piece in chess when your opponent has defeated you.

Checkmate.

Fingers shaking, I lifted the edge of the folder, slowly at first, and then fast, whipping it open, like ripping at a Band-Aid, or pulling the baby tooth that's desperate to come out.

At first, he looked peaceful – I swear to god.

Eyes shut tight, lips pressed together, he looked like he was asleep. Like he used to look when I would watch him sometimes, wondering if he ever dreamed about us.

And then, like one of those magic images I used to look at in elementary school, it shifted, and I saw it for what it was.

The pallor of his skin – vampirish, edging on blue.

The dirt smudged across his neck – grimy, unclean.

The spots of blood all over his denim shirt.

And beneath his head, on the ground and the brush and the leaves.

The blood. Not as much as I'd seen at the edge of the woods, but blood all the same, framing his head like some sort of noir halo.

That's when it hit me fully.

The blood I'd found. The blood that had been lining my nails.

It wasn't Diana's blood.

It was Harry's.

I turned to the side and abruptly threw up.

I didn't hear the knock on the door if there was one. I could barely focus, pulse pounding in my head, bile sour in the back of my throat, my stomach still churning in protest.

Before I could truly process it, Conway was back in the room, sitting opposite me, another bottle of Poland Spring on the table. An officer who barely looked more than twenty-two wielded a bucket and a mop and was cleaning up my mess, replacing the scent of sick with some sort of pine-tinged chemical aroma.

Then he was gone, and the folder and the photo had

disappeared, too, and the second bottle of water was in my hand, and I was sipping on it, slowly, Conway watching intently.

'I'm sorry to do this, Ms Lochman, but we need to go back to my earlier questions.'

I nodded, sipping again at my water. It hardly mattered now. Harry was dead. Harry had never had a chance to call me, to text me; he was gone before we could have our fresh start.

'When was the last time you saw Harold Brant?' she asked.

'Friday night,' I said. 'At the bar.'

Conway nodded and made a note on her pad. 'And was that a planned meeting?'

I shook my head. 'It was a surprise to me that we wound up in Catskill, where Harry was.'

'Did you tell your friends this?'

'No,' I said. 'I thought it would just be one night and then we'd be on our way to Saratoga Springs. None of this was supposed to happen.'

'Did you contact Mr Brant, ask him to meet you?'

'No,' I managed. 'But I did post on Instagram. I checked in at the bar. He could have seen it from that. Later on, I went to the back to have a cigarette with Diana, and he was just . . . there. I never saw him come in.'

Conway nodded. 'What did you do when you saw Mr Brant?'

My eyes flashed with rage. 'What would you do?'

Conway ignored my outburst, simply folded her hands in her lap.

'I hadn't seen him in two months,' I said. 'I approached him.'

'Were you angry?' she asked.

'Of *course* I was angry,' I said. 'He'd left me for another woman —'

I froze, wheels turning, as I suddenly realized what this was.

'Hold on,' I said. 'I didn't kill him, if that's what you were thinking. I was angry, yes, but I didn't —' My voice choked. 'God, I couldn't. I love him.'

It occurred to me that the present tense didn't apply to Harry anymore, but I didn't correct myself.

'Please tell me what happened,' Conway said.

I felt a flush in my cheeks as I imagined it, as I had so many times since it had happened. Shame.

But along with that shame, the knowledge that that was the last time Harry and I would be together. I couldn't bear to regret it now.

'We went back in the woods where it was private . . . to talk, but we ended up having, you know . . . relations . . .'

My eyes found Conway's, but her expression remained blank.

'Sexual relations?' she prompted, after a moment of quiet.

'Yes,' I said.

'And then?'

'And when I could see that this didn't change anything and it had been a mistake, I went inside.'

'Just like that?' Conway asked. 'You have your big reunion, and then you walk off?'

I looked up, catching her eyes, and I hated her in that moment. Hated her more than I'd ever hated Harry. It was one thing for me to judge myself. It was another for her to judge me. Harry was gone. My love was dead. Fuck.

'Yes,' I said. 'The whole thing felt wrong. Nothing like I wanted it to.'

'What happened next?' she prompted.

'He texted me,' I said. 'He said he was sorry, and then I saw the dots like he was going to say something else, but they disappeared. I never got another message.'

'And that was the last contact you had?' Conway asked.

'Yes, I was inside,' I said. 'I thought about going to talk to him again, but then I saw Diana, and she said she was going to see if he was still out there, scope it out.'

'Back where Mr Brant was?'

'Yes,' I said. 'In that direction.'

'And then?'

'Then she never came back, and I got drunker, and Margaret couldn't find Diana, and then that Alex guy drove us home.'

Conway stared at me, wheels turning.

Finally, she spoke.

'Is there anything else?'

'No,' I said quickly.

But it was there, niggling at the back of my brain, the knowledge that there *was* something, something that might help her find out what happened to Harry.

'Ms Lochman?'

'I went to see Harry the day before yesterday. I wanted to talk to him and ask him if he saw Diana, but Elizabeth was there. The woman he left me for.'

Conway nodded me on.

'She was upset. She told me he wasn't there. She sounded like, somehow, she knew what had happened between us. I thought maybe he'd told her, but he couldn't have, he would have been . . .' I swallowed back the word. *Dead*. 'I mean, he never would have come home on Friday.'

'And?' Conway prompted.

'So she must have found out another way. She said "You've already won" like she knew what had happened. And she . . . she didn't seem worried. She just said Harry wasn't home, like she'd thrown him out or something.'

Elizabeth. With her perfect home. With her stunning beauty.

Elizabeth, who in the end, he'd chosen over me.

Elizabeth, who was supposed to be out of the picture when we said our vows, who I'd spent the last months wondering if she ever was.

Elizabeth, who would always hate me, no matter how fair it was.

'If she saw what happened between us, she might have, god, she might have been angry enough to kill him.'

Conway's eyes widened.

'She's not just another woman. She's Harry's ex-wife.'

24

MARGARET

Two Friends Brewery.

It was smack-dab in the middle of town, taking up space along Main Street, only two short blocks from where I'd met up with Lars.

I parked in front and opened my phone, checking the finder app, but Lars's location was no longer being shared. Had he realized I'd checked on him and shut it off? I turned my location off as well, praying he'd agreed to what I'd asked of him and left.

Turning back to the brewery's glass windows, half covered in the bright green logo that had been lurking in the back pocket of Diana's jeans, I tried to make out Alex, but the sun was too bright, the glare too strong to see much of anything at all.

Had Diana been a regular here? Did she know Alex? Had Alex only been there to distract me so Diana could – could *what*? I pictured us on his sofa, and I wondered if I could have been so very wrong about him.

Inside, I spotted Alex right away, standing dead center behind the bar, the bandana tied around his head.

'Margaret,' he said.

I took a quick breath, orienting myself in the space. Unlike Eamon's, which had been run-down and dive-y, this place was trying, and very hard. Raw wood, stainless steel, and crisp white walls. There were even hops arranged artfully in glass apothecary jars. Behind the bar sat three enormous metal vessels, pipes snaking every which way like some sort of science lab. 'We used to spare the customers from seeing all that mess,' my dad, a restaurant manager who longed for the good old days of white tablecloths and silver ice buckets, had ranted. 'Now it's all open kitchens and unfinished spaces. And these places charge four bucks for a couple of extra slices of avocado.'

'I tried to call you,' he said. 'I didn't want to bother you, but, god, I'm so sorry.'

In moments, he'd hinged up one end of the bar and was in front of me, wrapping me in a hug. It felt so good, so warm and safe, that I thought I might be crazy, I might have this all wrong, but then my eyes caught the matchbooks scattered across the bar, and I forced myself to pull away. 'I need to talk to you.'

There were a few guys in the corner near the window, flights arranged before them, two-ounce glasses tucked neatly into skinny wooden slabs, filled with liquids, golden and clear to coffee black. Lars and I used to love sampling everything, the array of colors and flavors, bitter and sour and sometimes even a little sweet.

'Charlie,' Alex called without hesitation, and a guy stood up from behind the bar. 'I'm going to go out back. Watch the bar.' He turned back to me. 'This way,' he said, pushing open a door and nodding for me to follow.

Outside, the patio was huge. No smoker's station, by any means. It was closed off, surrounded by other buildings in town, but the expanse of concrete was packed with colorful picnic tables and umbrellas that hadn't yet been opened, all with that same damn logo.

The sun was shining strong, but there was a decent breeze, and I pulled my jacket tighter, the smell of Sam's puke long gone now. 'This place must get packed in the summer,' I said off-handedly, and, unable to help myself, I imagined Diana here, forgoing the flight and going straight for whatever on the menu went down easy and had the highest ABV content. Grabbing a pack of matches when she wanted a cigarette.

'Did you – did you have to see her?' Alex asked, ignoring my comment and getting straight to the point. He placed a hand on my arm, but I tensed up, and he whipped it back.

'No,' I said. 'Sam's still at the station, but . . .' I let my eyes lift to his, and I tried to imagine him conspiring with Diana, lying to me. I found I couldn't.

'When you saw us on Friday, did Diana look familiar to you?'

'What do you mean?'

'Did you recognize her? Did you know her?'

'No,' he said, face scrunching up. 'No, of course not. I would have said something if I had. Why would you ask that?'

I dug in my pocket until my fingers found the matchbook. I turned my hand over, showing it to him.

204

'Did you get that from my house?'

'No,' I said. 'I found it in the pocket of Diana's jeans. She wasn't wearing them that night, but they were there in the ones she'd packed. She must have been here before.'

Alex blinked twice. 'Oh.'

'Oh?' I said. 'That's all you have to say?'

'I'm sorry,' he said. 'I suppose that's got to be . . . *alarming*. I just mean, everyone has those.'

'Diana doesn't even live here.'

'Sure,' he said. 'But it's a popular brewery. Yelp. Tripadvisor, all that. We get lots of people up from the city.'

'Okay,' I said cautiously. 'So she did come here, then?'

'I don't know,' he said with a shrug. 'Probably, I guess, if she had those in her pocket.'

'But you never saw her? She's kind of hard to forget, you know. She's quite . . . striking.'

'I didn't,' Alex said.

'You swear?' I asked.

'Believe me.' His voice was suddenly firm. 'Before Friday night, I'd never seen any of you in my life.'

'It's strange, no? We weren't supposed to be here, and then we . . . we lose the car key . . . and we wind up at Eamon's, and you sit right next to us. You and I start talking. It's a *lot* of coincidences.'

'It is,' he said. 'But I promise you, I never saw her. I never heard her name. I barely even saw her that night. I spilled that drink on her, but after that, she was gone, remember? Out smoking.'

I bristled. 'How did you know she was out smoking?'

Alex laughed. 'Because you told me.'

205

'I did?'

He nodded. 'Plus, you and Sam were talking about it. I was right there next to you at the bar.'

'You were listening to us?'

'Margaret,' he said, reaching out for my arm again. This time, I didn't shake him off. 'Of course I was listening. The second you walked in, I knew I wanted to meet you. I was trying to think of a way to start talking to you. Who knows? Maybe my spilled beer was even some sort of Freudian slip. But I don't know your friend. I swear.'

I looked at his eyes, at his mouth and his chin, seeking out a narrowing, a tilt, a twitch, in the same way I had come to look at Lars when I questioned him about his drinking.

Alex wasn't lying. What's more, he didn't seem the type to lie. Not only to me but to anyone.

'I believe you,' I said as warmth swam through my blood. 'And I'm sorry. You should get back to work. Thank you for reassuring me.'

Alex's hands found my shoulders. 'Margaret, I don't care about work. I'm worried about you, with everything that happened. You must be losing it. I would be. Your friend.'

I lifted my eyes to his, and though the tears didn't come, my voice was thick, wavering with emotion. 'It's horrible, isn't it? It's . . . it's unthinkable. Detective Conway called Sam last night and told her they'd found a body, and that was it. They left us with that information, stewing in it.' I paused for breath, and his hands fell, a bit awkwardly, away from my shoulders. He shoved them in his pockets, as if he wasn't sure what to do with them. We weren't a couple, not by any means. We hadn't figured out the choreography that every couple does – how to hold each other, to console each other just right.

As if reading my mind, he stretched a hand back toward mine, our fingers lacing together, then resting like that, a single point of connection. 'I can't even imagine,' he said. 'It's so callous.'

I gazed at him, catching the stubble on his cheeks, stubble that had scratched across my belly, over my scars, his eyes, large and round, like two full moons, eyes that hadn't judged when he'd seen my body as it was. A good man is hard to find, but here he was, and I believed it: he was good.

'We went down there this morning, only –' The words caught as I pictured Sam, still there in the station. Were they grilling her? Was she scared? I'd thought myself the mother of the group, but I couldn't protect her *or* Diana. I couldn't stop any of us from getting hurt.

Alex unhooked his hand from mine and wrapped his arm around my shoulders instead. His muscles pressed against my skin, defined and strong.

I leaned into his chest, and I didn't fit like I did with Lars, it was a different fit altogether – but it felt so good all the same, his body human superglue, as if holding all the patchwork pieces of me together.

Carefully, he stroked his fingers through my hair, drawing parallel lines in my scalp. My pulse kicked down another notch, and I imagined escaping with him. Not having to pick up Sam, not having to return to Brooklyn – ever – or to the advertising rat race I'd never really liked but that had been worth it when I'd thought we were starting a family – to the bitter loneliness of staring at the cracked plaster of my prewar ceiling while stretched out across a queen bed — to all the damn babies I had to interact with to get through my day. Toddling up to the counter at the coffee shop. Lounging in their strollers as their moms pushed them through Fort Greene Park. Bouncing along with their heavenly baby laughs as their dads carried them like joeys, baby backpacks strapped over their tattooed arms. Instead, I'd be here, with a man who knew what it was to long for a child, to miss out on so much. We could sip IPAs while he worked, and the only decisions we'd ever have to make were how long of a hike we wanted to take on Saturday, whether our eggs should be scrambled or sunny-side up.

'Only what, Margaret?' Alex asked carefully.

His words broke my fantasy, and I straightened, disentangling myself from his arms. I turned to him, arranging my features back to neutral. 'When we got there this morning, they didn't want to speak to me. They only wanted to speak to her. And it was clear from the way Detective Conway was talking that it wasn't going to be a quick conversation, either. She all but told me to leave the station and come back later.'

'But you don't think . . .' Alex asked. 'I mean, Sam's your friend, right?'

'Of course I don't,' I said. 'Still, I don't know what to make of it. Yes, she found the blood on the ground, but that was it. Other than that, there was no reason to talk to her and not to me. I'm the one who officially made the first report.' The anxiety kicked up again, rippling. 'That night, Sam and Diana disappear to the back patio, and then Sam's drunk out of her mind. What if something happened between them? Something maybe

208

Sam doesn't even understand. Hell, maybe something she doesn't even remember. She's – she's important to me. We've known each other for years, even if we only got really close these last couple of months. I want to protect her, but I don't know how to . . .'

I can't fail Sam, too.

'I don't know, Margaret,' Alex said carefully. 'I see what you're saying, but I'm sure there's an explanation. She did discover the crime scene, and she was out on the patio a lot more than you were that night. They're probably just being especially thorough with her. What exactly do you feel you need to protect her from? I can hardly imagine her attacking your friend and then, god, dragging a body somewhere and coming back and ordering a beer.'

'No,' I said, because Alex had voiced what I was afraid to. 'I didn't mean that. I don't think she *hurt* Diana. I don't even know what I think.'

'Did you ask her why she was there so early when she found the blood? She told the detective she'd lost some jewelry, right?'

'Yes,' I said. 'Her ex-husband was there, well, her current husband, because they're not officially split yet. He lives here –'

Alex caught my eyes, raising another eyebrow. I hadn't even told him about Lars showing up like he did.

'I know, it's crazy, and I guess they hooked up, and she lost her wedding rings, which she wasn't wearing but she had with her in her pocket. In all the chaos of what happened with Diana not coming home, she completely forgot them.'

'And you believe her. Right?' Alex asked.

'Of course,' I said. 'She's completely distraught about Diana. I know she would never hurt her intentionally. Still, I can't shake this, this *feeling* the police know something I don't, something that ties her up in all this. Conway is smart. She doesn't seem like one to chase what's not there. It's unnerving.'

Cautiously, Alex reached for my hand again. I let him take it, let him squeeze it, as his other hand came to my cheek, tucking a bit of hair behind my ear, then resting on the back of my head. 'I hate how hard all of this is on you. And for it all to happen on the weekend, well, the weekend your son . . .' His voice trailed off, and I looked down, tried to still my quickly beating heart. When I looked back up his eyes were open, understanding. 'But I wouldn't jump to conclusions. It's far more likely that it was some creep, some attack, than it was in any way linked to Sam, even accidentally, right? Didn't you say Diana had a stalker ex?'

For a second, it was so easy to believe it. Something casual. Unplanned and drunken. The kind of thing that happened to women in bars, on the edge of the woods, in the shadows, all the time. Her ex, Brandon. Stalking her. Finding her.

'You're right,' I said. And then again, as if to force myself to believe it. 'You have to be right.'

His hand dug deeper into my hair, and my eyes caught his. 'Thank you,' I said.

He nodded without letting me go.

I had to have it, that escape, even if it was fleeting.

I leaned in and pressed my lips to his, craving his comfort, his sheer physicality, hungry for something that would take me away from all of this.

It was hard to know how much time passed before we

210

pulled away, but when he looked down, his eyes were naked, earnest.

'I'm so glad I met you, Margaret,' he said.

I blinked slowly, and in the chaos of all that had happened, I felt it truly.

'I'm glad I met you, too.'

25

SAM

I waited at the front of the station, chair hard beneath my butt, foot tapping against the linoleum, for Margaret to come get me. Tugging at a ragged nail, I couldn't help but see the look of judgment on Conway's face as I told her that Harry had been Elizabeth's before he'd ever been mine.

It's not like it was something I was proud of. Or something I'd ever intended.

I'd had so many rules after that first night Harry and I shut down the ad agency together, after the feelings had taken over, the crush that wouldn't go away, even though I knew he was married and, per the rules of not being a shitty person, off-limits. I wasn't that kind of woman, the one who hurts others to get what she wants.

At first, I told myself it was only talking. It was just friendly.

And then it was only texting. And after that, lunches outside the office. Our coworkers saw us leaving together. It's not like they were actual dates. Udon or a sandwich from a nearby deli a few times a week was harmless. Nothing more than a chance to unpack the project we were on, to talk strategy, to plan our next presentation.

I'd done the same with other coworkers – other guys, even – before.

It was nothing.

Only it wasn't, of course.

He talked about his marriage. I talked about my family.

It was friendly, if not outright professional. It was friendly, even if there was more there, brewing beneath the surface.

We still hadn't crossed a line.

And then that one happy hour. It was supposed to be the whole team, but a couple of people bailed out, blaming too much work. Just Harry and me at that bar near the office, the one that would later become my go-to spot with Margaret and Diana. Harry and me and a bottle of Cabernet. Harry and me and a drunken kiss.

But *just* a kiss. Nothing more.

A stupid, silly kiss that put it all into motion.

Elizabeth found out about that kiss. I'm not sure if he told her, or if she came down to the city and saw us, or what. But she knew.

And then, she was throwing him out. And it was easy to do, because he already had that apartment, his crash pad in the city, the one I would come to call my own.

And one night, he texted me, and he asked me to come over.

And it was nearing midnight, and I knew exactly what it meant . . .

Of course I went over. As he opened the door and ushered

me in and we looked at each other, the tension between us too fraught, too electric, not to pursue, I'd asked him: 'Are we really doing this?' And of course, he said yes.

It was already all in motion. It wasn't *because* of me. It wasn't my fault.

So that's what I told my friends, my family, anyone who'd listen. I'd met a guy who was separated – very nearly divorced – and we'd hit it off. It didn't matter if that wasn't *exactly* the truth to its truest letter, because no one knew but us. Well, us and Diana. I'd blurted it out to her the first night I met her: 'I have a crush on a married man.' She never judged me, even if she should have.

It's not like I didn't feel guilt. I knew the dissolution of Harry's marriage couldn't have happened without me. But at the same time, if it had been a strong marriage, could one kiss have destroyed it? What if it was bound to fail, I no more than the straw that broke the proverbial camel's back?

I opened Harry's messages again, looked at his last text.

I'm so sorry

My heart ached as I wished so badly that I could have another moment with him. I wanted to go back to that night out in the woods and never walk away. Or ask him, beg him, to come inside with me, to save him from whatever – whoever – awaited him out there.

I scrolled up through the texts, past the angry ones, the questioning ones, up to the ones from before, when things were good – the *xoxo*'s and the funny memes and the questions about what takeout to get that evening.

The tears came then, finally, slowly but steadily, water leaking through a sieve. I wiped them away and looked up to see Margaret entering the station, her eyes kind.

'Sam,' she said. She wrapped me in a hug, and more tears came, and when I finally pulled back, the words practically tumbled out:

'It's not Diana.'

In the car, Margaret's hands pressed into her thighs. 'I don't understand,' she said. 'I can't believe it. Harry. Your husband. I'm so sorry. I'm so very sorry.' Her words were tender, genuine, as they had been in the station, and again as we walked across the parking lot, and again as she opened the car door for me.

I'm so sorry I'm so sorry I'm so sorry.

None of those words would bring Harry back.

Margaret shook her head, as if refusing to process this new information. 'What about Diana? She goes missing the same weekend that your husband . . . I don't understand what happened to her or how she's connected to this.'

'Me either,' I said, feeling the heat rise to my cheeks. Picturing Harry's face, the blood around the crown of his head in that horrifying photo. 'Just drive me back to our rental, please. Before I get sick again.'

'I really am so sorry,' Margaret said again.

'I know,' I said. 'Please just drive.'

Hands clasped at her perfect ten and two, never going more than a few miles over the limit, Margaret did, not pressing me with any more questions as we made our way across the river,

215

the Hudson beautiful and mammoth, careening every which way you looked.

Back at the house, she fumbled with the keys but eventually got the door open.

I went straight to the living room, sinking into the couch.

'Water?' Margaret asked. 'Or I could open something stronger.'

'Water,' I said, my voice empty, cold as stone. I leaned back, let my head rest on the sofa's back cushion, and stared at the ceiling, every ding and nick in the plaster. I imagined how this all would have gone if we'd never come up here. Would Detective Conway have found me, called me, in Saratoga Springs – or maybe Brooklyn? Would I have been on the first train or bus or whatever to identify Harry's remains? Would my rings be in my possession, still, remnants of what was between us?

If Elizabeth killed him, it's all your fault.

If you hadn't come here, Harry might still be alive.

Margaret set a glass of water on the table in front of me, and I grabbed it, drinking eagerly. She sat next to me, her hands folded, waiting.

When I didn't speak, she reached a hand to my shoulder. 'You have to tell me, Sam. You have to tell me everything Conway said.'

Margaret's eyes locked on me the whole time, as if I might fall apart any moment, and I told her as much as I could remember. About the photographs I'd had to identify, the morbid vision of Harry, captured forever from behind a camera's lens.

I didn't tell her about Elizabeth, I couldn't. Not now. It wasn't her business anyway, and I wanted to preserve Harry and me, not sully it. I'd had to tell Conway, because Elizabeth

216

might very well have killed him. I didn't have to tell anyone else.

That secret was still mine.

'That's heartbreaking,' Margaret said, once I was done. 'And you had no idea before you got there?'

'None,' I said, taking another sip of water. 'He wasn't responding to me, after we – you know. I thought he was just being a dick.'

A laugh escaped me, and Margaret looked at me as if I'd finally lost it. I'm not sure why it was so funny, but it was. Here I was, Harry was dead, and I was calling him a dick. He *was* a dick, but he was my dick, and I loved him. The laugh quickly turned to a sob, and I sucked back more water, trying to put a stopper in the bottle of my grief.

Margaret reached out to hug me again, but I shook her away. Her comfort only made the tears flow stronger. 'I'm sorry, I'm just in shock.'

'Of course you are. Anyone would be. If something happened to Lars . . .' Her voice trailed off. 'It doesn't matter if they hurt us or if everything wasn't perfect. We still loved them. I loved Lars more than I've ever loved anyone in my life. I'm sure you felt the same way about Harry. I know you did.' She paused. 'I hate to ask this –'

'Go ahead. I've been asked everything at this point.'

Margaret nodded, but still, her face looked pained. 'Did they say anything about Diana at all?'

I blinked twice, slowly, trying to gather thoughts I hadn't had so much as a moment to process.

Harry was gone, but so was Diana, and I felt unbearably alone. Margaret was the only person still around who was even aware of what had gone on in my life the last two months, and I hardly knew her that well. I was thirty years old, and I had nothing to show for it. No one. Parents I'd lied to. A sister I'd hardly connected with. Friends I'd also been deceiving for months. Two women who knew the truth about my breakup, and one of them was gone.

More tears came, but I brushed them away quickly, getting back to the question at hand. 'As I was leaving, Conway said they're trying to figure out how everything fits together, but she didn't say anything more about Diana than that. She floated the idea that it might be a huge coincidence.'

Margaret leaned forward. 'What do you think?'

I glanced at the blemished ceiling, then back to my hands. 'I don't know,' I said, because I didn't. Even if Elizabeth had killed Harry, that didn't explain Diana. That didn't explain the man who was asking about us.

'What if someone killed them both?' Margaret asked.

My eyes flashed, and it was almost too terrible to imagine. How could someone have killed both Harry and Diana in one fell swoop? Christ.

'Brandon, you mean?'

'Brandon, or . . . *someone*. I'm sorry,' Margaret said. 'I don't mean to be so morbid. It could be entirely unconnected.' Her voice wavered, as if she didn't believe it herself. 'Did Conway mention any other blood, belonging to someone else?'

'No.'

But there, creeping into the back of my brain, a thought that was horrible, even more heartwrenching than both of them dying together. A thought beyond Elizabeth or Brandon or some frightening stranger.

Could Diana have had something to do with it? Could she have been pissed, furious that Harry had fucked me when he knew it wouldn't change anything? Could Elizabeth be as lost and confused as I am?

No. It wasn't possible.

Or was it the other way, as Margaret had suggested? Had Diana gone out, seen Elizabeth attacking Harry – had Diana tried to stop her? Had Elizabeth turned on her, too? Had Brandon found Diana and then somehow Harry got in his way?

'I need to lie down,' I said, theories turning to soup in my brain. 'I can't think about this anymore.'

'Of course,' Margaret said. 'You should.'

Slowly, I made my way up the stairs, past the locked door I'd tried to open in my hungover state on Saturday morning, oblivious to Diana's disappearance, past the bathroom where she had flat-ironed my hair, which Harry had said looked 'nice'. To the room I'd burst into on Friday, already scheming how to get Harry to come out and meet me.

As I was pulling the curtains closed and beginning to undress, my phone dinged.

A new text.

My heart leapt as I saw that string of numbers.

Elizabeth.

What have you done?

TUESDAY

MORNING

26 | MARGARET

I woke wishing for Alex, stretched across the spacious bed, longing to be near his nooks and crannies, the curve of his muscles, the feel of his bones. All those things that were so fresh, so exciting, like a new encyclopedia, waiting to be read. The doubts from that matchbook in Diana's pocket had been put completely to rest by yesterday's news: Diana wasn't dead after all, Harry was. Perhaps it all was a big coincidence, like Conway had said.

Alex had called last night as soon as he'd gotten off work, and I'd explained to him that Diana wasn't dead, that it was Sam's husband whose body had been found.

Sam and I passed the rest of the night quietly. We ate dinner and she went to bed. I loaded the dishwasher and set to work to find a manual, something that would allow us to contact the rental's owner. We'd checked all the typical spots, but I knew there had to be something, *somewhere*. I finally located a binder under the sink, buried behind a bucket holding a mishmash of cleaning products, a trove of plastic bags, and piping that was beginning to rust. Next to the binder, a Ziploc bag held match-books, Two Friends Brewery and Eamon's among them.

In the binder, a neat thing covered in canvas, were restaurant recommendations, a Wi-Fi code that didn't work (despite my trying multiple times), and a page in the back with an email address, contact@overtheriverproperties.com, and instructions to call Erin if there were any problems. By then, it was too late to call, so I emailed instead, explaining our situation, that we were still staying in the rental, and asking whether they had any info from the booking on Diana, anything that would help us find her.

Pushing aside the sheets and covers, I forced myself out of my empty, Alex-free bed and padded down the hall, past Sam's closed door and down the stairs. I brewed a big pot of coffee, added some more water to the cast iron, which was still coated with burnt bits of chicken, and checked my email for a response. Nothing. I dialed the number from the welcome manual, and it rang and rang, going eventually to a woman's voice: 'You've reached Over the River Properties. Please leave a message with the address of the property you're inquiring about, and we'll get back to you as soon as we can.'

I rambled off a message, then hung up the phone, took a sip of coffee, and grabbed a sponge, getting to work on the cast iron.

Sam was still upstairs, and I imagined she would be for a while. I wouldn't want to face the day, either, the tedious ins and outs of an altogether new way of life.

What people didn't get about tragedy, people who hadn't yet had the privilege of going through it, is that it could be so casual. When bad news came, it was never like the movies. No dramatic score building to a crescendo. No slow pan of the camera. It struck out of nowhere – a midday phone call while you were at work. A sentence uttered – 'It's probably fine' – that would replay henceforth on a loop. Bad news delivered while chicken breasts burned in a pan, leaving you forever wondering when the other shoe was going to drop.

I scrubbed the pan hard, until little bits of sponge broke off, bobbing up in the hot water.

Of course, if you were strong and resilient, you'd move past your bad news, process and grieve. You'd write a book, or at least an article or two, and you'd get involved with a nonprofit, and your loss would help others who were destined to bear the same pain. You'd make lemonade from lemons and look back on your life and say you wouldn't change a damn thing, because all of it brought you to where you were now.

If you were like me, however, you wouldn't do any of those things. You'd grow so scared it would be impossible to trust anything and anyone. You'd spend money on every alternative therapy you could find so you didn't have to face the facts of your new life. You'd watch your husband, the man you'd loved so dearly, become an entirely different person, turning to the bottle as a relief from your robotic coldness.

I hoped Sam wasn't like me in this way, at least, but I feared she was.

I was still scrubbing when Sam appeared in the doorway. Her gaze was intent, locked on me, and I knew in her eyes that things were about to change, yet again, the screw turning tighter and tighter in this awful place.

'Conway just called,' Sam said, and in her eyes, there was the grief, strong as yesterday, but it was wrapped up in something else now, fear. Emotional cellophane. 'She said she wants to talk to both of us this time.'

They set us up in separate rooms, as they had on Sunday. Only now, a thick black laptop sat perched in the middle of the table. Though it made no sense, I imagined credit card statements queued up, Conway raising a well-groomed eyebrow: *We know you needed money, Ms Cahill*.

There was a quick knock at the door, and Conway walked in. She was nicely dressed and made-up as usual, but there was a tiredness to her, too, a crimp in her normally smooth hair, hints of darkness beneath her eyes. I imagined her poring over documents, pinning photos to a wall, hair pulled into an elastic tie as she connected the dots with string like some kind of FBI profiler on TV.

'Thanks for coming in,' she said, all business. She pointed to the video camera, reminding me it was recording and that this was voluntary, then took a seat, her spine rigid. 'I thought it would be good to follow up with you. Clear up any misunderstandings. Anything you have to add about Friday night . . .' She paused, eyeing me. 'Or from the scene on Sunday morning.'

'Nothing like that,' I said. 'But I found the contact info for the owners of the place where we're staying. I left them messages, but I was hoping you could find out how Diana booked it and what name she gave? It could help you find her.' I showed Conway the email I'd sent, rattled off the number from my call log, and she made a few notes in her Moleskine.

'Thank you,' she said. 'And that's all the info you have on the rental, correct? At 12 Meadowview Road?'

'Yes,' I said. 'That's it.'

She stared at me a moment, as if assessing, then flipped a page.

'I'd like to get back to Sunday morning, if we can.'

'Okay.'

'Anything you'd like to add?' Conway asked.

'No,' I said. 'I thought the blood was Diana's. I was shocked when Sam told me yesterday that it was her husband's.'

'Her husband's?'

'Harry,' I clarified. 'I don't remember his last name. Sam kept hers.'

Conway opened the laptop and pressed the space bar to wake it. 'You and Ms Lochman are close, yes?'

'Yes.'

'And how long have you known her?'

'We've worked together on and off for several years. We're both in advertising. It's a small world. We've been at many different agencies at the same time.'

'And that's how you met Ms Holbein?' Conway still didn't look up from the laptop.

'No,' I said. Didn't they know this? 'Diana was – is – a social worker with a therapy practice. Her office was near one of the ad agencies. She and Sam knew each other before I met her. Sam and I were out one night, and we ran into her. We connected because we're all separated, going through the divorce process.'

Conway turned the laptop around so I could finally see it.

A video player filled the screen, frozen on a crisp color image. Patio and woods.

'Eamon's has a security camera out back. I'm not sure if you knew that?'

'No,' I said, stiffening. 'I didn't.'

Conway's face was stony, but I detected a hint of a smirk in her eyes. *Gotcha*.

I took in the video before me. From the bar on the bottom, I could see it was long, several hours, but it was paused in the middle, an arrow stamped across the image, waiting for Conway to hit play.

'Nothing fancy. Just your basic Wi-Fi-enabled camera, like many people have in their homes. The owners of Eamon's, a couple in their sixties, weren't big on it. One of their nieces set it up for them as a precaution.'

A drop of hope rippled through my chest, tinged with fear of the truth. 'So do you know what happened on Friday? What happened to Diana? To Harry?'

'Don't I wish I did,' Conway said. 'Unfortunately, given that the details of your friend's disappearance were so . . . shaky . . . none of the officers checked with Eamon's for CCTV. Through this particular system, the video only stays in the account for twenty-four hours. After that, it's deleted. Honestly, I can't say I blame them too much. What you put forth was unusual, to say the least. No photo. No real information. A name that didn't get any hits.'

'We went to the bar the next night,' I said. 'We asked if they'd seen her. The bartender didn't mention any cameras.'

Come to think of it, we hadn't asked specifically. Perhaps we should have.

'Maybe they were blowing you off,' Conway said with a shrug. 'Or maybe they didn't know. Regardless, I was able to get a day's worth of video. The coroner estimated time of death for Mr Brant between eleven p.m. Friday night and three a.m. Saturday morning, so there wasn't enough video to get back that far, but I could make sure Ms Lochman's story about discovering the scene checked out.'

Without further ado, Conway reached over, pressed the space bar again.

The video from Sunday morning began to play. At first, there was nothing remarkable, just the smoker's patio, the grass, the woods in the distance, a group of people clustered in the corner.

Slowly at first, and then all at once, it clicked into place. I recognized myself among the people. Sam and Alex, too.

In the video, I took a few steps away, then stood a moment, head dropped down, staring at something on the ground. I knelt, grabbing it, then held it in my hand, frozen like that for a good five seconds. The police officer approached me, and I walked away, my hand slipping into my pocket.

I looked so *obvious*.

Conway stopped the tape. 'Care to explain?'

I tried to keep my breathing calm. In and out, in and out, the way I'd forced myself to take control before an audition.

'When I first saw this part of the video, I did wonder if it was innocuous. If you'd dropped a tissue, or your phone, or a piece of jewelry. Only when I watched it again, I saw the way you jumped when the officer approached you.' Conway paused, finger hovering over the keys. 'Do I need to show you again? Because I can –'

'No,' I said, heart beating wildly. 'No, you don't need to show me.'

'Then tell me,' Conway prompted. 'What did you see? What did you pick up? And why didn't you tell us before now?'

I inhaled again, and as I did, it's like I could picture her, Diana, her face urgent, impatient, that day at the gas station.

Can I have the key, Margaret?

I grabbed my bag from where I'd set it on the ground and dug through it until my fingers connected with metal. Carefully, I pulled it out and set it on the table between us with a click-clack.

Conway tilted her head to the side. 'What's that?' she asked.

'The car key,' I said. 'To our rental SUV.'

Her brows knitted up. 'I thought you lost that key. That's in multiple reports.'

'We did,' I said. 'Well, we didn't. Sam thinks we did.'

Something flashed across Conway's eyes, like a dog on a scent worth chasing. She pushed the laptop aside and retrieved her Moleskine. 'Why don't you start from the beginning?'

I nodded, swallowing. 'She wanted to stop. She insisted.'

'Who's *she*?' Conway asked, making a note in her Moleskine.

'Diana,' I said. 'I was the driver, and she was the navigator. Sam was in the back. Diana made some joke about how I shouldn't question her official role as navigator. She was like that. Everything was an adventure to her. Even when we'd meet for drinks, she'd pick out the wine and call herself the "wine-master", that kind of thing. It's what made it easy to get so close to her so fast. She made everything more fun.'

Conway pursed her lips, waiting for the next part of my

story. She wore coral lipstick, and I imagined her reaching for it this morning, after the call from the officers. Her power lip, the one that helped her with cases of dead husbands and missing women.

'What was strange was, when I stopped to get gas, Sam went into the convenience store but Diana stayed. She went around to the back of the car.'

'Why was that strange?' Conway asked.

'Because Diana kept insisting it was the nicest rest area and that's why we had to stop. I figured she'd want to actually use it.'

Conway nodded. 'And then?'

'I pumped the gas and paid for it with my credit card.'

'Was Ms Holbein with you the whole time?'

Just give me the key, Margaret.

'No,' I said, pausing only momentarily. 'She was having trouble with getting the trunk to stay shut. She said she wanted the key to lock it. Which didn't make sense. It was a hatchback.'

'What happened next?'

'I checked that the trunk was locked – it was – then I told her she was being weird and we got back in the car and I drove it to the front, so the car wasn't blocking the pump.'

'And then?'

'She told me to go inside, get us some snacks and waters, move my legs a bit. That she'd watch the car.'

You're the one who's been driving all this time. You deserve a break.

'I was beginning to get freaked out, so I told her no. She

didn't take well to that. She said I was too worried about the rules and that I should have let her take a turn driving.'

It's always by the fucking book with you, isn't it?

'She told me to give the key to her.'

I need that key. Now. I don't have time to argue with you.

'At this point, she was practically wrestling it from my hand.'

Diana, what the hell is wrong with you?

Conway cocked her head to the side. 'Did she give a reason?'

'Not exactly,' I said. 'She told me she couldn't go to Saratoga Springs, but she didn't explain why.'

I can't be there tonight, okay? I just can't. We can go tomorrow. I promise.

'And then?'

'I told her that this was ridiculous, asked if this was a game or a joke. When she said no, I suggested we wait for Sam to return.'

'What did she say?' Conway asked.

It had happened so fast. She'd reached into her bag, pulled out an envelope. Counted out hundred-dollar bills. Fifteen of them.

I don't want to involve her. Now, come on. You need the money, and I need that key.

'She said not to bring Sam into it and offered me money,' I said. 'To give her the key.'

'And you took it?' Conway asked, on the edge of her seat now.

I'll give you more when we get back to the city. Five thousand. It's nothing to me.

Five thousand big ones. I know it should have given me pause, but it was a dent in my mounting credit card debt. It would mean so much to me, so little to her.

I would never see that money now, and I hated how desperate I still was for it.

'Ms Cahill?'

'Sorry,' I said. 'Yes, I took it. I'm caught up in . . . debt. Credit cards. I don't really talk about it all that much, but Diana figured it out. I thought maybe Brandon was going to be in Saratoga Springs. I didn't think, really. She had said it would only be for one night.'

'And you didn't tell Ms Lochman?'

'No,' I said. 'Diana said I couldn't. That was part of the agreement. When Sam came out, Diana claimed I'd lost the key.'

'And you don't know what Diana did with the key?'

'I figured she hid it somewhere on her. The next time I saw the key was Sunday morning. I wasn't looking for it. I was shocked to see it.'

'You didn't think it was something you should tell us?'

'I panicked,' I said. 'I didn't know what the key meant, and I'd lied to you about the whole thing when I made that first report. I'd already picked it up, and when the officer came up to me, I was worried he wouldn't even believe me that I'd found it. So I put it in my pocket, and I pretended to find it at the auto shop that afternoon.'

'And Ms Lochman didn't suspect a thing?'

'As far as I know, no,' I said. 'She's had other things on her mind.'

Conway closed her notebook. 'That's a hell of a story,' she said.

'It's true.'

She pressed her hands to the table.

'Are you protecting her?' she asked.

'Who?' I said. 'Diana?'

'No,' she said, shaking her head solemnly, the look on her face dead serious.

'Are you protecting Ms Lochman. Are you protecting your friend Sam?'

27

SAM

It was a half hour before Conway entered my room, a bright white cinder block box centered around a table that wobbled if you so much as breathed too close to it – no sofas or creamy pale yellow walls here.

I couldn't help it, I felt downgraded. Yesterday, I'd been put in the 'grieving spouse' room, the homey one reserved for people whose emotions needed to be handled with kid gloves. Today, I was in the suspect room, I would swear to it.

Don't be petty, Sam, I could practically hear Harry saying. *It isn't like you.*

Conway was wearing flats this time, nude ones, and there was no click against the linoleum. She looked tired, but still, she was beautiful, even beneath the shitty fluorescent light. I felt a stab of jealousy – to walk around every day looking like that – not cute, like me. Not photogenic. Not attractive.

But beautiful. Like her. Like Elizabeth.

Would you have left me, Harry, if Elizabeth hadn't been so irresistible? Would any of this have happened? Would you be alive? Would Diana be safe?

'Thanks for coming in, Ms Lochman. I appreciate your cooperation.'

'Of course,' I said, wondering if I sounded genuine. 'I'd do anything to help find who did this to Harry.'

'I'm sure you would,' Conway said as she pulled out a folder, set it on the table between us.

My stomach twisted. Not more photos of him. Please god, not more photos.

'I know we covered a lot yesterday,' Conway said, drumming against the file with her nails. 'I wanted to start by asking if you had any questions for me.'

'Am I a suspect?' I asked. The words rushed out, almost involuntarily, water gushing through a burst dam. Like the way they had after Harry and I first kissed: *Did that just happen?*

I wanted to take my words back, return to a second ago, play my role better, the grieving partner who wants to do anything she can to get justice. Not the self-serving ex who only cares if her own ass is on the line.

Conway, however, didn't look jarred by my question. 'The investigation is so new,' she said. 'We're still ruling people out. These conversations help us do that.'

'Because I loved him, I swear. I could never hurt Harry. Never.'

Don't lay it on too thick, Sam. Harry had helped me learn to present better, learn to go into a client meeting sounding confident but never too eager. We'd practice in the kitchen, while stirring tomato sauce. We would never have a conversation like that again, he and I.

236

'Unfortunately, Ms Lochman,' Conway continued. 'If we excluded everyone who loved a murder victim, we'd have to entirely rethink the way we approach homicide investigations. Love is far closer to a motive than an alibi.'

'So that's how it goes, huh?' I asked. 'Look to me, just because he left me.'

She raised an eyebrow. 'Your words, not mine.'

'I know,' I said, already regretting the turns this conversation had taken. 'I'm just pointing out that it's all caricature, the way you approach these things. It's based on statistics, on, I don't know, archetypes and anecdotes. You can look at the way things are – that we're split, all that – but it doesn't mean you understand me and Harry.'

'You're right,' Conway said. 'It doesn't. Ask anyone who's made a career out of homicide. It's by the book until it's not. People can *always* surprise you.'

I nodded, congratulating myself on making my point.

You always have to make your side heard, don't you, Sam?

Harry had found it sweet, the way I'd passionately argue a point, not let it go until I got my words out. He told me it was one of the things he loved most about me.

'Why don't you tell me about you and Harry,' Conway asked. 'In your own words. Because you're right, you know what went on between you better than anyone else.'

Relief, if only tiny and fleeting. The chance to stick up for me and Harry, for what we had.

'We were in love,' I said. 'We still were, even though he left.'

'Did he ever tell you precisely *why* he left, Ms Lochman?'

'He was caught between both of us,' I said. 'He said he'd

tried to stop his feelings for Elizabeth but he couldn't. She'd had a hard childhood. He was her only family. He said she needed him.'

'Wow,' Conway said. 'That must have been hard to hear.'

'Yes,' I said. 'It was.'

Conway raised both eyebrows this time. 'Humiliating, too. To be compared with someone else, and an ex-wife at that – and to not be chosen.'

'Of course it was,' I said. 'But that doesn't mean – that doesn't change – I still loved him. I'm not the kind of person who loves conditionally. I didn't go into this thinking it was temporary. I was in it through thick and thin, sickness and health, all that.'

'Leaving your –' Conway took a quick, sharp breath. 'Leaving the person you've made this commitment to for an ex-wife, that can hardly be called a disease, though. It's a choice, yes. A conscious one. It would make anyone furious. I know *I'd* be furious,' Conway added.

'I thought this was about me and Harry.'

Conway tapped her pen against the table. 'Yes. It is.' She flipped through her notes. 'So yesterday, you said you had very little contact after he left?'

'Yes,' I said. 'I wanted to talk more, but he didn't.'

'You called him a lot, yes?' she asked.

'Wouldn't you?'

Conway ignored my question. 'But he didn't really give you a chance to be heard, did he?'

'No.'

'Now, that must have made you angry. He leaves you,

without much warning. For his ex-wife. And when you ask him to talk, like anyone would, he brushes you off? I would have been fuming. I would have been wondering if he ever loved me at all, if the whole thing was nothing more than a lie.' Conway's eyes caught mine, and my heart raced mercilessly. 'Mr Brant's remains have been processed. Everything on his person has been logged into evidence.' Her hand found the envelope, then rested there. 'The official cause of death is blunt force trauma. Death does not appear to have been immediate but rather over some time, perhaps several minutes.'

I stared at her, my stomach roiling.

'You don't look all that surprised,' Conway said.

I gulped. 'I'm in shock.'

'I told you I've been through a divorce myself?' she asked, abruptly changing the subject.

'What?' I asked. 'I mean, yes. Yes, you mentioned it.'

'Right,' Conway said, even though it was clear she knew the answers, was just going over every last line she'd written into her script. 'The thing is, as someone who's gone through it, this whole situation begs believability a little, doesn't it?'

'How so?'

She lifted her pen, as if to make a note, then dropped it, letting it clatter against the table. 'Mr Brant leaves you high and dry for another woman – and not just another woman, his ex-wife. You're desperate to reconnect, but he doesn't want to. And then you happen to lose the car key in the exact town he lives in, putting you right in his path.'

'Margaret lost the car key,' I said. 'Not me. You can ask –'
You can ask Diana.

'You can ask Margaret.'

'Oh, I have,' Conway said, matter-of-fact. 'Don't worry. And I'm still trying to figure out how much she's covering for you.'

'She's not —'

Conway raised a hand. 'Let's leave it for now. Say you had nothing to do with that lost key. It was all Margaret and Diana.'

'Diana?' I asked.

'Either way, you find yourself in the same place as Mr Brant, and then, after not wanting to meet before, he suddenly shows up at your beck and call.'

'I think he saw my Instagram.'

'Yes,' Conway said. 'You mentioned that. Only we've been told that Mr Brant always went to Eamon's on Friday. Perhaps you knew that? Perhaps that's why you decided to go there?'

'No.' I shook my head. 'I didn't. It wasn't even my idea to go there.'

Conway shrugged me off. 'So you see him, and then, after all the anger and all the hurt between you, you end up . . . *reconnecting*. And you walk off. Even if all that is true, how am I supposed to know you didn't try to confront him, that you weren't upset you weren't good enough to stay with but *were* good enough to screw in the back of a bar?'

My chest seized up. She'd hit on everything I'd been feeling myself.

'Ms Lochman,' she went on. 'Can you tell me again how you lost your rings?'

I jerked back my head, surprised. 'My rings?'

'Yes,' she said. 'You mentioned you visited the scene of the crime because you'd lost your rings – an engagement ring and wedding band.'

My eyebrows furrowed. What was she getting at now? She kept going back and forth, zigzagging like an aggressive driver changing lanes. 'I told you,' I said. 'They were in the pocket of my dress, and when we . . . well . . . when he and I were together, they must have fallen out.'

'But you didn't find them?' Conway asked. 'That morning you went to look?'

'No,' I said. 'I didn't.'

'Rings are important to a marriage,' Conway said smoothly. 'Wouldn't you say?'

'I guess.'

'You know one of the worst arguments I ever had with my ex-husband, one of the last ones before he moved out, you know what I did?'

'No,' I said, my heart pounding steadily now.

'It was a real doozy. He was arguing that because I'd come home half an hour late for dinner for the fifth or sixth time in a row, something he really should have expected by that point, given my job and all, that I was checked out of our marriage. Had one foot out the door, if you will.' Conway sighed. '"I don't even know you anymore," he said. "I don't even see the woman I married." Do you know what I did, Ms Lochman?'

I shook my head slowly.

She smirked. 'I tugged my rings off, and I threw them at him.' She tapped her nails against the table. 'I'm not proud of it. It was childish, petulant, but it felt so *good* at the time. He wanted to tell me I was checked out – well, I could raise him

241

one. I could take these symbols, these pieces of jewelry we'd exchanged in front of all our friends and family, and throw them – quite literally – in his face. Do you know what my husband did?'

'No.'

'He picked them up and put them in his pocket. Said they'd cost thousands of dollars and I shouldn't risk damaging them – or losing them somehow. See, to women, rings are a promise. They're this beautiful thing we dream of. All these emotions wrapped up in a diamond or a sapphire. They're circular, infinite. Something you can touch every day to think of your partner, of what you've entered in together. They're the ultimate symbol.' She half laughed. 'But to men, they're an investment. They're proof of some sort of financial prowess, of an ability to be a caregiver. Ms Lochman, when the medical examiner was processing Mr Brant's remains, do you know what she found in his pocket?'

My palms began to sweat.

Conway reopened the folder, flipped through the autopsy report, grabbed a shiny photo.

She pushed it over to me, turning the photo around so I could fully take it in.

I couldn't help it, my jaw dropped.

There they were, the last bit of me and Harry. The promise we'd made to each other in shiny platinum and a cushion-cut diamond.

What I'd been looking for for days now.

My rings.

28

MARGARET

In the station's parking lot, waiting for Sam to finish, I again checked for Lars, but his location was still hidden. I prayed this meant he was back in Brooklyn, accepting what I'd been saying for months now: it's over.

Conway had sent me on my way, either taking my word for it that I wasn't protecting Sam or deciding there was nothing more to get out of me today.

I nestled my phone back into my bag, then jolted at the sight in front of me.

Alex.

His hands were shoved deeply into his pockets, and his mouth was set firm. He walked briskly across the lot to the truck I recognized. Before I could stop myself, I opened my door, rushed toward him.

'Alex,' I said, his name getting lost in the wind. 'Alex,' I said again, louder. He turned.

We were still ten or so feet apart, and I paused, only briefly, watching him watch me. He looked . . . surprised. He looked almost . . . disappointed. Still, he forced a smile, and I closed the distance between us, meeting him at the driver's side of his truck.

'What are you doing here?' I asked, completely thrown.

His eyes were bloodshot, as if he hadn't slept well. Alex opened his mouth to speak, then closed it again.

'Alex, what is it? Is everything okay?'

He ignored my question. 'I'm sorry,' he said. 'I'm just surprised. You said it was your friend, and then you said it was Sam's husband, and now it's . . . this is so hard to wrap my head around.'

'What is?' I asked, my eyebrows narrowing.

'The fact that all this time it was Harry Brant.'

Ten minutes later, Alex was unlocking the front door of the brewery with a set of keys on a large brass ring. I'd been full of questions, shocked to hear Harry's name, so familiar, on Alex's lips, but he'd insisted he had to get to the brewery and open up. So I'd driven over, tailing his truck, trusting Sam would call me when she was done.

Inside, Alex flicked on the lights and turned over two stools, setting them neatly in front of the bar.

'Sit,' he said.

'I'm sorry,' I said as I took a seat. 'I know you have to work. I just . . .'

'It's okay.' Alex grabbed two glasses and filled them to the brim with a golden ale.

'It's barely past noon.'

'I know,' he said, setting one glass in front of me, one in

front of him. 'But I need a drink. And from the looks of it, you do, too.'

I couldn't argue with that. 'When does this place open?'

'One,' he said. 'But don't worry. It's no problem. Opening is easy enough.' He lifted the glass to his lips, drained a third of it in one go.

I took a sip myself, savoring the earthiness of it. Grounding, somehow, among the swirl of questions weighing heavily on my mind. If there was a chance, any chance at all, that the man I'd slept with, the first man I'd done anything with since Lars, could be bad . . . if my trust was so ruined I couldn't give it to anyone anymore, I had to know.

'You know Harry?' I asked, just as I had in the parking lot.

Alex took another gulp. 'Yes,' he said. 'But just barely.' He turned, tapping an iPad behind him to life. There was no clunky point-of-sale system here, like I used to use when I waited tables back home, only a clean white screen and a minimalist credit card reader hooked to the side.

Alex took another sip. 'Harry used to come in a lot, when we first opened, a few years ago. He was friends with one of the owners from way back when. They grew up together.' Alex shrugged. 'Or something like that. I don't know all the details. But then he moved to the city and I . . . I didn't see him much after that. Until recently. A couple of months ago. Then he started coming back to the brewery.'

I nodded. That would have been around the time Harry left Sam.

'So that's it?' I asked, glass cold in my hands. 'You're no more than an acquaintance of his? And that's why the police wanted to talk to you?'

'Yeah, I don't know him well,' Alex said carefully. 'But the whole thing threw me. You and I were on the phone for like a second last night. I didn't want to bother you with questions with everything going on.'

'What do you mean?'

'I mean, I didn't even think to ask who it was. If it was someone I knew.'

'Oh,' I said.

Alex shook his head. 'That's what I still don't understand. You said that Sam's husband was killed.'

'Yes,' I said. 'They're separated. He left her to come back here.'

'I thought there was a short-lived thing in Brooklyn. That's all.'

Short-lived thing? That was Sam. Had to be. How awful to hear her referred to this way. Sam was Harry's *wife*. She wasn't some short-lived thing, damn it. What had Harry thought of her? What had he told his friends?

I took another sip, but nothing could quell the sour taste rising in the back of my throat. Everything felt upside-down suddenly. Topsy-turvy. 'You shouldn't say that,' I said, running my finger along the rim of my glass and temporarily breaking Alex's gaze. 'You shouldn't put it that way.'

'I'm sorry,' Alex said. 'That's how I understood it.'

'Maybe it *was* short, but it was still something, you know. Sam's completely alone. She had to identify him,' I said. 'And she's still down there at the station, being grilled about their last moments together. She was probably one of the last people to see him alive, you know. She meant something to Harry, however it ended. And he meant *everything* to her.'

'I'm sorry,' Alex said.

'After all, Sam's still Harry's *wife*,' I said finally. Forcefully. Because once you were one, once you weren't anymore, the word stuck with you, taunting you, needling at your own history. Four letters that always made you feel like a bit of a failure, no matter how stupid you told yourself that was.

Alex cocked his head to the side. 'How much do you trust her?'

'Sam?' I wondered briefly if Sam could have somehow misrepresented her relationship with Harry to us. None of us had been honest with each other. Diana was – who even knew? I'd only recently told Sam the truth about my baby, and she still didn't know about my mounting debt.

I shook my head. It wasn't possible. I'd seen Sam's wedding photos on Facebook. I'd seen her rings. I'd seen her crying in the bathroom. I'd listened as she'd opened up about her failed marriage.

It was all real. Undeniably so.

'She's his wife,' I said finally. 'I know that much is true.'

When Alex spoke, it was so matter-of-fact, so chillingly firm.

'That's the thing,' Alex said. 'I'm almost positive she's not.'

29

SAM

Conway wasn't done yet. I could see it in her eyes. She still had another trick up her sleeve. A surprise or two as she circled closer and closer to the truth.

We'd spent the last half hour going over the details of the rings. Where, exactly, I'd had them, when, exactly, I'd noticed they were gone, why I hadn't picked up on their being missing before. Whatever she was looking for in that department, she wasn't going to get it. I didn't know any better than she did. Harry must have picked them up. It was the only explanation, unless . . .

Conway cleared her throat. 'The problem with your story, the problem with all your stories over this whole long weekend, is how much you hold back. You were there looking for jewelry, but actually it was a wedding set. You were out there with a guy, but it wasn't just any guy, it was Mr Brant. The blood was your friend's, except you found it exactly where you and Mr Brant had your encounter and didn't think to mention that. Elizabeth Wren was just another woman, until she wasn't. The car key was lost until it wasn't.'

I shook my head forcefully. 'What are you talking about? The key *was* lost.'

Conway ignored me. 'Now about Ms Holbein,' she went on. 'I am very, very sorry that she hasn't turned up. But we've got no photos, no address, nothing. We have, at most, a couple of eyewitness accounts of a middle-height, mid-thirties silver-and-brown-haired woman out with you at a bar. That's it.'

'What are you saying? That we made her up?'

'I'm saying there isn't very far we can go with the information you've given us. I'm saying that we have a situation where you and your friends were supposed to be somewhere else. Friends who admittedly haven't known each other all that long. But then, somehow, the key "disappears"' — Conway made dramatic air quotes — 'and you wind up here. At the same bar Mr Brant always goes to, even though he's resisted contact since leaving you. Suddenly, he wants to talk to you. More than that, he wants to make up. You supposedly have relations. And he happens to turn up dead, with your rings in his pocket, that night. Your friend, the one allegedly responsible for getting you up here on this little detour, is missing without a trace. Your other friend, she tells us that the car key was never lost at all. You understand why this doesn't add up for us?'

The white walls looked suddenly sickly, anemic, and the air felt stale, as if there were only so much of it to share between Conway and me. 'I don't know what you're talking about. The key *was* lost. That's what they told me.'

'Did you ask Ms Holbein to intentionally lose that key?' Conway asked.

'What? No,' I said, dumbfounded. 'No, of course not.'

'I'm only asking because Ms Cahill alleges that Ms Holbein hid it away intentionally, that she wanted to avoid Saratoga Springs for whatever reason. Had she agreed to help you out?'

'Margaret?' I asked. 'You mean, she and Diana . . .'

Had Margaret been lying to me this entire time?

Conway was looking at me, waiting.

'If I wanted to come up to Catskill, I would have. Period. If I wanted to show up on Harry's doorstep, that's what I would have done.'

Conway scooted her chair forward, clearly changing tactics. 'Like you did before? According to Ms Wren, you did show up on Harry's doorstep. You went to their house.'

Heat rose to my face. 'That was only once,' I said. 'I just walked by. I didn't even knock on the door. I wanted to see where he was living. It's not a crime.'

'It's not a crime outright, no. But if it's part of a pattern of harassment, then it could be.'

'A pattern of harassment? Are you serious? He *left me* without any warning. If you ask me, I could have handled it a whole lot worse.'

'Worse how?' Conway asked.

I sighed in frustration. She was trying to trap me, catch me in a snare set up carefully with her perfect fucking nails. I hated her for it.

But in a way, I hated myself even more. I should have had some goddamn self-respect. I should have been furious when Harry left, refusing to answer his calls instead of the other way around. I should have taken the rings off immediately, told everyone. I should never have gone through with his stupid idea in the first place. Only I hadn't. I'd been hopeful, pathetic, and look where it had gotten me.

But Harry . . .

Harry had told me he missed me.

He'd said he was sorry.

He'd been about to say something else, before someone killed him.

It was hard to imagine trading those brief moments, painful as they were now.

'Ms Lochman.'

'I'm sorry,' I said. 'What were you asking?'

'How could it have been worse?'

'It's a figure of speech,' I said. 'I didn't mean anything by it.'

Conway swallowed, then caught my eyes. She had something else to ask me, I was sure of it. Another serve coming my way. She was rearing the racket back, getting it ready . . .

'You know, I'm in a hell of a bind because of you. My supervisor is furious. You're not even next of kin, and here I had you identifying the body. It should have been Ms Wren. It should never have been you.'

My heartbeat quickened. I began to feel sick.

'Why did you lie, Ms Lochman? Why are you *still* lying? Why in the world did you lead us to believe you were married to Mr Brant when you weren't?'

My chest seized up, and for a second, it was like the world stopped spinning. The double life I'd been living was suddenly out there, laid bare, and probably detailed in her notebook, too, for her to examine, to pore over – another detail of her fucking case.

There were some things you told no one. Absolutely no one. Some things you clutched, you buried so deeply, so no one else could see. Why? Because they were too humiliating, too pathetic, to bear. Because if you let anyone in on the truth, you'd never be able to hold your head high again.

What was sadder and more pathetic than a soon-to-be-divorced woman?

A soon-to-be-divorced woman who was left for someone else.

And what was worse than that?

When that someone else wasn't just another woman, but an ex-wife.

But let's keep going for a minute. What would be even worse than that, so terrible, so embarrassing, it was impossible to put into words? Not to your closest friends. Not to your sister. Not to your parents. Not even to the two women who knew about your situation, the only ones you'd opened up to.

What was so terrible that it was impossible to admit even to yourself?

If that woman he left you for – if she wasn't an ex-wife at all.

And if you, you weren't soon to be divorced.

How could you be, when you'd never been a wife in the first place?

When you'd never even gotten to wear that title, not for real. Not where it mattered, in the end.

You couldn't get divorced if you'd never been married at all.

'Ms Lochman?' Conway prompted.

'I didn't lie,' I said finally. 'I never actually said he was my husband.'

It was Conway's turn to look shocked.

'I didn't,' I went on. 'I talked about our union, our commitment. I never used that word. I promise.'

'You told me about your wedding bands.'

'Yes,' I said. 'What else would you call them?'

'You're going to have to explain, Ms Lochman. Because I don't think I understand.'

No one ever intends to have a fake marriage, and I didn't, either. Harry proposed, Harry bought the rings, Harry let me shop for dresses and set the date and plan it all in North Carolina so my dad could be part of it.

Harry. Not me. I never asked for any of this.

I knew things were complicated with Elizabeth, but I didn't nag him about it. When I asked about their divorce, he said they were working out the details. He said not to worry and that it would be taken care of. I trusted him: Weren't marriages supposed to be about trust?

I didn't get the sense that things were really wrong until about a month before the wedding. We were getting ready to book our plane tickets – last minute – and I'd been researching how far ahead of time you needed to get a marriage license in North Carolina. He'd come behind me, kissed me on the shoulder like he always did, and spoken calmly: 'We need to talk.'

After all that's happened, I can see now that it was excuses, but then? He didn't want to call off the wedding. Their divorce wouldn't be ready by our date. Elizabeth had money, and money made things complicated, so we couldn't get married – not legally, at least – but we could still go through the motions. No one had to know but the two of us. When I called to delicately explain the situation to our New Age officiant, she wasn't remotely thrown. 'Don't worry about it,' she said. 'I've been doing gay weddings since long before they were legal. It's the ceremony, the promises you make, that matters. The rest is between you and whoever you do or do not pray to.'

I never in a million years thought that we wouldn't actually marry. Harry had even said it would be fun to go down to the courthouse – the beautiful one in Manhattan – and do it in secret, just us. It wasn't ideal, of course, but what was the alternative? To wait (and hope) that my dad outlived the ins and outs of Elizabeth and Harry's complicated divorce proceedings? That didn't even feel like an option. By then I was hungry for Harry, for our union. I was bound to make it happen, piece of paper or not.

'Ms Lochman?'

'Their divorce got held up,' I said. 'My dad was – is – sick. We didn't want to wait. So we had the wedding. We always planned to get married at the courthouse as soon as their divorce went through.'

'How do you know they ever planned to get divorced at all?' Conway asked. 'According to Ms Wren, their lawyers weren't very far along.'

Her words struck me, a weight in my gut.

'I don't think you propose to someone and make vows to them in front of their whole family if you don't intend to divorce.'

'Was Mr Brant's family there? At your ceremony?'

I blinked slowly. 'He's not close with his family.'

Conway raised an eyebrow.

'His best friend was there. James. He lives in San Francisco. He flew in for it. I'm not making this up, okay? I can show you our photos, for chrissakes. I didn't *invent* a wedding.'

Conway threw her hands up in the air. 'I never said you did. I'm only pointing out that the lack of legal status sure was convenient for Mr Brant when he decided to make amends with his actual wife.'

Conway stared, waiting for me to react, to fall apart, to blanket myself in shame, but I wouldn't give her the satisfaction.

'I don't care how it sounds when you lay it all out like that, it was real. He loved me, and I loved him. I didn't hurt him.'

Conway sighed. 'Where are you staying again?' she asked, changing tack.

'At a rental. Why?'

'I mean the address,' Conway said. 'It's 12 Meadowview Road, correct?'

My eyes narrowed. 'Yes. I think so. Why are you asking if you already know?'

'Why did you choose that place exactly?'

I shook my head. 'Diana did. Not me.'

'Is there a reason you chose to stay at a place owned by your fake husband's wife?'

I reared back. 'What?'

'12 Meadowview Road is a property owned by a company called Over the River Properties. That company is co-owned by Elizabeth Wren. You're telling me you didn't know this?'

What in the world? What in the ever-loving fuck?

Conway went on. 'We're working on getting the booking information from Ms Wren now. To try to get a lead on the real name of your friend, whoever she is.'

I shook my head, my mind spinning. We'd been staying in Elizabeth's place? All this time?

'I didn't know that,' I said. 'I swear.'

Conway folded her hands together.

'Is that it?' I asked. 'Are we done?'

'Almost,' she said. She flipped open the folder, flicked through a few papers, let her fingers land on one.

Something wasn't right. Diana had pretended to lose the key. Margaret had gone along with it. They'd taken me to a town where Harry lived, to a house connected to him, too.

What the fuck is going on?

'You ever find your license, Ms Lochman?'

'What?'

'Your driver's license. You didn't have it when our officers tried to log you in to our system.'

'I know,' I said. 'I don't know how I lost it. Probably at the bar.'

Conway lifted a paper from the folder, a photo, and placed it in front of me. 'That your ID?'

'Where did you?' I asked, as I took it in, a photo of my license, set off by dirt and earth. 'Where did you find that?'

'A few feet away from Mr Brant's body,' she said. 'In the woods.'

I shook my head. 'That's not possible. I was only ever on the edge of the woods with Harry. I wasn't any deeper in. I wasn't . . .'

Even as I was saying it, the realization struck me, like a slap across the face.

This was more than coincidence. This was more than chance.

Diana and Margaret, the women I'd trusted with my secrets, the women I'd relied on these last two months, they'd brought me here, they'd thrown me into both Harry's and Elizabeth's path – and it had resulted in Harry's death.

And now this. The rings could be explained away, but this very much couldn't.

Harry was dead, and my things were near his body.

Someone was setting me up.

30

MARGARET

I left the brewery an hour later, once it had opened and Alex was busy with work.

In the car, I checked my phone for word from Sam. Nothing. Diana was not who she said she was – fine – but Sam? I'd known her for years. She wouldn't simply create a marriage out of thin air. Would she? Alex had been adamant: Elizabeth was Harry's wife, and they'd never legally split. Another marriage simply wasn't possible.

Main Street looked exactly as it had yesterday, or perhaps slightly busier, two or three more cars peppered across the otherwise-abandoned stretch. I looked north, and I could see, a couple blocks up, the chalkboard sign of the coffee shop where I had met up with Lars. I checked the finder app, but his location was still turned off.

I slipped the key into the ignition, then decided to change course.

Back outside, I shut the door with a thud. I walked down Main Street, storefront by storefront, until I was nearly in front of the coffee shop. Lars was a creature of habit. In Brooklyn, on his days off, he'd go to the same fancy coffee shop almost every morning, order a latte and this muffin-shaped egg scramble that didn't have any carbs. He'd read the Arts section of the *New York Times*, and if we weren't in a fight about his drinking, and sometimes, even if we were, he'd text me at work for help with clues on the crossword.

If he was still in town, and I prayed he wasn't, he would be here. Nowhere else.

He's not, I told myself. He's back in Brooklyn, where I should be, too. He listened, finally. He got it.

I approached the shop, braced myself, and then I saw it, his long hair pulled into a ponytail. My heart sank.

I pushed through the door quickly. 'Lars,' I said.

He looked up, momentarily startled, then composed himself. 'Peggy.'

'What are you doing here?' I demanded. 'I told you to leave.'

His shoulders stiffened, and I saw him glance to the barista, the same girl who'd been here yesterday. 'You want me to get you something?' he offered.

'No,' I said, working hard to stop myself from making a complete scene. 'We need to talk,' I said. 'Outside.'

'But I –'

'*Now.*' He didn't move. 'I swear, Lars,' I said, my voice rising. 'If you don't –'

'Okay, okay,' he said. 'Christ. Okay.'

Outside, the door clanged behind us. A gust of wind blew by, shaking the leaves of a maple tree that lined the sidewalk. Within me, anger surged to the surface, bubbling like lava, ready to explode. Molten and hot, and only a few drops could kill you, or at least burn and disfigure, eating you up. 'You can't do this, Lars,' I said finally.

'Peggy,' he said, stepping closer, and I smelled stale booze on his breath. 'It's okay.'

'No, it's not okay,' I snapped. 'None of this is okay. Don't you get it? We're *over*. We're getting a divorce. This is done. Finished. Just *leave*.'

'Don't say that, Peggy,' Lars said, his voice cracking. 'Come on. You're angry. Don't say things you're going to regret.'

'I regret nothing, you know that. I don't regret the choice I made, the choice only *I* was brave enough to make, even though you've spent every day since making me feel guilty about it. I don't regret pulling away from you, because neither of us are the same people we were before all this happened.'

'No,' Lars said. 'You don't mean that. We work together. We make sense. We know each other better than anyone.'

'You're an alcoholic,' I said. 'You barely even know yourself. And me – you don't know me at all anymore. I've opened four credit cards in the last year and a half – did you know that? – I've completely ruined my finances and who knows how I'm going to afford to rent a new apartment or a lawyer for the divorce. I've spent all this time doing personal development courses and buying crystals and doing Reiki and finding anything I could to help dull the pain, because you left me to bear it all on my own, Lars. *You* shamed me and guilted me and then you fucked right off to your booze.' There were tears in my eyes now, tears that were so rare for me, but they were angry tears this time. 'And you think you can follow me and pretend to care because it's the anniversary? You think this is helping me? It's about you, Lars. It's always about *you*.'

I lifted my hands, and I wanted, so badly, to push him, but I dropped them just as soon, forcing myself to take a breath.

Lars seemed to read my mind, seeing what I was about to do, and it alarmed him, but he pressed his lips together, forcing calm. 'We can work through the debt,' he said. 'I can go to rehab. All of this is still fixable, Peggy. You *haven't* moved out yet. And I haven't, either. There's a reason for that,' he said. 'Because we belong together. You and me.'

I shook my head, the tears spilling down. Nothing would do it. Nothing would break him out of these delusions, these fantasies.

'I lied to you,' I said finally. 'Bitterly. It wasn't a one-night stand. His name is Alex, and he's wonderful, and I care about him, and we're going to see each other after this weekend. I like him. He makes me happy, happier than you have in a long, long time.'

It was only then that the hurt, the desperation, turned to anger, flashing in his eyes. 'You really are a slut, aren't you?' he spat. 'And after I tried so fucking hard for you.'

He turned, pushed open the door to the coffee shop so hard it slammed, so hard the barista abandoned all pretense of pretending not to stare.

I turned away, racing back to the car. Hating myself for what I'd said, but knowing I had to say it. Knowing there was no other way.

31

SAM

When Conway was finally finished with me, nearly an hour later, when the ins and outs of Harry and me had been picked over so viciously our love was beyond recognition, I didn't call Margaret. I let a cop take me back instead, blood boiling the entire drive.

I'd trusted Margaret, I'd trusted Diana, when I shouldn't have trusted anyone. Margaret and Diana had *pretended* to lose the keys. Which made no sense. Why in the world would Margaret lie about that? Even if it had all been Diana's idea, why would she have gone along with it?

I found her in the kitchen, back to me, wiping down the counters. She couldn't clean or organize her way out of this one.

'What the fuck?'

Margaret jumped, turned around and pulled out two earbuds.

'Sam,' she said. 'You scared me. Why didn't you call me to pick you up?'

'Why did you lie to me?' I snapped. 'Conway told me about

the car key. About what you and Diana did. She thinks I some-how put you up to it. She thinks you're *covering* for me, for fuck's sake.'

Margaret's eyes widened in shock, but just as quickly she composed herself. She rubbed her hands on her jeans. 'I told her you had nothing to do with it.'

'With *what*, Margaret? What happened between you? And why here? This rental, this is owned by Elizabeth, Harry's ex.'

She stiffened, but I continued. 'Why did you bring us here?'

'I didn't,' Margaret said. 'I didn't know that. I swear.'

'You better tell me everything,' I said. 'Now.'

Pushing past me, Margaret rushed up the stairs. I followed her into her room. She sank down to her knees, unzipping her suitcase. She pulled all the clothes out, tossing them haphaz-ardly on the hardwood floor, in a way that was completely un-like her, until her hands found an envelope. She handed it to me, an offering. Carefully, I opened it. A stack of bills, fresh as daisies.

She told me Diana had offered her the money – and more, too – with the caveat that she pretended to lose the key and never tell me what happened. She told me she was desperate. Credit card debt, kept secret from Lars. She told me about the key, finding it, hiding it, and pretending to find it again.

'Jesus, Margaret,' I said when she was done. 'We could have avoided all this.' My voice was cold. Steely. 'Harry might not even be dead.'

'No,' Margaret said adamantly. 'You don't get to do that. You don't get to put that on me.'

'Why not?' I demanded. 'If we'd been in Saratoga Springs,

263

none of this would have happened. If you hadn't fucking *lied* –'

'Oh, like you didn't?' Margaret said. 'Alex says you aren't even married to Harry.'

I reared back as if I'd been slapped.

'He swears up and down that Elizabeth isn't someone Harry left you for, that she's his wife, and they never split up. Current wife. Present tense.'

'Alex should mind his own business,' I said. 'How does he even know Harry?'

'Harry used to go to his brewery. Does that matter? Is he wrong?'

My face went hot as shame filled me up. My secret was about to be out. Not just for Conway but for Margaret, too.

'It was just a piece of paper,' I said bitterly. 'It doesn't mean, because we didn't have it, that I was nothing. We made vows to each other. Promises. Just because it wasn't legal doesn't mean it wasn't real. Harry's divorce wasn't finalized, and my dad was dying. We did what we had to do.'

'I'm sorry,' Margaret said, her jaw agape. 'I didn't know about your dad.'

'Yeah, well, you obviously don't know a lot of things about me,' I shot back, and without another word, I turned around and bolted down the stairs, didn't stop walking until I reached the road, until she couldn't see me anymore. Then I called a car.

Twenty-five minutes later, I was in front of their house once again. It looked so different at dusk, even more beautiful, more open, airy, and light, its windows wide and all-encompassing, inviting nature in, its lines clean and parallel to the ground.

My phone buzzed as I walked up the stone pathway. It was Margaret.

Where'd you go?

I ignored her. I didn't have the patience for her right now, for all the what-ifs and questions that were rushing through my head.

I'd spent the rest of my interview with Conway trying to convince her that Elizabeth had orchestrated all of this, that Elizabeth had taken my ID, from a property she owned, apparently, and planted it on the scene.

But it had been no use. It seemed I was the suspect, not her. The cops weren't going to give me answers, Margaret wasn't going to give me answers, so I had to get them myself. I knew it was a risk, going to see her, but I had to know something. Anything.

Grief weighed me down as my feet drew me closer. Harry's last days on earth had been spent here, with her, so far away from me. His last months had been here, loving, living with, fucking a woman who was not me.

She needed me.

And for whatever reason, Diana had brought me here, too.

I remembered the joke Diana had made on Friday evening, when she was trying to get Margaret to let her drive, despite her not being on the rental agreement. 'We might have to buy off Sam's silence, but I hear she comes cheap.' Even then, Diana had been making plans, figuring out how to buy off Margaret, not me.

There was a pickup truck at the top of the driveway, navy blue. It looked somehow familiar. Was it Harry's? Elizabeth's? It didn't seem to fit either of them. People who have expensive modernist houses nestled in the woods do not clutter up their driveways with mud-spattered pickups. They buy luxury SUVs – Subarus if they're pinching pennies. Not cars like this.

I rang the bell.

No answer. I waited a few minutes and rang again.

Finally, I couldn't take it anymore. I pressed the bell, over and over, like I used to do as an impatient kid, until I saw her, hair swept off her shoulders, swooping down the staircase, coming to the door.

Her voice was cool, clipped. 'You have some goddamn nerve coming here.'

'I need to talk to you,' I said. I pushed past her before she could turn me away.

'Hey,' she said, but I kept walking, into the foyer, past a pair of strappy sandals and scuffed-up sneakers. My stomach twisted again – were those Harry's shoes? I used to kick them out of the doorway every night when I came home. It was annoying, the way he'd leave his shoes lying around, even though we had a fancy shoe rack I'd impulse bought from an Instagram ad, but now I wished so badly for just one evening when I could kick them away again.

'What the hell are you doing?' Elizabeth demanded. 'I'm calling the cops.'

'The cops are going to figure out what you did. Maybe they

haven't already, but they will. It's so obvious. My ID. My rings. Did you think you looked smooth?'

'I have no idea what you're talking about.'

'I'm staying at your house,' I said. 'The farmhouse, a few miles out of town. Green clapboard siding. Red shutters.'

'I know one of my own houses, thanks.'

One of? Christ, how rich is she?

Elizabeth took a quick breath. 'I had nothing to do with that. I don't even manage the rentals. My colleague –'

'How convenient,' I said. 'My ID goes missing and turns up next to Harry and *you* own the house where I'm staying. Harry doesn't come home to you on Friday night but I see you on Saturday and you don't say a word about him missing. Conway will figure it out. She has to.'

'I had nothing to do with your ID,' she said. 'And how could I have known what happened? I didn't want him to come home. I told him to stay away from me, after what I saw. Now can you please –'

What I saw.

You've already won.

'I knew you saw us. I knew. Did you confront him? Did you –?'

'You think *you* get to question me?' she asked angrily. 'I'm his wife. I'm the one who's left to put the pieces back together. Harry chose *me*,' she said. 'No matter what you got him to do while he was drunk out of his mind. No matter what ill-reasoned promise he made to you. One phone call from me last summer, and he was walking back all of it.'

'You called him?' I asked, momentarily thrown. 'When?'

'When our divorce was about to go through. I said I'd changed my mind, that I'd acted hastily.'

I shook my head, hardly understanding her. 'Harry said it got held up by lawyers.'

'That's one way to put it. But he was never good at owning up to bad news.'

My mind reeled. Had he been thinking of going back to her, even then? Even when we'd flown down to North Carolina, made our promises in front of everyone?

Jesus.

The thought struck me quickly, awfully.

I could kill him.

Elizabeth was throwing me off. Who knew if she was even telling the truth? I had to stick to the facts here. I had to focus on what I'd come to find out, how this all came together. 'How do you know Diana?'

Elizabeth closed her eyes. 'I don't know any Diana.'

'Diana Holbein,' I said.

She took a quick, sharp breath, as if someone had singed her with a hot iron.

'You do know her.'

'I *did* know her. There's a difference. What does Diana have to do with this?'

'She brought me up here, to your place. She's been missing since Friday. Did you put her up to it? Did you do something to her?'

There was something there, something running through Elizabeth's head, something she wasn't about to share with me.

'What is it?' I asked.

268

'Nothing,' she snapped. 'I told you. She's got nothing to do with this.'

Questions raced through my mind – What wasn't she telling me? How was Diana connected to all of this? – but there was no time to ask them. There was a sudden sound of tumbling, of something falling, upstairs.

I jumped, and Elizabeth did, too.

'Who's up there?' I asked.

'No one,' Elizabeth said, but already, I was running, taking their modern open stairs two at a time.

When I got to the top, I could feel it, so strongly, that sensation in my gut, that there would be answers now. That Diana would be there, waiting. That at least I would know that she was okay. At least I would know who she was – and *why* she'd conspired with Elizabeth to bring me here.

Only it wasn't a woman – it was a man.

He turned, and my chest clenched up.

I didn't understand, *couldn't* understand.

How many cogs had been set into place before we even arrived at that bar?

And why?

There he stood, that stupid bandana tied around his forehead, his shirt rumpled.

He seized up, as if caught. 'What are *you* doing here?' I asked.

He took a few steps forward, and I realized, as my eyes adjusted, that he was coming out of her bedroom. That his feet were bare. That his shoes were downstairs. Not Harry's.

His.

'It's not like it looks,' he said sheepishly.

But it was. That was beyond clear.

For once, I had a feeling it was *exactly* like it looked.

'Alex,' I said.

Without another word, I turned and fled.

32
MARGARET

After Sam left, I got in the car and drove to the brewery. I wanted to see Alex. I craved his warmth, his calming energy. I wanted a distraction from all of this, and he'd told me I could come by if I needed company. Now I very much did.

He wasn't there: his coworker told me he'd headed home early, so I went to his house instead. No sign of him. I parked in front and retrieved my phone.

> You ok? I tried to find you at work but your coworker
> said you left. At your house now. Would love to talk.

He started typing almost immediately.

> Got tied up with something but be there soon.

I tossed the phone into the passenger seat and pressed my hands against the steering wheel. Ten minutes passed, then fifteen and twenty. Around me, the sunlight was changing, late afternoon merging with evening, and then, eventually night. What would happen then? Where would Sam and I be?

I heard a pitter-patter first, then saw droplets speckling the window. I hadn't even thought to bring an umbrella.

Two figures in my periphery made me jump: police officers, walking up to Alex's door, knocking, their caps their only protection from the drizzle. The cops waited, then knocked again and turned toward me. The woman waved.

She approached my car, and I put the key in the ignition, turning it halfway so I could roll down my window, droplets splashing into the car.

'Can I help you, ma'am?' she asked.

I cleared my throat. 'Can I help *you*?'

The officer smiled at me. She had dark brown hair that was graying around her temples and a mole beneath her right eye. Her hair glistened in the rain. 'You're an acquaintance of Alex Hart's? Or you just felt like taking a break on this particular patch of road?'

'I'm meeting him here,' I said. 'He's on his way.'

'You know where he is right now?'

'No.'

'At work, maybe?'

'He wasn't there when I checked.'

The woman raised her eyebrows. 'Yeah. For us, either.'

'Is this about Harry?'

She lifted a hand over the bill of her cap. 'You know about Mr Brant, then.'

'It's a small town,' I said. 'Doesn't everyone?'

'People who live here, yes. But you're in a rental car.'

I gripped the wheel of the car tighter, then let it go. 'My

272

friend discovered his crime scene,' I said. 'I've been in touch with Detective Conway. I was at the station this morning, giving my statement.'

'And you are?'

'Margaret,' I said. 'Margaret Cahill.'

She stared, unblinking. The fact that she didn't seem to immediately recognize my name was comforting, like I could leave all of this behind if I wanted to.

'And how do you know Mr Hart?' she asked. There was a familiarity there, in her voice, in her words, and I found myself wondering if she knew him, too.

'We just . . .' I felt the blush come on, giving myself away. 'We're friends.'

There was a beep on her walkie, and then the other officer came around to my side. 'Another call. We gotta go.'

She nodded. 'You tell Mr Hart we need to talk to him,' she said, turning on her heel.

She wasn't two steps away before she turned back.

'And tell him it's important.'

It was another twenty minutes before Alex showed up, his pickup pulling into the driveway. He stepped out of the car, and I did, too, lifting my cardigan over my head to protect myself from the rain. Without hesitation, he walked up to me and wrapped me in a hug, squeezing me tight. He pulled back to kiss me on the lips. 'Are you okay?'

I nodded weakly.

'Come on,' he said. 'Let's get out of the rain.'

Inside, Rosie jumped up to greet me, trying to lick my face.

'Down,' Alex said firmly, but I gave her a pat on the head anyway.

I shook myself off, hanging my damp jacket on a hook.

He took his jacket off, too, then leaned in for another kiss. 'I'm glad to see you,' he said. 'But we should talk.'

'Okay,' I said carefully. Only something was off. His bandana was there, tight on his head, but there was a smell on him, too. Something sweet almost, floral. *Perfume*.

'Wait, were you with someone?' I asked.

He hesitated. 'Margaret . . .'

My jaw dropped. 'I didn't,' I said, stumbling for the words. 'I didn't expect you to . . . I'm not saying we were exclusive or anything, but, damn. I thought you'd wait until I left town, at least.'

'It's not like that,' Alex said. 'Give me a second to explain.'

My phone vibrated in my pocket, but I ignored it.

'Where *were* you?' I asked.

Alex bit his lip, hesitating.

'That was your second,' I said as Alex paled.

Meanwhile Rosie, seeming to sense the tension radiating through the room, began to whine, her tail dropping between her legs.

'I should go.'

I grabbed my jacket and moved for the door.

'Come on, Margaret,' he said. 'Come on, just wait. She wanted to talk. Elizabeth –'

'Elizabeth?' I asked. 'Harry's wife?' I shook my head. 'I thought he was only an acquaintance.'

'He is,' Alex replied. 'He was.'

'This is getting too complicated,' I said, reaching for the handle.

Alex followed me. 'I can explain everything. I promise. Please stay. I didn't mean it like that. You waited all this time for me. And it's nasty out there.'

It was too much, all of a sudden. Too complicated.

'I have to go,' I said again. 'I shouldn't have come.'

'Margaret,' he said.

I turned back, feeling suddenly bold. 'You know when I told Sam what you told me about Friday night, about breaking a glass, taking it out to your truck, she said it sounded strange to her. "Weird," she said. I defended you, of course. Should I not have?'

'Come on,' Alex said. 'You know I would never hurt anyone.'

'Do I?' I asked.

I reached for the door and felt my phone vibrate again.

'Please, don't go,' Alex said. 'Please stay.'

For a second, the lilt in his voice, the way he was almost begging, he reminded me of Lars.

'I'm sorry,' I said. 'I don't know who I can trust anymore.'

I pulled the door open and the rain droplets pattered hard against his front porch. I walked quickly toward the car.

'You can trust me,' Alex called.

I turned back, raindrops on my cheeks.

'I really wish I could.'

33

SAM

I was still damp by the time the car pulled into the driveway of our rental – Elizabeth's driveway – she owned it, after all.

I shivered at the thought.

My eyes scanned the drive, the porch, for any sign of Margaret, but no one was there. Where was she? Was she waiting to meet Alex? Was he already with her? Fuck. I'd tried calling her, but no luck.

Bolting out of the car, I ran up the remainder of the driveway, onto the porch, then twisted my key in the lock. It took a couple of tries, my hands were so slippery.

Inside, kicking off my shoes, tossing aside my soaked button-down, I took a deep breath, trying to figure out what to do next.

The second I'd seen Alex, I'd freaked out.

Were they having an affair? Had they killed Harry together? There were too many coincidences. Too many connections.

I locked the door behind me and pulled out my phone,

rubbing it against my jeans to rid it of raindrops. I hated how I'd fought with Margaret earlier – it was a stupid thing to do. I didn't really think – I couldn't believe – that she had wanted to hurt me, even if she had agreed to go along with Diana's batshit plan. Diana, who'd led me straight to Harry, straight to Elizabeth. Straight to Alex, who'd been hanging around all weekend, pretending to be someone we could trust. Taking advantage of Margaret's heartbreak to provide comfort. It made my stomach turn.

The grumble of a car in the driveway shook me out of my thoughts. I rushed to the front window, relieved to see our rental car pulling in and Margaret dashing up the steps, her hair plastered to her face, the rain awfully strong now.

I ran to meet her, untwisting the dead bolt and opening the door wide.

'You must be freezing,' I said.

She was out of breath as she walked into the foyer – and dripping like a drowning rat.

'Are you okay?' I asked.

Margaret nodded, kicking off her shoes, tossing them over to where mine were sitting, wet and musty. 'Are *you* okay?' she asked. 'I'm sorry about before. I shouldn't have questioned you like that. I'm so sorry about your dad.'

'It's okay,' I said. 'I'm sorry, too.'

We found our way to the sofa, our bodies still damp, leaving marks against the pale gray fabric, thumbprints on clean white paper.

'Were you with Alex?' I asked.

'Yes,' Margaret said. Her cheeks were speckled with tiny

flecks of mascara. 'I didn't want to be alone, and I didn't know where else to go when you left. I didn't see your texts until after I'd already left.'

Around us, the wind rustled, and above us, there was a groan of wood, an old-house sound.

I reached for her hand, cold and clammy, taking it in mine, and I told her what I'd seen. Elizabeth and Alex, the intimacy of the scene. My rings, my ID, and how I was sure someone had planted them next to Harry. For her part, Margaret told me the police were looking for Alex, that they wanted to talk to him.

When we'd brought each other up to speed, Margaret shook her head, as if unable to believe it. 'Do you really think they were . . . that the two of them . . .'

'I don't know what to think, but when I saw Alex today, he looked –' I paused. 'He looked caught.'

Margaret blinked slowly. Her eyes turned down, unbearably sad. She cared about him – she did. He had her in his hooks already.

'Did he ever mention having a relationship with her?' I asked.

'No,' Margaret said. 'He said there hadn't been anyone since his ex. Damn it, I feel so stupid. I don't know why I tried to convince myself it was anything more than a casual thing. But the way Alex spoke, the way it felt when we were together, it didn't seem like that at all. It felt like maybe I could actually move on. Not get past it but at least *try* to feel something for someone else.'

I reached my hand to her shoulder, pulling her close to me, our bodies still damp, smelling of ozone, wet earth. 'It's not your fault,' I said. 'Of course you thought that.'

Margaret pulled away. 'He said this felt different to him. Lord, I'm like a teenager at junior prom.'

'You think you're bad,' I laughed bitterly. 'I slept with the man who left me in the back of a bar because I wanted to feel close to him again. People don't realize, when your world breaks apart, you'll do anything for the chance to put it back together.'

When Margaret spoke, her voice was soft. 'I'm sorry that you ever thought I would judge you. And I'm so sorry for what I did to bring us here. But I swear, I never thought it would lead to this.'

'I know,' I said. 'I believe you. Whatever this is, whatever happened, it's not our fault.'

My phone rang, and I jumped.

I stared at the number, a local one. I imagined Conway, calling me to ask more questions. Conway, getting ready to make an arrest.

'You have to answer,' Margaret said. 'It could be important.'

And so I did. 'Hello?'

'Ms Lochman?'

I felt a rush of relief. It wasn't Conway. 'Yes?'

'This is Officer Ramos,' she said, and for a moment, I flashed to that first phone call from her, learning that Diana as we knew her did not exist at all. My heart ticked up a bit. Why was she calling now?

'Is Ms Cahill with you?' Ramos asked. 'I tried to call her first, but I didn't get an answer.'

'Yes,' I said. 'She's right here with me.' I set my phone on the sofa between us and put it on speaker.

'Great,' Ramos said. 'Look, I'm sorry this took me so long

to communicate. Things got slowed down over the weekend, like they always do, and then with the murder investigation, it fell through the cracks.'

I was desperate for her to be out with it, whatever it was. 'What?' I asked urgently. 'What fell through the cracks?'

'We got a hit for a Diana Holbein in California. Same age as your friend. The right spelling. And a New York connection, too. Lived for a time in Poughkeepsie.'

I racked my brain, trying to think of whether Diana had ever mentioned California.

'But there's a hang-up, too,' Ramos said, and her voice had that same tone as it did in that first phone call. That same hint of curiosity, of perplexity, of being almost excitedly stumped, the way you'd sound when you were describing a *Twilight Zone* episode.

'What?' Margaret asked.

Ramos cleared her throat.

'Diana Holbein died three years ago.'

TUESDAY

NIGHT

34

MARGARET

'We have to go,' Sam said. 'We have to go now.'

I glanced at the front door, listened to the rain lapping against the house, seemingly from all directions, and I tried to imagine Alex plotting with Elizabeth. I found I couldn't. It was impossible to picture, like a thumb in front of a lens, a blank spot where there should be details.

'We don't know who Diana is,' Sam went on. 'She lied to us, she . . . she doesn't even exist. She brought us here. She, or Elizabeth or even Alex, is setting me up. We can't stay here.'

'What about Detective Conway?' I asked. 'I thought she wanted you to stay.'

'I don't give a fuck about Conway,' Sam said. 'Or the stupid fucking rules. If she wants to arrest me, she can come down to Brooklyn.'

The tenor of Sam's voice scared me, but at the same time,

maybe leaving now was for the best. We were never supposed to be here anyway.

'Okay,' I said finally. 'We'll go.'

Up in our rooms, we packed our bags. It didn't take us long. We left Diana's things behind, not sure what to do with them.

Soon, we were back in the foyer, changed into drier clothes, umbrellas in hand, ready to go.

'You okay to drive in this rain?' Sam asked me.

'Yes,' I said. 'I'll go slow, and if we need to pull over and stop, it's fine.'

'We can get a hotel if we have to,' Sam said.

'Yes,' I said, bristling at the thought of even more money, even more debt. 'Yes, I guess we can.'

We did one last check, walking through the kitchen and the living room, making sure we hadn't left anything important behind, and in spite of Sam's protestations, I flipped through the manual that had taken me forever to locate to find checkout instructions, unable to help myself. The rules calmed me. Following them felt safe and secure, even now.

On the porch, the overhang protecting us from the downpour, rattling and percussing like a drum kit, I locked the door, then opened the lockbox and placed the house keys inside, shutting it tight.

'Ready?' I asked. 'I left the car unlocked.'

Sam nodded. 'Ready.'

We ran, pulling our suitcases behind us, rushing down to the car, umbrellas overhead but not doing much. Sam's inverted from the wind within a few steps.

Fingers slipping against the handle of the trunk, I pulled it open and took cover beneath the hatchback, tossing my suitcase in.

Sam set hers on top of mine and then, quickly, I closed it, ran back to the front and got inside.

Our umbrellas brought gushes of water into the car, but it didn't matter, we were inside, and we were about to be gone. We pulled the doors shut, and I let out a long sigh.

'Jesus,' Sam said. 'You sure you're good to drive?'

'Yes,' I said. 'I'll be extra careful.'

On my phone, I loaded up directions back to Brooklyn. Two hours and forty-five minutes, and I'd be away from this mess.

Into a new mess. Back in the apartment with Lars. Barely enough money to even think of moving out.

I rubbed my hands on my jeans, drying them off, then reached into my purse for the car key, but when my hand found the pocket where I kept it, there was nothing there.

Suddenly frantic, I retrieved my wallet, a pack of tissues, a reusable water bottle, a pill box full of Advil, which I never traveled without.

'What is it?' Sam asked, the pitch in her voice already rising.

'The car key,' I said, my heart beginning to race. 'I checked as soon as you said we should go, before we packed our bags. I unlocked the car from the window, so we wouldn't have to pause to do it in the rain. It was here, I know it.'

'Until someone fucking took it,' Sam said.

'No,' I said. 'She couldn't. She —'

Sam grabbed my bag, flipping it over, shaking receipts, two pens, and a tin of mints onto her lap. 'It's not here,' she said, a vanquished tone to her voice. 'It's not fucking here.'

Back in the house, I dug my fingers into each and every pocket of my purse, praying it wasn't true.

Sam was upstairs, trying to figure out our options. A bus. Another rental car. A cab to the city at an exorbitant cost.

I reached into my purse again, fingers poking at the seams, until I felt a hole in the lining. Perhaps the key had dropped through. Pushing my finger into it, I pulled – hard – tearing at the silk lining of the bag I'd gotten years ago in Italy with Lars. Same trip he'd bought me my red leather jacket. It came apart with a satisfying *rrrrrrrip*, and with both hands I shoved the pieces of lining aside. Nothing.

I tossed my bag down, then knelt next to the coffee table, looking underneath, moving onto the TV stand next, tugging it away from the wall.

There was an awful crack of thunder, and I jolted up quickly, banging my head against the edge of the TV stand. I rubbed my hand against the spot, the pain sharp and hot.

I stood up, walked slowly into the kitchen. At the counter, I steadied myself, taking a few deep breaths, my throat suddenly parched. I whipped open the cabinet, but there were no water glasses on the shelf. I opened the dishwasher, where I'd loaded everything neatly. I grabbed a glass, filled it from the tap, drank it down in a couple of gulps. Then I grabbed a wineglass, too, and the bottle from the other night, eager to take the edge off, just like Lars. I twisted the opener and popped the cork out, then poured the wineglass three-quarters full, took a sip, savoring the warmth, then started to close the dishwasher.

Something was bothering me. Something was *off*.

A tickle at the top of my spine, sending shivers all the way down. I let the door of the dishwasher fall with a heavy clank. There had been four of everything. Four wineglasses. Four coffee mugs. Four water glasses. It had been meticulously organized, the type of setup I'd envied.

I glanced to the cabinet. Two wineglasses sat on the shelf, one in the top rack of the dishwasher. One in my hand. On the next shelf, I found two coffee mugs, two in the dishwasher.

No, it was the water glasses that bothered me. Those didn't make sense.

There were three glasses in the dishwasher and the one I'd just used. Four.

Alex had made it sound so matter-of-fact, the hole in his alibi, his absence from my bed on the night Harry had been killed.

I broke a glass. I had to clean it up. I took the pieces out to my truck because I didn't want you to find out.

Today, he'd doubled down when I asked him about it.

You know I would never hurt anyone.

The truth was taunting, hard and real and impossible to ignore: Alex couldn't have broken a glass.

There were four glasses, perfectly intact, staring me in the face.

He'd lied to me. He'd been lying from the very beginning.

35

SAM

Diana's room felt eerily, unbearably empty, the space a shell of her, not offering a single clue to who she really was.

The cell service wasn't even that much better up here, but I didn't tell Margaret that. I needed to get away from her, to have a moment to think without her denial driving me insane.

The rideshare apps had been useless. Normally there were only one or two drivers in the whole area, with the waits for a car twenty minutes or more, but with the storm, there wasn't a single person out. I'd called local cab companies, too, but between my spotty service and theirs, it was useless. I'd finally gotten through to one after five minutes of trying, only to have the call drop just after the man said hello. I'd called back right away, receiving a busy signal instead.

And so now I was here, in Diana's room, desperate for answers. Desperate to know how she and Elizabeth were connected.

I tore into Diana's fancy suitcase, lifting up the whole thing and flipping it over, her clothes scattering all over the floor. I'd looked through it on Saturday, but that was before I knew that everything about her was a lie.

There was a flash of lightning, brightening the room. About five seconds later, a crack of thunder. I stood, momentarily abandoning my work, and looked out the window. The rain was angry, coming down in buckets. We were so goddamn stuck, dolls in a dollhouse, waiting for whoever was pulling the strings to come back.

If it came to it, we could run, run down that driveway and to the road, keep on running until we came across a car, someone who could help us, until our phones worked again, until we could call for help . . .

No, I thought. It was *not* going to come to that. The storm would pass, and the cell service would return, and the cab companies would answer, and someone would come get us, and we'd be out of here for good.

I tried my phone again, but the call wouldn't connect.

There was nothing useful in her clothing, so I moved on to the rest of the room, yanking open the top dresser drawer.

It was empty, and I slammed it shut. I whipped open another drawer. Then another.

Alex and Elizabeth were sleeping together, they had to be. But if they wanted to be together, they could have. Harry was with me by then – maybe not married, but well on our way to it. Everything was settled. Why bring him back? Why have Diana bring me here? Why did Elizabeth need to kill him when she could have let him go?

More than anything, why did Harry listen to her? Why did he choose her in the end?

One phone call from me, and he was walking back all of it.

I abandoned the dresser and went to look under the bed, but kneeling down, I finally lost it. My face fell to my hands, and I felt tears on my palms.

Fuck, Sam. Don't fall apart now.

It was too much.

How was I meant to mourn a husband I hadn't known at all?

How was I supposed to mourn a husband who wasn't ever really my husband – and never would be now?

Beyond Diana, beyond the missing car key and Elizabeth's rental property, beyond the drunk sex in the back of the bar, my puke on the porch out front, the questions and the police reports and the fights with Margaret and the visits to Elizabeth's gorgeous, perfect house. Beyond a twentysomething man who'd used my friend because she was vulnerable, who'd pretended to help her and had done anything but.

Beyond all of that, Harry, the man I'd loved, the man I'd promised to stand by, through sickness and health, till death do us part . . .

He was dead. I would never see him again.

Another bout of sobs rocked my body, and as if the world somehow understood what I was feeling, the thunder crackled then, louder, bolder, more insistent than ever.

It crackled again, so hard it shook the house.

Then a buzzing sound, followed by a flickering . . .

All the lights went out.

36

MARGARET

Thunder vibrated through the kitchen, rattling the glasses in the dishwasher.

When it stopped, the digital clock on the oven flickered and went out. Darkness, pure and terrifying, invaded the room.

'Sam,' I called, but I knew it was no use. The rain was far too strong now – between the wind and the thunder, there was no way she'd hear me upstairs. Still, I tried again. 'Sam!'

Lightning illuminated the kitchen, and there was my phone, plugged into the charger. I lunged for it, the lightning quickly disappearing and my hand missing it by inches, banging into the counter.

'Damn it,' I said, but with my other hand, I felt around until I found my phone.

I grabbed it, quickly tapped the home button and entered in my passcode. The glow of the screen was a welcome relief, until I saw the battery, only six percent.

It hadn't even been charging. It must be a dead outlet. Old houses were notorious for those.

I checked the cell service. What had been one and a half bars now was zero. Fear and relief washed over me in equal measure. I couldn't call Conway and tell her what I'd discovered, that Alex had lied to me.

At the same time, I didn't *have* to call Conway. A part of me, however foolish, still wanted to trust Alex. Or maybe that part of me simply didn't want to contend with the fact that I couldn't trust anyone.

Meeting Alex had made me think that it *could* make sense again, but now I feared that all I was doing was rebounding – not even from Lars so much as from that entire phase of my life, the forked road and the path I thought I was meant to go down.

A few years back, I could never have imagined Lars becoming an alcoholic, coming home from bars with a busted lip or a bruise at the top of his head. I couldn't have pictured him following me, stalking me, watching me. Calling me a slut. He had been my refuge, my safe, secure space, until he wasn't.

Had I seen Alex and simply imagined that he could fill in all the holes Lars had left? Had everything he said to me, in all those still, small moments, had they been nothing more than lines? Yes, I was desperate to hear all those words from someone, to imagine that with another person I could pick up the broken pieces of my adult life, build something new with someone else.

Still, I thought I had more sense than that.

On my phone, I swiped up to find the flashlight, then tapped it on as another bolt of lightning filled the room. On the kitchen island, I found the binder. I flipped through it as fast as I could, past the check-in and check-out instructions, restaurant recommendations, bars, including both Two Friends Brewery and

Eamon's, that godforsaken place. I skimmed through more pages and saw what I was looking for on the second-to-last page of the book.

'In case of inclement weather, a power outage or another emergency, there are candles, matches, flashlights, two gallons of potable water, and an AM/FM battery-powered radio in the closet in the upstairs bathroom.'

'Sam,' I called again as I made my way to the hallway. 'There should be flashlights in the bathroom upstairs.' I checked my phone again. Only three percent left.

My hand was on the bannister when I heard three loud knocks on the door.

'Sam,' I called again, but she didn't answer.

Bang bang bang.

Slowly, I crept to the door.

Maybe it's the cops, I thought, and Conway only wants to see that we're okay. Maybe I'll tell her what I know about Alex, seal his fate. Maybe, *maybe*.

I took another step and peered through the window in the top of the door.

He held a camping lantern, one of those LED ones that charge by USB, and it illuminated his face, his round cheeks, his hint of stubble, the signature bandana wrapped tightly around his head.

Alex.

37

SAM

I pawed around, feeling that childish jolt of fear that comes with darkness, with thunder and lightning, with being someplace you know you're not supposed to be. The house, Diana's abandoned room, looked even creepier now in the absence of light. The bed, the nightstand, even her suitcase cast awful shadows as lightning lit up the room. I rushed into the hall – I needed to find Margaret.

But at the top of the stairs, I paused. One of the doors that flanked the bathroom was cracked open. My eyebrows scrunched up. It had been locked, hadn't it?

Yes, it had. When I was so hungover that first morning, I'd turned the knob accidentally, thinking it was the bathroom.

Had Margaret found a key? Was it a supply closet? I would have heard her, wouldn't I?

I grabbed the handle, pulled the door open, and my heart kicked up a notch. It wasn't a closet at all. I stared at a rickety staircase, leading up to what looked like another room.

I took a careful step forward, feeling drawn, magnetized,

that strong sensation in my gut that this room, this cordoned-off space, had answers.

At the top, I found another door. It was old, heavy, and wooden, with peeling paint at the bottom and an ornate antique knob.

I reached my hand toward it slowly, as if it might singe me, and then I gave it a good turn.

Unlocked.

I pushed the door open and stepped inside.

The light on my phone revealed an expansive room, tall enough to stand in, built into the eaves of the house, walls rising to a point at the top, dropping to acute angles at the sides.

It was wide open, maybe twenty feet by twenty feet, with a rough, uneven plank floor and beams that covered the walls — taken together, the lines had an almost dizzying effect.

My flashlight illuminated spatters of water on the planks of wood, and the wind whistled through what must be a very old roof. It was colder up here, and wetter, too, with bits of insulation peeking out from between the beams — cotton-candy guts.

Hands shaking, I shone the light around the rest of the room. Sheets of drywall were propped along one wall next to a giant bucket of Spackle with a palette knife on top. It looked like Elizabeth was renovating. Perhaps turning this place into a proper room, upping the bedroom count for rentals.

I kept turning, illuminating the other side of the room, then stopped, rooted to the spot.

There in the corner was a small cot, dressed in sheets, and a nightstand, an old lamp on top of it, the lampshade bent and askew.

My eyes strained to take it in, but finally I did.

The sheets, the duvet and blankets, even the pillow – they were rumpled.

Almost as if . . .

As if someone was living up here, stowed away beneath the eaves, batting the chill away with a mess of blankets.

Someone who could have been watching us this whole time.

38

MARGARET

I couldn't see a damn thing, barely the outline of my own hands. Through the window, Alex waved, as if this was normal, as if he'd never lied at all. My phone was dead now. The only light came from his lantern.

'What do you want?' I yelled.

His eyes scrunched up, like he couldn't hear me. He said something, but I couldn't make it out.

'What do you want?' I asked again.

Alex shrugged, obviously confused.

He was under the cover of the porch, raindrops dripping from his temples.

I turned. 'Sam!' I called, but there was nothing. No answer in the darkness.

I was terrified at the thought of letting him in, but at the same time, I was terrified of being alone, trapped in the dark.

'Sam!' I called again.

Where is she?

I grabbed the door handle, twisting it quickly.

Alex stepped forward, but I pushed him back, moving out onto the porch instead, pulling the door shut behind me.

'What are you doing here?'

Alex's face fell to a frown. 'I . . .' he started, the wind half eating his words. 'I . . . I know you were upset when you left. I know you think that Elizabeth and me . . .' His voice trailed off.

'Save it,' I said. 'I know your alibi from that night was a lie. I lied to the cops for you. You never broke a glass,' I said, the words tumbling out now. 'Elizabeth keeps the cabinets meticulous. There aren't any extras. Nothing is missing.'

Alex shook his head.

'So that's it,' I said. 'You have nothing to say? How do you expect me to trust you?'

His eyes flashed, catching mine, and for a second, I worried I'd angered him. That he really wasn't the man I thought he was, that I'd gone too far.

In an instant, his demeanor changed. 'You're right,' he said, his words deflating the intensity around us, popping it like a balloon. 'You're totally right.'

'So where *were* you?' I asked. 'Why did you leave? What's your story now?'

He ran a hand over his forehead, pushing moisture away — rain, sweat, I wasn't sure. 'It's so stupid, and when you asked me that first morning, I was embarrassed, and I clammed up. I didn't want you to think that I actually left, that I didn't care about you . . .'

I crossed my arms, waiting.

Alex looked up, catching my eyes. 'Rosie,' he said.

For a second, I didn't catch it, I wondered who Rosie was, how she fit into all of this. Then I stared at him. 'Your *dog*?'

His eyes didn't break from mine. 'I told you, she has terrible separation anxiety. I never, *fuck*, I never do what I did on Friday. I never leave her alone all night. Even when I was . . . when Elizabeth and I were . . . well, it was casual. I always went right home. So on Friday, I woke up at three a.m., and I panicked. I could have just left, but I felt so bad – you guys hadn't even found your friend – and I didn't *want* to leave. I liked you, and I knew what it would look like if you woke up and I wasn't there. So I drove to my house, and I checked on her.' He laughed. 'She was fine. I guess I should have given her more credit. Anyway, I topped off her food and changed her water and scratched behind her ears, and then I came back.'

I stared at him, wanting so badly to trust him but at the same time incredulous. 'You really expect me to believe that?'

There was a rustle nearby, cutting me off. It sounded like it was coming from the bushes on the side of the house. 'Did you hear that?' I asked, pointing.

There was a crack, a breaking branch, and in the light of Alex's lantern, it was undeniable: I saw the foliage shake.

'Lord,' I said. 'Someone's here.'

39

SAM

Someone was living here. Someone was fucking living here.

My heart raced, and I knew I needed to find Margaret, to get the hell out, but I couldn't. Just a few feet from the cot, on the back wall, I spotted a tiny storage door, halfway open. Possibilities knit themselves together in my mind.

Answers, finally answers. An explanation I craved so desperately.

I knelt down, whipping the door open to find cardboard boxes marked by year. Taxes and records. 2009. 2010. 2011. 2012.

Elizabeth was organized, as Harry had said. They were lined up neatly, but on top, my flashlight caught something shiny, black-and-gold leather, nestled in the back. Something that didn't fit. An album.

Hairs standing straight on the back of my neck, I propped up my phone so the flashlight lit up the space and grabbed the album with eager hands.

I sat, ignoring the dampness of the wood on my jean shorts,

the splinters digging into my bare calves, and pulled the book onto my lap.

It was bound in black leather, with words printed in gold on the front.

ELIZABETH + ERIN

I found a newspaper clipping and an envelope on top of the first page. Fingers shaking, I unfolded the clipping: an obituary for Diana Holbein. What the *fuck*?

My eyes read over it, hungry for new information. California. A bike accident. Survived by her husband, Brandon.

Brandon. That's the name of Diana's ex.

I pushed the clipping aside and grabbed the envelope instead.

I turned it around so I could see the front properly. It was addressed to Erin Wren, a Tenth Avenue address in Manhattan. Right near where Margaret and I used to work, where I'd first met Diana.

Fingers still quivering, I opened the letter.

The handwriting was neat, as if whoever had written it had done so very carefully.

Erin,

I know you prefer to discuss in person, but I can't seem to get through to you that way without you or I getting so upset. It's impossible to communicate properly, so I'm writing you everything I need to say.

I'll start with the most pressing news: I'm taking Harry back. I know you don't want to hear this. He made an awful mistake, and I am unwilling to throw away all these years of marriage when I can choose to forgive instead.

You've always been my hero. After Mom and Dad died, I know you worked so hard to keep it together for me. I don't think I could have ever handled living with Aunt Cora if not for you. You've been more than a sister to me but a mother in some ways, too, but as we've gotten older, your protectiveness has become obsessive and controlling. Harry helped me see that. He helped me set boundaries with you.

I never imagined you'd react the way you did, just because I wanted some space. I can't believe you interfered to break up my marriage. I can't believe that you knowingly pushed Harry toward her.

I don't want to see you. I don't want to interact any more than we have to for the business. And ideally, we will soon find a way to disentangle that.

I will always always love you, but I can't forgive you.

– Elizabeth

Frantically, I flipped through the album. There were photos, loads of them. Two little girls, each with brown hair, one maybe a couple years older than the other. Doing all the sorts of things little girls did. Playing in the sprinklers. Building sandcastles at the beach. Blowing out candles on chocolate cake. Under each was a caption.

Best vacation ever

I'm pretty sure this cake made me sick.

6th birthday!

I kept flipping pages, discovering more of the same. The girls sitting together on a plane. Playing Monopoly at a big oak table. All decked out in mismatched outfits. Dolled up for what could have been a dance recital.

I flipped another couple of pages, found what must be a middle school graduation. An awkward photo from high school, the girls' hair in barrel curls, arms wrapped around each other, another girl between them.

Elizabeth, Diana and Erin
take on homecoming!

The answer was there, already coming to focus in my mind, but I had to see it, there on the page. Had to hold the truth in my hand.

Heart threatening to pound out of my chest, I turned another page, and on this one I only saw Elizabeth. Dressed in a gown from her Bard graduation. A tiny figurine walking across the stage.

I flipped another, and it hit me like a gut punch.

Elizabeth and Harry. Adults now, but younger. Harry's hair free from even a speck of gray. His face clean-shaven.

His wedding photo, he and Elizabeth leaning in, smiling for the camera. They looked like two of the happiest people in the whole wide world. Crazy and stupid and completely in love.

Next to it, I spotted a message written in neat handwriting.

I can't believe my favorite person in the world has gotten married! I know you have Harry now, but remember, I've been with you since day one and I'll be with you through thick and thin — forever.

Love always,
Erin

I turned the page again, and there was Elizabeth, resplendent in her dress. Standing next to her, a woman in a satin lilac gown, a floral clip nestled in her prematurely graying hair, a smile so easy to recognize I could never forget it if I tried. Her lipstick red as blood.

Quickly, I flipped back a couple of pages, to the photo that must have been from high school.

I lifted the album closer, studying it.

The woman on the right looked so much different than the Diana I knew. She was easily twenty or thirty pounds thinner, for one, and her hair was an even chocolate brown, no hints of gray at all. Free of the makeup — the thick mascara and bold red lipstick Diana always wore — she looked fresh-faced, almost boyish. She was pretty, sure, and certainly not plain, but she was a far cry from the striking silver-haired siren, the voluptuous woman she'd grown into. Diana was one of those women who got more beautiful every year.

In the photo from high school, the two looked very much like sisters, two different expressions of the same genetic pool.

Only Diana's features were a bit sharper, more pronounced. The bridge of her nose a little wider. Her eyes set farther apart. The sort of difference in looks that feels cavernous in high school and silly in the years to follow.

I turned back to the last page, studied the photo of the sisters at Elizabeth and Harry's wedding. There was the Diana I knew, her body grown curvy, her hair already nearly half-silver. Standing next to Elizabeth, in the lilac bridesmaid dress, there was some resemblance still, if you really looked for it, but the two looked less like sisters and more like friends. As adults, they'd developed so differently – if you knew them both independently, you'd never spot the resemblance.

It explained, if anything, why I hadn't.

I flipped back to the photo from high school, then back to the one at the wedding, proof staring me straight in the face.

There was a sound behind me, a terrible clattering, loud enough to hear over the rain and the wind and the chaos raging around outside.

I jumped, slamming the book shut, and turned. Another clatter, like furniture being turned over.

I tossed the book aside, grabbed my phone and rushed down the attic staircase, back into the hallway. Another sound. It was coming from my room.

'Margaret!' I called, rushing toward the sound, yanking the door open.

'Margaret, are you okay?'

My flashlight revealed the wrong set of eyes, the wrong hair, the wrong proportions.

The silver hair. The eyes that I'd found striking but now seemed almost haunted instead.

Here in my room was the woman who'd picked me back up when I was at the lowest point in my life, who'd shared many a glass of wine with me, who'd been a shoulder to cry on, who'd never failed to make me laugh.

Here was the woman I'd been desperate to find since Friday.

Diana.

40

MARGARET

'There's no one out there,' Alex said.

He was soaked by now, hair matted on his forehead, raindrops wet on his cheeks.

'You're sure?' I asked, my heart racing brutally, my hair standing on end. 'I know I heard something. I saw the bushes shake.'

'I'm sure,' Alex said. 'Reached into every bush myself, but I saw something scuttle out. A raccoon or a cat or something. I couldn't tell in the dark. Don't worry,' he said. 'It's okay.'

He reached out to me, his hand damp on mine, but I shook him away. 'Don't.'

'What I said is the truth, Margaret,' Alex said. 'I really did go home to check on Rosie. I promise you. I *swear*.'

My eyes locked on his, and when I spoke, my voice was thin. 'Then why didn't you say that? Why make up such a ridiculous lie about water and a glass and —'

'Because I'm a bad liar,' he said. 'I made it up on the spot. It seemed harmless, but then after everything happened, how could I have told you that I lied? I didn't want you to think the worst. That I'd had something to do with Harry's death or Diana's disappearance.'

'Even if you weren't lying about that,' I said. 'What about Elizabeth? You told me you hadn't been with anyone else. You were so convincing.'

His eyebrows knitted together. 'It wasn't like that, Margaret.'

'Oh yeah?' I asked. 'Then what was it like?'

Thunder rocked around us, shaking the old porch.

Alex let the lantern drop to his side, its light casting harsh shadows across his face.

'When I said I hadn't been with anyone in a long time,' he said, 'I meant, I don't know, in a real way.'

'You're only saying that now,' I retorted. 'You're only saying that to get yourself out of a sticky spot.'

'I'm not,' he said, his head tilting to the side. 'If you knew her, if you knew them, you'd understand. She and Harry used to come into the brewery together sometimes, and after he moved to Brooklyn, she kept coming. One night, when I was closing, she told me she wanted to check out this sushi place in Hudson. We went out, and then we went to a bar after that, and then . . . it just kind of happened. But she was always clear it wasn't anything serious. She said it was a rebound, and it would only work if I was okay with that. She always thought Harry was going to come back. She knew he was. But she wasn't going to wait for him to come to his senses "like some chaste Victorian wife." That's what she said.'

'And that's how you felt, too?' I asked. 'That you didn't want anything serious?'

'Yes,' he said. 'I was still too caught up in stuff with Luke's mom. I knew it was over, it wasn't that, but I was an emotional wreck. All of it was a distraction – for me and for her. I know I should have phrased it differently, and I should've told you, once we found out it was Harry who had died, not your friend, but I was scared you'd take it the wrong way. I was scared I'd lose you and this would end before it had even begun.'

In the light of the lantern, I saw, for the first time, faint acne scars arcing across both of his cheeks. I had a sudden sense that I was seeing Alex now, as he really was. An imperfect man. Not a fantasy. 'I really want to believe everything you're saying,' I said finally. 'But it's hard to know what to trust now.'

Alex's eyes turned down at the corners, hurt. 'I had no idea that you and Sam were connected to Harry and Elizabeth at all. I swear. And with you, I thought, I really thought we hit it off. I thought you understood what it was like, with my son . . . I care about you, Margaret,' he said, reaching out a hand to cup my cheek. 'No matter what else happened, I never ever lied about that. I promise you, I would never – I could never – hurt anyone. It's not who I am.'

I sighed. I believed Alex hadn't killed Harry – in truth, even when I was looking at those glasses, lined up in the dishwasher, I'd never really believed he had. But it wasn't enough. Lars never wanted to hurt me, but he did all the same. Alex was still caught up in all of this, and I needed to know how much.

'Why were you at Elizabeth's today?' I asked cautiously. 'Why go see her now?'

Alex lifted his lantern higher again, and the harsh shadows disappeared into the night. 'I thought that I saw her at the bar that night. She walked by so quickly, and it was while I was talking to you, so I wasn't sure. I saw her from behind, but she was wearing this dress, this green one with these straps that crisscrossed in the back that she always used to wear. I needed to be sure, before I said anything. I didn't want to get her in trouble if I'd been mistaken — I knew it wouldn't look good for her. I went over there to ask if she'd been at the bar that night. She said no, but she was always a terrible liar, and when I pressed, asking whether anything happened with Harry, she told me that he'd cheated on her again, that everything had gotten messed up, that it was her sister's fault, not hers. She was so *angry*. When we heard a car outside, she rushed up the stairs, leading me to her bedroom. She said she didn't want the police seeing us together in case they got any ideas. When she went down to see who it was, I found the green dress, bunched up at the bottom of her hamper, as if she'd just worn it. Then Sam came upstairs, and she saw me coming out of Elizabeth's bedroom. But I swear, I was only there to try to figure out what happened that night. That's *all* it was.'

Alex's eyes met mine. 'I lied to you, and I shouldn't have. And I should have been up front about everything with Elizabeth. But this is over now. That's why I came here. I wanted you to know first.'

'Know what?'

'After I left, I called Detective Conway and I told her I'd seen Elizabeth at the bar that night. I said that I'd seen her from the back, that I was ninety-nine percent sure it was her. She said another witness had seen her, too, but that my statement would help as confirmation. She said an officer would come by in the next few days to take a proper statement. Afterward, I couldn't think straight. I needed to know if . . .' His voice trailed off.

My pulse raced even faster now. 'If what?'

'I needed to know what was going on with the investigation,' he said. 'So I called one of my friends – this guy who comes into the brewery most afternoons – his brother's a cop. It's a small town, Catskill. He got back to me just now, right before I came over.'

Alex cleared his throat, and his face looked painfully, undeniably sad.

'They arrested Elizabeth for Harry's murder tonight.'

41

SAM

Diana stood in front of me, once missing, now here.

Like the car key, materializing out of thin fucking air.

Diana who wasn't Diana at all. Erin.

'Sam,' she said, walking closer to me, her voice warm and caring, like it had been so many times over the short course of our friendship. 'Sam, I'm so glad it's you.'

There was something in her hand, but she dropped it, and before I had time to look at it closely, she pulled me into a hug. She was so fast, so smooth, that I didn't even have a moment to resist.

And the truth was, it felt good, even if only briefly. Diana, my friend, was safe. Diana was here. I hadn't lost everyone after all. On Saturday morning, I'd been sick with worry, sick that something could have happened to her, to my friend. On Sunday, I'd recoiled at the thought of her blood on the ground.

'I'm so sorry,' she said softly. 'I'm so sorry for scaring you. For everything.'

But she's not Diana, I could practically hear Harry saying.

She's not your friend. You trust people too easily, Sam. You love too quickly.

I shook my head, pulling away from her. 'Stop it.'

'Don't be mad,' she said. 'I know you must hate me, for making you and Margaret worry. But you have to understand: I didn't have a choice. Brandon found out where we were going. I *had* to bring us here. But it didn't work. I think he saw me at Eamon's. I've been hiding out, up in the attic. I didn't want him to find me. I'm sorry I didn't tell you. I'm sorry I took the car key. I'm sorry for everything. I was so scared.'

For another brief moment, I felt it, that gravitational pull of Diana's and my friendship. We had talked and laughed and told each other our secrets, even if none of hers had been true, and it had all meant something – it felt as if it had meant something, at least. Not a bit of our friendship was real. Elizabeth's letter had said as much.

I can't believe you knowingly pushed Harry toward her.

Harry always thought I went too easy on people. I could be tough as nails at work, but in my personal life, I was always letting things go. A friend an hour late for brunch? NBD. A cutting comment? Who really cared, in the end? Harry pushed me not to idealize people, to demand to be treated better by friends and acquaintances. Ironic, when you thought about it, because he had treated me worse than anyone.

Don't see her for what you want her to be. See her for who she is, Harry would say. *And see* me *for who I was.*

And there it was, the truth, so real: I'd seen Harry, I'd seen my fantasy, and I'd wanted it all, and I hadn't cared about the consequences.

Now those very consequences were staring me in the face.

She was Erin, and she'd brought us here. If she hadn't killed Harry outright, she'd made it so Elizabeth and Alex could.

'Don't bullshit me,' I snapped. 'I know you're not Diana.'

She paused, pursing her lips. 'It's easier not to give my name with new people. You and Margaret.'

'No,' I said. 'Stop with the fucking lies. I *know*.'

Erin cocked her head to the side, and the light of my phone's flashlight made her look ghostly. 'What do you want me to say, Sam? I'm still me. I just needed to lay low is all. I'm sorry.'

I wanted to believe it: That there was a reason for everything. That she had been my friend. That Harry had loved me just as much – more – than he'd ever loved Elizabeth. That the cancer that would always live inside my dad's body would disappear.

But those were fairy tales, weren't they? Not based in reality but delusion. The desire for the world to be a way it wasn't.

'You must think I'm so stupid,' I said, and as I did, my phone slipped from my hand, and the flashlight illuminated the floor beneath us.

There, tossed on top of my suitcase, was a denim shirt. My eyes caught the label. It was from a small shop, one we'd come across in Williamsburg. Harry had paid one hundred and twenty dollars for this basic denim staple. He'd told me later he'd rather pay a lot for something good than a little for a lot of things he'd end up throwing out anyway.

It was his, no doubt about it. It both horrified me and broke my heart.

The shirt was Harry's, and it was covered in blood.

She hadn't just brought us here so Elizabeth could hurt him. She'd killed him herself.

42

MARGARET

I believed Alex.

I trusted him, this man I hardly knew standing on a porch I didn't belong on.

More than anything, I trusted myself. I believed that I hadn't been wrong about him, and I deserved a second chance as much as the next person.

'Do you really think Elizabeth did it?' I asked.

Alex paused a moment, then shrugged. 'She was so angry after Harry left. Whatever happened between the two of them, I think it built to a breaking point. I don't know if it was on purpose. Harry could really put back the drinks. Maybe she pushed him, and he stumbled. If the way he fell . . . I don't know. I don't *have* to know. It's all beyond our control now. I told the truth about seeing her. It was the right thing to do.'

Relief coursed its way through my veins. I still didn't know what Diana had to do with it, where she was, or even *who* she was, but the investigation was over. It wasn't Alex. Sam wasn't going to be wrongfully prosecuted. We could go home now. We could move on.

My life might be a mess, my relationship with Lars might still be terribly entangled, and I might be up to my ears in credit card debt, but I had gotten one thing back, one thing I'd lost: trust in myself. It would see me through this next season, no matter how hard it was.

'I'm so glad,' I said. 'I'm so glad it wasn't you. I thought, I thought that – you have to understand – since we lost my son, I haven't felt like I could trust myself at all. But deep down, I didn't think it was possible that you would hurt someone. I believed you were good.'

'I am,' he said. 'Good, I mean. Or I try to be. I try to do the right thing.'

I felt it then, that prickle of affection, of infatuation or love or whatever you wanted to call it, because when you were in it, when you were deep in that pool, whether you'd jumped in or waded, letting the water slowly rise to your chest, it felt the same either way. Here was this person, here was this person whom I'd found, and that made me so lucky.

After so long of feeling so incredibly unlucky, it was such a strange feeling. New, but so very delightful. So very deserved.

Alex stepped closer. 'I wasn't bullshitting, you know. We can make this work. I'll come down to your apartment in the city. You'll come up here.'

I laughed. 'I don't even know where I'll be living in the city,' I said. 'My ex is still there. He's sleeping on the couch, but . . .' I hesitated, for a moment, the shame filling up my insides, but I knew I had to build this, whatever it was, on a foundation of truth. 'I'm in credit card debt. So I don't know how I'm going to afford to get a new apartment or even if my credit will hold up for a renter's application in the city. It's a bit of a mess.' I sighed. 'Sorry,' I said. 'Apparently mid-thirties women come with a lot of baggage. Or I do, at least.'

'There you go with the age stuff again,' he said, but he was smiling now, and his hand was on the small of my back.

'Margaret,' he said, and his voice was earnest, with that bright, vibrant inflection that's there so strongly in your twenties. 'I don't care if your life is messy. Mine is, too. All that matters is you. I like you. I like you very much. I think I could maybe –'

'Stop,' I said. 'Don't say it. It's too soon.'

'Okay,' he said, but the knowledge of what he wanted to say, what he thought he could maybe feel someday, it warmed me, deep in my bones.

And since he couldn't say it, he showed it. He leaned in and kissed me hard and long, while the rain carried on overhead.

But when he pulled back, I heard it, faintly, behind the wind and the rain and the walls of the old house.

Voices. Yelling. Sam.

317

43

SAM

Erin stared at me, the denim shirt clutched tightly in her hand. She'd pounced on it before I could, grabbed it in her claws like a cat.

I felt suddenly sick, remembering all those moments we'd shared together. All those moments I'd bared my soul to the woman who would take a hatchet to my life. 'You killed him,' I said. 'Not Elizabeth. You.'

Erin's hand clutched the shirt even tighter. 'I didn't kill him.'

'Stop lying,' I spat. 'I know you're Elizabeth's sister.'

She smirked. 'And so what if I am?'

'You lied to me,' I said. 'You lied to us. About everything.'

Erin pursed her lips. 'Oh, and you didn't? You pretended to be going through a divorce when you weren't even married at all. You knew Harry was married to my sister, and you let your family and all your friends think he was yours. The only people you even told that he left you were me and Margaret – and you couldn't even be honest with us.'

My face flushed. 'We were as good as married. It was just a piece of paper. He loved me,' I said, my voice cracking. 'I loved him.'

'Harry loved himself,' Erin said. 'If you didn't know that, well, then I have to say you didn't really know him at all.'

The night I'd met her began to replay in my mind. It wasn't long after Harry had started at the agency. She'd been so enthralling, so open, so kind, head kicked back in laughter, that I'd opened right up. 'You targeted me,' I said. 'You followed me. That first night we met – it was no accident.'

'Can you blame me?' she asked. 'You think you know heartbreak? I do, too. Watching the person you love walk away from you, cut you out of her life, all because her all-knowing husband says so. Elizabeth and I were everything to each other.' Erin's voice wavered. 'So what if I was a little protective? Our parents died when I was fourteen. She was twelve. Do you know how hard I worked to make a nice childhood for her? Our aunt resented our very presence. I held it together. I kept us a family. I protected her so she wouldn't have to grow up as fast as I did. And then, after so many years of caring for her, Harry swoops in, and he wants her to set *boundaries*, he starts tossing words around like a freshman right out of a Psych 101 course. Codependent? Of course we were codependent. We depended on each other. We were all we had.'

'Life is short,' Diana – Erin – had said to me that night. 'Life is too short not to go after what we want.'

'Why didn't you try to stop me?' I asked, horrified. 'She's your sister. But instead, you . . . you *encouraged* me.'

'Don't you get it?' she asked. 'I wanted him to be with you. I wanted you two to work it out. I wanted my little sister to finally be free of him. As long as Harry was around, she would always be wrapped up in him, no matter if he respected her or not.'

Elizabeth's letter flashed into my mind.

I can't forgive you.

'What exactly did you do?'

'Nothing,' she said. 'I merely talked to you to see what was going on, and when it was clear that something very much *was* going on, I told my sister.'

'But we didn't – not until they separated – it was only a kiss. An accident.'

'Go ahead and keep telling yourself that,' Erin said, judgment seeping into every word. 'You knew it was bound to be much more than a kiss. So did I. Elizabeth needed to know herself.'

'But why did you lie to me?' I asked, trying to make sense of it all. 'Why did you pretend to be someone else?'

'I couldn't very well tell you it was me, Harry's own sister-in-law, could I?'

My mind reeled. Erin had pulled the strings, pushing me and Harry together even more than we already were. It suddenly made sense. Elizabeth had thrown Harry out so quickly I'd always wondered why, but now I knew: Erin had pushed her to. 'I still don't understand,' I said. 'Why did . . . why did he go back?'

Erin sighed. 'Because my sister, much as I love her, never did know what was good for her. She lost her resolve. She changed her damn mind.'

'And that was it?' I asked. 'That's all it took?'

'Harry was a piece of shit,' she said. 'You should know that by now.'

I shook my head. 'He wasn't.'

'Oh, but he was,' Erin said. 'He was happy to bounce between the two of you. Always so spineless. Sure, I helped move things along a bit, but he was the one who went through with it all. He was the one who left his wife and went running straight to you. Harry always wanted to have his cake and eat it, too.'

'So you thought it was okay to show up in my life again? To run into me and Margaret and *pretend* to have a whole sordid breakup of your own. Pretend to be a dead woman.'

'Don't talk about Diana,' Erin said. 'You know nothing about her.'

'Did you kill her, too?' I asked.

Erin shook her head emphatically. 'I didn't kill *anyone*. I loved Diana. She and Elizabeth are the two best friends I ever had. It's not my fault they both had terrible taste in men.' She glared at me. 'And you know, for a while, I thought – hey, maybe I was wrong. Maybe Harry really has changed. Maybe he's back with Elizabeth for good. I doubted myself, I did, especially once Margaret insisted we go fucking four hours north for our little escape from the city, nowhere close to where he was. I was *planning* on giving up on getting you and him together. I was going to try to find another way to get my sister to kick him out again. I was going to skip the trip and disappear from your life, be done with the whole damn thing. But then you told me about that text he sent you – 'I miss you' at two a.m. – and I knew I'd been right. I knew I had to give it one last shot. Make my sister see the truth of who he was.'

I shook my head, tears swimming in my eyes. 'You were there for us. You comforted me. You were at my apartment anytime I needed you. You pretended to be our friend – Jesus, you pretended to be *your* friend, your dead friend, like it was nothing. You could have pretended to be anyone, but you picked her.'

'I missed her,' Erin snapped. 'You know nothing about it. Don't try to understand. You don't know what it's like to care for someone like that. You're too weak-willed, too crazy about shitty men to care about anything, or anyone else. You aren't even honest with your own friends, your own family.'

'That's not fair.'

'You care about Harry, and you care about yourself, and fuck anyone who gets in your way. And you proved it to me, didn't you? That night at the bar, I was expecting a conversation – maybe even another drunken kiss – but boy, you two really pulled out all the stops. *You* did that. Not me. You made all this happen. All I did was document the evidence.'

'You, you watched us,' I said. 'You –'

'Filmed you, yes, not that it matters. I knew she wouldn't believe my words, not again. I knew she needed actual proof.'

Her hand still clutched Harry's shirt.

Tears cascaded down my cheeks. 'You killed him,' I said. 'It was always you. Not Elizabeth. *You.*'

'It wasn't me,' Erin said, her voice a shriek. 'It was *you*. You're the one who brought all of this mess upon yourself.'

My eyes once again found the shirt still grasped in her hand. 'What are you going to do with that?'

Then I spotted my suitcase, and it all made sense. Yet another thing to plant. The final straw. Between the rings, the ID and now this, it would be enough. Enough for Conway.

Hell. Maybe in some twisted way Erin didn't even believe that she killed Harry. Maybe she'd rewritten it all in her mind so she could find a way to live with herself. But here she was, the blood literally on her hands.

'Give that to me,' I said. Suddenly I couldn't handle it, the way she held so tightly the last thing Harry had ever worn.

The way she'd used me – and Margaret, too.

Erin backed away.

'Give it to me,' I said again. 'Now.'

'No,' she said, her eyes lighting up with rage. With both hands she pushed me so hard I stumbled back.

'*You* got him killed,' she said again, stepping forward, pushing me again. '*You* brought all this on yourself. Perhaps if you hadn't gone so crazy, if you hadn't fucked him in the back of the bar like a fucking *whore*, maybe none of this would have happened.'

Before I could say another word, she rushed at me.

The woman I thought I'd known, the woman I'd thought was my friend.

The woman more tied up in all of this than I ever could have imagined.

Diana – no, Erin – lunged.

44

MARGARET

I knew it as Alex and I scrambled inside, as he bolted up the stairs, his lantern lighting the way. Diana was here. Diana was going to hurt Sam.

I followed him as quickly as I could, taking the stairs two at a time.

The door to the right of the bathroom, the one I'd assumed was a closet, was wide open, revealing a staircase, but the voices were coming from Sam's room, in the front of the house.

Please don't let us be too late.

Alex didn't hesitate, he ran down the hallway, bursting through the door, revealing a scene, so awful, so hard to comprehend. Diana was on top of Sam, straddling her, one hand batting Sam's away, the other holding something, something that looked to be covered in blood.

'Stop it!' I yelled. 'Diana, stop it!'

Alex was quick. In moments, he was on top of both of them, pulling Diana off Sam, dragging her away.

'Margaret,' Sam said, sucking in breath. 'Thank god. She attacked me. She was, she was . . . she has Harry's shirt. She killed him . . .'

Words spilled from Diana's mouth as Alex held her back. 'Just try to prove anything. You're all over that crime scene. Your rings, your ID. The video of you two together. The police will arrest you, they'll get you for Harry's death, you won't get away with what you've done to us. It will all come back to haunt you.'

Alex gripped Diana even tighter.

'It was her,' Sam said, her voice cracking. 'It was always her —'

'But the police,' I said. 'They arrested Elizabeth tonight, they —'

The sound was so pained, so shrill, like a small animal being tortured, that at first I didn't know what to make of it, and it was only after a moment, after we all seemed to wake from the situation we'd found ourselves in, that I understood that the sound was coming from Diana's mouth.

A cry of pain, of hopelessness, of loss.

'No,' she said. 'You don't mean that. There was no evidence. Nothing to tie her there. Nothing.'

'There was,' Alex said. 'I saw her, and I told the police. Other people did, too. This is over. It's done.'

Diana shook her head, tears streaming down her cheeks. 'No,' she said. 'No no no. It wasn't supposed to happen like this. No no no.'

Then, so quickly, none of us expected it, she lifted her foot and stomped – hard – on Alex's. He cried out in pain, and she took her chance, wriggling out of his grasp and bolting away, the bloody shirt still in her hand.

'No,' Sam said, her eyes wide, terrified. 'It wasn't Elizabeth. It was her.'

Sam flew down the stairs, chasing Diana through the dark. Alex grabbed his lantern, rushing after her, his gait uneven, his foot obviously hurt. I followed, bumping into bannisters, my toes getting caught on protruding floorboards.

Diana bolted through the front door, and there was just enough light from Alex's lantern to see it:

Sam, tripping, missing the last stair.

Sam, falling forward.

I raced down the stairs, kneeling next to her.

'Sam,' I said. 'Sam – are you okay?'

She turned over. Her nose was bloody.

I heard Alex's breaths, heavy next to me.

'Go,' Sam said, eyes on Alex. 'Go. Stop her, please. Before she gets away.'

Alex jolted up as best he could on his injured foot, making for the front door. The lantern dropped from his hand, but he didn't pause to get it. He rushed through the door and out onto the porch.

I wanted to tell him to stop, to let Diana go. Too many people had been hurt, and I didn't want to see him hurt, too.

But he didn't.

Then, among the rain and the wind, I heard it.

The grumble of an engine.

326

'The car,' I said. 'Damn it. Diana had the key. She's getting away.'

Sam shook her head.

'That's not Diana.'

She took a deep breath.

'It was never Diana at all.'

45

ERIN

Over the river and through the woods.

Elizabeth and I used to love that song when we were very small. Our mother would sing it to us, her voice bouncing over each new note, happy and sweet as a bird's chirp, only she would replace 'to grandmother's house we go,' with 'to Aunt Cora's house we go'. Elizabeth and I didn't have grandparents. Our parents were older when they had us, and their parents had died either before we were born or when we were too young to remember, but we had Mom and Dad, until we didn't. Four of us in our own little cocoon. Plus Aunt Cora, who liked us then, before she had to be responsible for us on her own.

I'd sung it to Elizabeth on that first drive down to Cora's in Poughkeepsie, even though we were too old for it then. I'd sung it to her in those early days, when Elizabeth's anger had gotten the best of her. The song reminded us of our mother. Of a time when we'd felt safe. We'd only stopped singing it, really, when we'd met Diana, Aunt Cora's neighbor two doors down. Then it was the three of us, during the day, at least, when we were away from Cora's bitter resentment, building Rollerblade ramps in Diana's paved driveway, getting lost in the woods on her property, blasting music loud in Diana's unfinished basement.

The song played on a loop in my head as I drove, over the Hudson River, to the police station on the other side. Going fifty miles an hour, then sixty. Seventy.

Over the speed limit and through the woods.

In spite of everything, I laughed.

Mom used to say we would understand when we had kids of our own, why she felt the way she did. Why she had to come into our rooms late at night to check that we were breathing, even when we were way too old for that.

But Mom, wonderful as she was, was wrong.

I didn't need to wait until having children of my own to feel it. I felt it with Elizabeth, from the very first moment the cop came to our front door, telling us our parents had died.

I knew it then. *This is all on you now. You have to protect her. She's all you have.*

I knew it as true as any mother does. I will love her forever, no matter what.

I will do what's best for her, no matter what.

When people hurt her, it hurts me. I will harness the rage she's too powerless to follow through on. I will act.

No matter what happens, I will protect her, like I promised myself that very first day.

The car, the stupid SUV that Margaret had insisted on driving all on her own, swerved onto the shoulder, a rumbling sound rocking through the vehicle. Any farther, and I'd be flying off the bridge, which wouldn't do me – or Elizabeth – any good.

329

Into the river and not through the woods.

I veered back, took my foot off the gas.

I would get there, only a few more minutes now.

I would get there before they could get very far with Elizabeth.

I would do what I knew I had to do to save her. It was a dreadful prospect, but the alternative was even more so. Nothing was impossible when you loved like a mother did.

I'll bear this pain so you don't have to.

Elizabeth said she'd always love me, but that she'd never forgive me.

A smile crept to the corners of my mouth, a smile that morphed into a grin as I pressed my foot back onto the gas – hard – speeding through the rain. High on the rush of it all. Hardly able to believe I was about to do what I was about to do.

She said she wouldn't forgive me, but she'd surely forgive me now.

TWO
MONTHS
LATER

46

SAM

The Amtrak ride was beautiful, hugging the Hudson, the river framed by lush greenery, verdant trees. The thick of July, the most beautiful part of summer.

My phone buzzed in my purse, and I pulled it out. There was a text from my mom.

> Can't wait to see you next week! Dad and I are
> thrilled you're staying for a whole week this time!

I put it away, then rubbed, absentmindedly, at the white sliver of skin on my finger as I watched the trees – the river – roll by.

I had gotten my rings back after all. Conway had delivered them to me when the investigation was over, a few weeks after Erin had been arrested. A case had brought the detective to Manhattan, and she said she'd rather return something so valuable in person.

Over burnt Starbucks coffees on Broadway and Forty-Eighth

Street, Conway had filled in the gaps that Margaret and I hadn't been able to put together ourselves from what the officers told us when we gave our statements that night.

On that last night in Catskill, they'd arrested Elizabeth. Motive spoke for itself. Apparently, she had a video of me having sex with her husband behind a bar, one that had been sent to her by Erin. But more than that, there were threatening texts from her to Harry that same night, just after the video was sent. There was the fact that she'd never reported him missing when he hadn't come home on Friday. Together with Alex's statement that she was at Eamon's, as well as evidence that had turned up at the scene – blood matching her DNA on the bottom of Harry's undershirt – they felt they had more than enough to make an arrest. Truthfully, all the wheels had been in motion, even while Conway was interviewing me and Margaret. Besides, she told me, even though she'd never said as much in our discussions, she'd always felt that the rings and my ID seemed planted. The fact that we were staying at a property Elizabeth owned gave her access to these items.

Of course, that had all changed after I found Diana-slash-Erin in my room that night. After the chaos of our confrontation, after Alex pulled her off me, she'd taken the car key (the one she'd filched from Margaret's purse) and driven straight to the police station, delivering a full confession, with evidence to prove it. Harry's denim shirt, what she was going to use to frame me – proof positive she'd killed him.

Elizabeth had been at the bar that night, but she'd never found Harry. She'd come, looked for him in the back, and left. In the threatening texts she'd sent him, she told him she didn't want to see him anymore. That's why she didn't call anyone

334

when he didn't come home. Of course, by then, Erin had already attacked him, smashing a beer bottle over his head until he began to bleed, before dragging him into the woods where he wouldn't be found and covering his body with brush. No easy feat alone, but Harry was only five foot eight – and he was slim, one hundred and fifty-eight pounds, to be exact – and a rush of adrenaline had apparently given Erin enough strength to drag him back.

Erin had returned to the house she and Elizabeth owned together, one of a portfolio of houses up and down the region that they rented out through their company, Over the River Properties. This one wasn't currently being rented – they were renovating the upstairs attic apartment – which is how Erin had known we wouldn't be bothered with any other guests on our little trip.

What's more, though Erin co-owned the property in Catskill, unlike Elizabeth, she had never lived there herself. She'd grown up in Hurley, a town about an hour south, then spent high school in Poughkeepsie, college and after between Poughkeepsie and the city. She did visit Elizabeth up in Catskill sometimes, but those visits had dropped off after she and Elizabeth had their falling-out. Erin knew she wouldn't be recognized in town. The only people who knew who she was were Margaret and me, and we didn't have her name or even so much as a photo to tie her to us at all.

From the attic, Erin had kept an eye on me, pinched my things, done her best to make me look guilty. The bloodied shirt, which she'd intended to plant in one of my bags and tip off the police with an anonymous phone call, was meant to be the final straw. Evidence planted, Erin would go back to her life

335

in Manhattan, no one the wiser that she'd ever been in Catskill at all.

It was a perfect murder, complete with a perfect escape – it should have been, at least.

Perhaps it would have gone her way had the power never gone out, had she not found herself stumbling around my room, waiting for me to find her.

Conway had left me in that shitty Midtown Starbucks, staring at the rings that had once meant so much to me, that I now knew were a promise Harry had never been sure of, even from the beginning.

Even now, I didn't doubt that he loved me, in his way. When Elizabeth had thrown him out, I was the one he turned to. When my dad had gotten sick, he'd been eager to jump in and do anything he could to make it better.

Erin had been wrong about Harry. She said he loved only himself.

But now, two months gone, Harry long buried in a ceremony arranged by Elizabeth up in Catskill that I had attended, even if for only ten minutes, I felt differently.

It wasn't that Harry loved only himself.

It was that he loved being the hero.

He cared for both of us, in his way. If Elizabeth needed him, he was there, even if it pained him to hurt me. And if I did, he was ready to drop everything and plan a last-minute wedding.

These two forces, Elizabeth and me, had tugged him back and forth, even to the end. Not because he wanted to have his cake and eat it, too.

But because Harry was so bad at saying no. He was so bad at not swooping in to the rescue whenever he had the chance.

There was this one time, on our honeymoon, while we were waiting to go on a boat excursion. Two American tourists had rented a car for the day on the island, and when they'd told us they had a flat, Harry had insisted on fixing it himself. They'd already called their rental company, and someone would be on the way, but Harry knew how to do it and he wanted to.

We'd missed the excursion, one I'd very much been looking forward to, but how could I be mad? Here was my Harry, my hero.

Over the last two months, I found myself going back to that memory, seeing it differently. Not a positive quality so much as a compulsion.

He should have chosen me on our honeymoon, not a random couple who had help coming anyway.

He should never have offered to save me, to make my dad's dream come true, when his heart, when his lifelong commitment, wasn't free to give.

I hated him for it. But at the same time, I missed him.

I wasn't a widow, because our marriage had never been real, but my heart still felt widowed all the same.

I stared out the window as the train passed a small pedestrian bridge. I was almost at my stop.

I texted my mom back.

Can't wait to see you, too!

It had taken time for me to get the guts to do what I needed to – and what Margaret kept urging me to. I had canceled my parents' visit to New York, claiming I wasn't ready to see anyone so soon after losing Harry, but eventually I made the phone

337

call, told them the truth: it wasn't just that Harry was dead, it was that he'd left me months before for another woman – and not just any woman, his wife. I'd had to repeat it three times to my parents before they properly understood. Our ceremony had been just that – ceremonial.

When I'd first met Erin, there in that bar, when I'd drunkenly spilled my secret, told her of my crush, I'd been so naive. I'd thought love could conquer all. I didn't know that love could be as selfish as anything else.

I knew I couldn't blame myself for Harry's death – that had been Erin – but I couldn't totally absolve myself, either.

Erin was right. Though she'd stretched the truth to Elizabeth, what happened between Harry and me had felt inevitable. Because deep down, I hadn't cared at all. I'd wanted Harry. I'd wanted him all to myself.

The train slowed, and the conductor came to a stop.

I stood, grabbing my bags.

It had taken all of this, my supposed friend's disappearance, Harry's death, for me to finally be honest with my friends, my family.

For me to finally be honest with myself.

But it wasn't over – not yet.

There was still one thing I had left to do.

47

MARGARET

My stomach did somersaults as I paced back and forth in the tiny kitchen. I'd done my best to organize it. I'd put all the pans in one cabinet, all the pots in another and given the space a good, thorough scrubbing, something Alex hadn't done in what looked like years.

I was still a guest, technically speaking, and I liked to earn my keep. Nothing had been properly arranged.

After Diana – or Erin – left, we'd tried to take Sam to the hospital, but she'd insisted she was okay. So we'd grabbed our bags, and we piled into Alex's truck. We took Sam back to his place. She was too afraid to spend even one more second in Elizabeth and Erin's house.

Only a handful of hours later, we were getting our rental car from the police station, where Erin had left it, giving our statements, and then, eventually, on the road, Alex caravaning behind us the entire time.

In Brooklyn, I turned the key in my door, heart beating at the thought of seeing Lars after all I'd said to him, but I was lucky to come home to an empty apartment. I asked Alex up, and I grabbed as many of my things as I could.

The choice had been so easy, so natural. 'I can't stay with Lars anymore,' I'd said.

'So you'll stay with me instead,' he'd replied.

And here I was, two months later, still living with Alex. Or crashing with him, at least. Lars and I had texted some and had a couple of phone calls, but that was it. I hated that we hadn't had a proper goodbye, and there would be one at some point, but too many lines had been crossed that weekend for me to live with him again. So Alex and I had been floating along, cocooned in the bliss of new love, new bodies to explore, new routines to establish.

Until now, of course.

I jolted, hearing the grumble of Alex's truck.

I rushed to the bathroom, splashing some water on my face, then back down the hallway, passing Luke's room on the way.

Alex's son would be coming to stay in a couple of days. I hadn't met him, but we'd talked some on FaceTime. He was a cute kid. Boisterous and rambunctious, the way a kid should be at that age. Unafraid of anything. Ready to take the world by storm.

Lord, this could change everything.

I heard Alex's steps on the porch, and in the living room I waited, shifting my weight from foot to foot.

'Hey, baby,' Alex said, as he always did when he came in.

It had been a crazy couple of months. Trying to work out the logistics of the lease in Brooklyn that was still in my name. Keeping up with Sam as best I could, helping her get the courage to tell her family everything. Trying to figure out what my

340

life looked like in Catskill. Working out payment plans with all my creditors. Vying for freelance assignments that could be done remotely.

Even so, today, what had happened this morning; it was a whole different realm of chaos. One I hadn't expected or been the least bit prepared for. One I'd thought I'd never have to face again.

'You okay?' Alex said, pulling back. 'Something's off.'

I blinked slowly, felt heat rise to my face.

'Margaret,' Alex said. 'God, what's wrong?'

I turned on my heel, then walked to the bathroom. I opened the cabinet, pulled the little white contraption from where I'd stored it, plastic cap still on so my pee didn't get everywhere.

I could hardly believe it. We'd been so careful. And I was thirty-six, for god's sake. It wasn't supposed to be this easy.

I hesitated, knowing this would blow our world – my world – apart – and handed the test to Alex.

He looked down at the two pink lines, then back up at me. 'Seriously?'

I nodded, ill at the thought. 'I don't know how, I took the pill every damn day. I don't get it. I –'

'Margaret,' he said, a grin spreading across his face. 'Margaret, this is wonderful. A baby. Oh my god, a baby!'

My breaths came short and shallow. 'I can't do it again,' I said. 'I can't roll the dice. I can't bear to . . . I can't bear to lose someone I love again.'

Alex took a few steps toward me, placed his hands gingerly on my shoulders.

'Margaret, babe, if you don't want this, if you can't –'

'No,' I said. 'I *do* want this. More than anything.'

341

The thoughts had been running through my head all day.

I want this I want this I want this.

I want to meet you, my child.

My second chance.

'I do want it. I wish I didn't, but I do. I'm just scared,' I said. 'I'm scared it's all going to happen again.'

Alex shook his head firmly. 'It won't,' he said.

'You don't know that,' I argued. 'You *can't* know that.'

'Okay,' he said. 'Maybe I can't. But we're in it together, right? You and me.' He let his hands fall to my belly. 'You and me and another little person in there.'

'What about Luke?'

'Are you kidding?' he asked with a laugh. 'He's been begging for a baby sister or brother for as long as I can remember. He'll be thrilled!'

'Really?' I asked. When I caught his eyes, I saw that his were glistening with moisture. 'Because I'll be a mess,' I said. 'I'll be anxious. I'll be paranoid. I'll be so scared that it's all going to happen again.'

Alex stepped forward, kissing me lightly on the lips.

'And I'll be with you. Every step of the way.'

342

48

SAM

It was twenty-five minutes across the river to Elizabeth's house.

I spotted her as I walked up the driveway, sitting on one of the gorgeous modern sofas. Beautiful, as always.

I knocked at the door, and in moments, she was there.

Her face scrunched up as she opened it. She stared at me.

'Can I come in?' I asked.

'Why?' she said. Her words were careful, hesitant.

'It won't take long,' I promised. 'I just want to apologize.'

We sat on her sofa, two glasses of Perrier with lime on the coffee table before us, and I took a breath, knowing I needed to do it right.

'I don't want to offer any excuses,' I said. 'I'm sorry, truly sorry, for what I did. The way Harry and I spoke to each other, the closeness we developed, the one time we kissed, it wasn't right. Not when he was married to you. I know I knew that, deep down.'

Elizabeth looked caught off guard.

'I mean that,' I said. 'I was so in love, I was so blind, I

didn't care who Harry and I hurt. I didn't really even think of you as a whole person, just an obstacle to getting what I wanted.'

Elizabeth remained silent. She'd changed since the last time I'd seen her. Her anger seemed to have subsided, replaced by the calmness of acceptance, of grief. She hadn't just lost her husband. She'd lost her sister, too.

'I know that maybe that's not how Erin portrayed it, but that is how it happened. I swear.'

She took a slow, careful sip of Perrier. 'That's what Harry said when I confronted him. He said it was a stupid kiss and nothing more.'

I cringed at the word *stupid* but forced myself to go on. 'He was telling the truth,' I said. 'I have no reason to lie to you. Not anymore.'

She set her glass down, then stared at her hands. 'Thank you for telling me that. Can I ask you a question?'

'Of course,' I said. 'Anything.'

'Did Erin encourage you?'

I nodded without hesitation.

Life is short.

'How far along was the – er, the *flirtation* – when she did?'

'Early stages,' I said. 'I met her at a bar. I had no idea she was connected to you at all. She told me her name was Diana. I confessed after one too many cocktails that I had a crush on a married guy. I said what people in my position always say, that he wasn't happy and he was looking for a way out. I'm sorry,' I said again. 'I know it was wrong.'

Elizabeth sighed. 'That's what I thought.'

'What did Erin tell you exactly?' I asked. 'About Harry and me?'

'Oh, you know. That she'd run into Harry in the city and was about to say hello when she saw him with you. She had a photo and everything. That you were incredibly intimate, all over each other, in fact. That there was definitely something going on. She said she followed you, that he took you into a hotel room on the West Side. She had the location and everything. She said she'd suspected Harry for a while. That she thought there were other girls before you.'

I shook my head. 'That never happened. I swear.'

'Harry denied sleeping with you and everything about the hotel room – he admitted the relationship had become inappropriate, that he'd slipped up with the kiss. I was convinced he was lying, trotting out a more palatable version of the affair so I wouldn't leave him. I was wrecked. I went down to stay in the city with Erin, and we came up with a plan. I told him to leave, that he better have his things out of the house by the time I got back. She was my big sister, and she'd always looked out for me. I didn't think she'd ever go so far as to lie to break us up. I didn't think she had it in her. But after Diana died –'

'Diana Holbein?'

'Yes,' Elizabeth said. 'You see, we were good friends for so long, and at such a pivotal time, the three of us. High school together, hung out all through college. Erin and Diana were the same age. They were so incredibly close – they even lived in the city together for a couple of years. Then Brandon came along. There was nothing wrong with him, per se. He was just a little quiet, a little reserved. Erin didn't like him from the start. She tried to convince Diana that he wasn't good for her, that she could do better. When he said he was moving to California and he wanted her to go with him, Erin begged her not to go. She said she'd seen Brandon with another woman. Of course, I believed her then – just like I believed what she said about Harry. But Diana didn't listen. She asked Brandon if he ever cheated, and he said no. She basically told Erin to fuck off before she left for California. The whole thing sent Erin into a deep depression . . .' Elizabeth took a hesitant breath. 'I think she never got to grieve for our parents, because she was trying so hard to protect me. When Diana left, it was like she pulled out the stopper in whatever was holding Erin together. She lost the job at the restaurant.'

'The restaurant?'

'Yes,' Elizabeth said. 'It was the only work she ever had. Waiting tables at high-end places. Besides the business we started together. Why? What did she tell you?'

I gulped. 'That she was a social worker.'

Elizabeth's lips turned down at the corners. 'No,' she said. 'No. That was Diana. Anyway,' she said. 'It doesn't matter. Erin was a wreck after Diana went to California. I had her come back up. I was living in Poughkeepsie at the time – not here. We hadn't started the rental company yet. Anyway, she came up, and she lived with me, and everything felt like it was going so well. We bought our first property. We got a good deal, and we worked together to make it nice before we started renting it. We used the rest of our trusts to buy some other properties in the area, the place where you stayed included. I mean, we had so much to start with, but still, we used it wisely.'

She grabbed her water again, took another sip. 'I know it

was codependent, looking back. But it was what we'd always known, and it worked for us, in its way. Erin would have these depressive episodes, and I'd pull her through. Do whatever I could to help her. If that meant staying up all night with her, talking it out, so be it. If that meant holding her in bed, telling her it would be okay, that was fine, too. Yes, I let my social life flounder, and I didn't spend a whole lot of time dating, but we were each other's people. And she did care about me. I know that.'

'So what changed?' I asked.

'You can guess, can't you?' Elizabeth asked, pressing her palms to her thighs. 'I met Harry. And he blew my world right open. I was in love, and Harry and I were traveling – weekends here and there – and we were going down to the city more, planning a wedding, all that. Things came to a head when it was time to arrange our first vacation after we were married. Erin wanted to come, and I didn't see why she couldn't. Harry and I were going away for two weeks – what if she got depressed? What if she needed me? Harry put his foot down. He helped me – well, he helped me see that it wasn't healthy. After that, it was always a battle. Harry would want to do things with just me, and Erin wasn't okay with it. We got in this huge fight one Christmas, and Erin said she was moving back to the city. She got an apartment in Hudson Yards, and Harry and I moved up here. We still talked and everything, but it changed between us.' Elizabeth sighed. 'But then Diana died, and it all started again.'

I pressed my lips together, needing to know, as awful as the thought was. 'Did she kill her? Did Erin kill Diana?'

Elizabeth jolted. 'Oh god, no. Erin would never –'

'But, Harry,' I said. 'How can you say that when she killed Harry?'

Elizabeth shook her head firmly. 'You don't understand. She wanted to protect us, not hurt us, and she wanted to hurt anyone who got in the way of that. She never would have hurt Diana.'

'Is there any way that Brandon killed Diana?' I asked. 'Because when Erin told us she was Diana Holbein, she said her ex, Brandon, was obsessive and controlling. She said that's why she wasn't on any social media, so he wouldn't find her. Was that another lie?'

Elizabeth sighed. 'About their relationship, I honestly don't know. There may have been . . .' She paused, as if choosing her words carefully. 'There may have been some nuggets of that, it's possible. But Erin always exaggerated things, she always wanted to believe that the women she loved were wronged by the men they loved. In regard to Diana's death, no, it was a bike accident, truly. Neither Erin nor Brandon had anything to do with it.'

Elizabeth folded her hands in her lap. 'Still, even though it happened so far away, Erin was sick with guilt about it. She felt that she never should have let Brandon come between them and that she missed all those precious years with her best friend. Diana's death *unraveled* her. Erin and I fell into our old patterns, and the closer she got, the more Harry tried to keep our boundaries clear.'

Tears filled Elizabeth's eyes. 'I wanted us to have a normal adult relationship. I didn't want her to be constantly battling my own husband for affection. I said some things I probably shouldn't have. And every fight I had with her, I blamed Harry for it. I knew he was trying to do the right thing, and I knew deep down I needed some space from her, but I resented him for making me see it so clearly, for coming between us. I think that's around the time . . .' Elizabeth's voice trailed off.

'That he met me,' I said.

She nodded.

'And Erin told you about us, and you threw him out.'

Another nod. 'I had no idea she was exaggerating so much.'

I took a sip of water, then trained my eyes on hers. 'But then you changed your mind. You wanted Harry back.'

'I went down to the city to visit Erin, and we were talking one night, about everything that had happened with Harry, and she kept slipping up. The story kept changing. First it was in a hotel. Then she'd seen you two go back to his crash pad in the city. I started to wonder what really had gone on. I began to remember, way back in the early days of Brandon and Diana, when she was so intent on convincing Diana not to go to California. She said to me, "I would do anything to keep her from leaving. Anything." When I was back home, I called Harry to tell him what I suspected, and he told me about his proposal to you. I told him no, absolutely no way was he marrying someone else when our own breakup had been orchestrated by Erin. But he told me it was too late, and I really thought it was. The divorce still wasn't final, but he was making this commitment to you. I was sure it was over. But we stayed in touch. He kept changing his mind. He said he didn't know what the right thing was, and he said he missed me. I sent Erin a letter saying I didn't want to see her anymore. One night, when Harry and I were talking, I told him, "I don't have anyone. My parents are dead. My sister is willing to destroy me to get what she wants.

I have no friends. I need you." He came back shortly after that. He never could leave me hanging when I needed him.'

Fucking Harry. Just had to save the day. With me. Then with her.

'I'm sorry,' I said again, though it wasn't nearly enough.

Elizabeth stared at me. 'I'm not going to say it's okay. I'm not going to say I don't have days when I hate you, when I blame you for everything, but I know, deep down, that's not fair. Erin did this. She set this all up. She killed him.'

I bit my lip, finally ready to voice the thing that had been bothering me for two months now.

'Why did Erin send you that video? If her plan all along was to kill him and frame me, it would only make you look more suspicious. The angry wife, all that. It doesn't make sense. She's so much smarter than that.'

'I don't think getting him out of my life was enough,' Elizabeth said.

'What do you mean?'

'I think it was crucial that she have me hate him, too.'

I swallowed. 'And do you?'

Elizabeth laughed. 'Some days I do. Some days I don't.'

I found myself smiling back, the tiniest bit.

'Me too.'

49

MARGARET

I was walking home from town, a bag of groceries in each hand. Sparkling water and lemons, gummy candy, sharp cheddar cheese, pancake mix and Log Cabin syrup, like I used to eat when I was a kid. It was more than a month since I'd told Alex I was pregnant, and I was nearly fifteen weeks along; the pregnancy cravings had fully kicked in.

Alex's house was only a half mile from the supermarket, and I enjoyed the walk.

I heard the steps behind me as I neared the house. Slowly, and then faster, as if they were intent on overtaking me. I picked up my pace and tried to stay calm. Catskill was safe, and it was broad daylight, but it was hard not to imagine Erin lurking in a corner, angry and unhinged.

'Margaret.'

I jolted, one of the sparkling waters falling out of the bag, and turned.

Lars leaned down to pick it up. He stood, offering it to me.

'What are you doing here?' I asked.

He looked altogether different. His skin pink instead of pale, his face completely clean-shaven, his hair, normally unkempt and thrown into a ponytail, cut neatly. He looked good. Like the man I'd fallen in love with, what felt like a lifetime ago.

'I was driving around the block, trying to get the nerve to come up to the door, when I saw you. I parked up there.' He gestured behind me. 'I'm sorry. I didn't want to scare you. Looks like I freaked you out anyway.'

I looped both bags over one hand and took the sparkling water back from him. 'It's okay,' I said. 'But, Lars. I've moved on. I have a new life now. We've talked about this. I can't –'

'No, no,' he said, shaking his head. 'That's not what this is about.' He reached into his pocket and retrieved a cheap plastic medallion, golden in color.

'AA?' I asked. 'Really?'

Lars nodded. 'Twenty-eight days at a recovery place in Albany. Beautiful, really. I didn't want to tell you until it was done, until I had completed it, but I thought of you the whole time.'

'Lars,' I said.

'No,' he said. 'I don't mean like that. I mean, I thought you'd be proud of me, for finally doing it.'

'Oh,' I said, adjusting the bags on my arm.

'Here,' he said, reaching out. 'Let me help you with that.'

I hesitated only a moment. 'Okay.'

Together, we walked across the threshold of Alex's place, Rosie bounding up to greet us.

In the tiny kitchen, we set the bags down. I glanced at the clock. It was five o'clock. In thirty minutes, Alex would be home, having just picked up Luke from day camp.

'Can I get you – er – water? I have sparkling, as you can see.'

Lars shrugged. 'I'm okay.'

We sat down, right there, at the table that Alex and I had shared so many times now. Lars sat straight, rigid. Rosie put her chin on my knee.

'I'm sure you know,' he started, 'that you're supposed to make amends.'

I nodded.

'I've been over and over it in my head, Pegs, but there's no good way to say it, except that I'm sorry.' He sighed. 'For everything. For wanting to try again so soon after we lost the baby. For needing you to grieve the way I did. For turning to alcohol instead of therapy or you or my family or anything that could have actually helped.'

'Lars –'

He held up a hand. 'Let me finish. Please. And I'm most sorry for that last weekend. I'm sorry I followed you up here, and I'm sorry I got so drunk, and I'm sorry about acting like I did and calling you those names. Maybe I could have handled it better if I'd just known you were with someone else, but seeing you, out there in the back of the bar. It was too much. I'm sorry for how I reacted. I'm sorry for what I did.'

I stared at him, my eyes narrowing. 'You mean inside? With Alex?'

Lars paused. 'No,' he said. 'I mean when you were in the back.'

I was about to correct him, but Lars went on. 'I know you were drinking, and I know it was dark and you didn't think people could see you, but to see it happen like that, in the back of a bar. It just . . . it's like something inside me just . . . snapped.'

Already I could feel the ground beneath us moving. I could feel that nausea – but it wasn't from morning sickness, it was from this. What Lars was saying. Right now.

'You were outside the bar that night?'

'Yes,' Lars said. 'I wanted to see you, and I did see you, in the bar, but you looked so happy with your friends, and I couldn't bear to make you upset. I was already pretty drunk. So I wandered out back, but then I needed to sit down, so I leaned against a tree and drank. I had my flask and a half-drunk beer I'd found on the patio. I figured I'd go in later, and maybe I'd catch you on your own, when your friends weren't right on top of you, but I kind of . . . blacked out, I guess, but when I came to, there you were, you and that guy.'

'No,' I said, my heart suddenly racing. 'No, Lars. That wasn't me.'

'It was,' he said. 'I know it, and you don't have to pretend with me. You were wearing your jacket. The red one I gave you. That's half of what made it hurt so much. To see his hands on you. On this piece of clothing that had meant so much to you, to us. I'm sorry. As soon as you walked away, I couldn't help myself. It was like I was someone else. An animal. I just, I just rushed at him.'

I felt suddenly like I couldn't breathe.

It couldn't be. It *couldn't* be. It was Diana – Erin. It had to be her. She'd *confessed*.

'You . . .' I could barely find the words. 'You hit him?'

Lars pressed his lips together. 'Like I said, I'm not proud of it. It just . . . happened. The bottle was in my hand, and it just, it connected. He fell backward and I freaked out, and I ran back into the woods. I was afraid he'd chase me. I tripped and fell and I, well, I passed out again.'

'Didn't you worry?' I asked. 'Didn't you worry you hurt him?'

Lars shook his head. 'He was okay. I woke up later, when the bar was closing, and I pulled myself together and I found my way back to where I'd hit him, and he wasn't there. I went inside and asked about you and your friends, but the bartender said you guys had left. And then I just . . . I had to talk to you, so I stuck around, and I didn't leave until you told me that it wasn't a one-night stand, that you cared about the guy. I went back to Brooklyn, and, god, it was my worst bender ever. I'm lucky . . . I'm lucky I'm alive and not lying in a gutter somewhere. I'm sorry,' he said. 'I'm so so sorry.'

My stomach roiled, and I felt sick inside. This couldn't be happening. This couldn't be real.

Unless . . .

Unless Erin had never intended to kill Harry. Sam had called me the other day to tell me about her conversation with Elizabeth, about the lengths Erin would go to keep Harry from her.

Was it possible?

Was it possible that Erin had only wanted to get Harry and Sam in the same space, to get some sort of evidence to take back to her sister and break them up for good?

But then it had all gone wrong: I'd given Sam my jacket, and Lars had seen them in the back of the bar, too drunk to realize it wasn't me. He'd attacked Harry, and he'd run, and —

And —

And Erin, she must have found him back there. She must

have assumed it was Elizabeth who killed him, Elizabeth, angry, driven to a mad rage after receiving that video.

She'd dragged him deeper into the woods, and she'd taken his shirt, and she'd planted those things of Sam's.

When Elizabeth had been arrested, Erin had jumped into her role. The big sister. The always protector.

Only she was covering for the wrong person.

She wasn't covering for Elizabeth.

She was covering for Lars.

My god, I thought. The man I'd loved for so long –

He was a murderer.

He was a murderer, and he didn't even know it.

'Pegs?' he asked. 'Are you okay?'

I should tell him the truth. I should call Conway, explain everything. It would be manslaughter, at most. It wouldn't carry that much of a sentence, would it?

'Oh,' I said, and on instinct, my hand reached to my belly.

'What happened?' Lars asked.

Already, he was putting it together, taking in the curve of my belly beneath my oversized top, something he hadn't noticed before. I was only just showing after all.

I took a deep breath. 'I think I felt a kick.'

Lars's eyes looked unbearably sad. 'You're pregnant,' he said.

I nodded. 'I'm sorry.'

He stared at me a moment, and then he picked the chip up, grasped it in his hand. 'It's okay,' he said. 'I'm glad for you.'

His eyes looked down, then back up at me. 'Anyway,' he said. 'What were you saying? That that wasn't you back there?'

I stared at him, my love, my Lars.

There was so very little I could do for him now. I couldn't give him the baby he always wanted. I couldn't be the wife he'd needed.

But I could do this.

'No,' I said. 'I did go back there. I forgot. I'd had a lot of margaritas,' I said. 'I'm sorry you had to see that.'

Lars nodded, then stood up, pushing his chair back. 'I should get going. Take care of yourself, Pegs.'

I followed him to the door. 'You too.'

His eyes glanced down to my stomach. 'And take care of that baby.' He forced a smile. 'I always knew you'd make a wonderful mother.'

He walked through the door, and I closed it behind him, and my fingers tingled.

In quick strides, I walked back to the kitchen, found my purse set neatly on the counter.

I took out my wallet, dumped the contents on the table, flipped through credit cards until I found what I was looking for.

Conway's card, the one she'd given me months ago.

There was that tingle in my fingers again, and I reached back in my bag, retrieving my phone.

Then I shook my head, set the phone down.

I ripped her card in two.

ACKNOWLEDGMENTS

An enormous thanks to all the people who made this book possible.

To my passionate and dedicated agent, Elisabeth Weed, thank you for the endless phone calls, guidance and pep talks as I took this book from a one-line idea to a fully fledged novel. Also, for being there for me during the early days of parenthood with cute outfits and practical advice. A huge thanks to the entire TBG team, and especially to Hallie Schaeffer, who kept everything running smoothly even through the chaos of 2020.

To my incredible editors at Putnam, I owe this book to you. To Danielle Dieterich, thank you for jumping in enthusiastically and finding so many ways to make this story better. To Sally Kim, I appreciate all of your incredible support – it's amazing to know I have your whole team in my corner. And to Margo Lipschultz, many thanks for your fantastic early notes. Thanks, as well, to Alexis Welby, Kristen Bianco, Emily Mlynek, Nishtha Patel and the entire marketing and publicity team for working so hard to get this book out there!

To Joel Richardson, Grace Long and everyone at Michael Joseph, I have the best UK team on earth, and I mean that from the bottom of my heart. Joel, your plot suggestions are brilliant, and I owe at least one or two twists and misdirections to you. Thanks to the entire team for always finding ways to get eyes on my books, even during a shutdown.

To Jenny Meyer and your team, I am beyond thankful for the care you've taken in pitching this book around the globe – and Jenny, thank you especially for our masked coffee in Woodstock after I hadn't seen anyone in ages.

To Michelle Weiner and everyone at CAA, thank you for continuing to fight for my books even in the most trying of times. I hope we can meet in person one of these days.

This book would have a lot of glaring plot holes if not for the ingenious notes of my two longtime beta readers, Andrea Bartz and Danielle Rollins. Thank you both for all the plot-doctoring it took to make this story what it is today.

The Perfect Escape deals with the very sensitive issue of pregnancy loss and the stressors of noninvasive prenatal testing (NIPT). A very heartfelt thanks to all the friends and family who shared their own stories of pregnancy loss, as well as all of the doctors, counselors, therapists, kind internet strangers and real-life friends and family who helped me through my own NIPT scare. Pregnancy can be a joy but can also be extremely tramautic, and too often we feel pressure to put on a smiling face and ignore both physical and mental suffering. My sincere hope is that conversations around the difficulties of pregnancy become normalized, both in and out of medical settings.

No book of mine would be possible without the lifelong support of my mom, dad and sister. You all have been my biggest fans (and my most enthusiastic book-promoters) from day one. Thank you for always believing in me, even when I doubted myself.

Finally, to Thomas, thank you for being such a wonderful partner, giving me loads of baby-free time to write, coming up with the title and watching all those old noirs with me. To Farley, thank you for sitting on my lap through many a writing session. And to Eleanor, I can't wait for us to read and write together. You're my reason for everything. I love you so much.

THE PERFECT ESCAPE

LEAH KONEN

A CONVERSATION WITH LEAH KONEN

DISCUSSION GUIDE

A CONVERSATION WITH LEAH KONEN

The Perfect Escape is your second novel for adults, following your debut thriller All the Broken People. How was the process of writing your sophomore novel different than writing your first?

I do feel like I learned a lot writing *All the Broken People*, especially about how to set up a mystery, seed different twists and turns, and (hopefully!) surprise some readers along the way, but the funny thing is, what you learn for one book doesn't necessarily apply to another. I still had to work very hard to get the twists just right, to make the characters feel whole and round and different from one another, and to uncover their unique stories, especially when handling two points of view. Every book is its own puzzle, and it often feels like you have to relearn how to write a novel each time around.

And how does writing adult fiction compare to writing fiction for young adults?

The process itself is very similar. Craft is craft, no matter your target audience. However, I would say that writing a mystery or thriller is very different from writing a contemporary romance, which is what I wrote in YA. I had to really work to be able to get my head around the unique pacing and plotting of a mystery.

Where did the inspiration for _The Perfect Escape_ come from? And which came first – the idea of the plot, or the characters themselves?

Normally, my characters come first, but for this book, it was all plot. It was based on something that actually happened to us: My husband and I were driving down to Tennessee for the Bonnaroo music festival and our car broke down on the side of the highway. We had to call a tow and ended up spending the night in this incredibly cute town, Staunton, Virginia. We had a lovely time exploring the downtown and checking out the local dive, and I started to imagine a book set there. What if a group of friends got stranded in a quaint little town, but something went horribly wrong? The whole idea felt very _Twilight Zone_ to me, and I knew I had to run with it.

The novel is narrated primarily from two points of view – those of Sam and Margaret. Why did you choose this narration style? Was one of the perspectives easier to write than the other?

When I first started writing, the book was only from Sam's point of view, all about a woman going through the end of a marriage and wanting to get back with her ex. But as I was writing, I experienced something life-changing myself: I became pregnant. I had a really difficult early pregnancy, mainly due to the results of non-invasive prenatal testing (NIPT), which indicated the possibility of a potentially dangerous chromosomal condition. I eventually learned (after two invasive procedures) that the condition was not present, but the experience shook me. I decided writing was the best way to process it, and I added Margaret's point of view, who in the book deals with the grief of making an incredibly difficult decision when going through pre-natal testing. It was very important to me not only to process what I'd been through but to help destigmatize the difficulties of pregnancy and normalize these experiences. Margaret's point of view was, as a result, much easier to write because I had a lot of personal anxiety and trauma to borrow from.

The small town of Catskill feels so atmospheric and vivid on the page – why did you choose to set the story in this location? Is it personal to you?

Yes. I live part-time in Saugerties, New York, about a half hour away, and have spent time in the adorable town of Catskill. I love that it's not quite as busy as some of the other towns in the area but still vibrant and full of that small-town Hudson Valley spirit. Plus, its proximity to the highway made it a perfect place for Sam, Margaret and Diana to break down in.

Can you share a bit about your writing style? Do you dive in, or begin with an outline? Did you uncover any unexpected surprises as you wrote, or were the twists and reveals mapped out ahead of time? Where and when do you prefer to write?

I am a plotter through and through, and I live for my outlines. I can't begin until I know where I'm ending up, but of course, there are plenty of surprises along the way. Although I typically know how my scenes are going to play out, I do find that I always uncover some parts of the mystery as I go along – especially when it comes to key twists and reveals. As for writing, I am a relatively new mother so I get my word count in whenever and wherever I can, often at my desk during nap time.

Do you like to read suspense fiction in your free time? If so, are there any particular books or authors that you have loved or been inspired by lately?

Yes! Suspense is my favorite genre, and the reason I always wanted to write it is because I love it so very much. There are so many authors who've inspired me, but a few favorites in the mystery, crime and horror space include Ruth Ware, Oyinkan Braithwaite, Tana French, Lisa Jewell, Jane Harper, Silvia Moreno-Garcia and Lucy Foley.

So much of *The Perfect Escape* is rooted in the complexities of female friendship. Was the novel influenced by any of your own relationships or friendships?

I'm happy to report that none of my friends keep these sorts of secrets from each other (at least, I believe we don't!). That said, I definitely find female friendship powerful and fascinating, and the many friendships I've been blessed with in my life have definitely informed some of the close and intimate friendships I've portrayed in my novels.

Do you have a favorite scene or passage from the book that you would be willing to share? Why is it special to you?

Yes, my favorite passage is when Margaret begins to open up to the reader, as well as her new love interest, about what happened during her pregnancy. I love it, and the chapter that follows, because I think it is honest about some of the difficulties of pregnancy and the pressure that exists to keep quiet about them or put on a strong, resilient attitude for the world.

'No one ever thinks the world is going to implode, the ground sink right out from under where they're standing, and that the one in however many thousand will ever apply to them. I hadn't, either. If they did, no one would ever try to craft a life, try to build these absurd castles in the sky.'

All of the characters in *The Perfect Escape* make questionable choices at times – they feel incredibly human, and, like all of us, make some big mistakes. Why do you think it is important to write in this gray area between 'good' and 'evil'? What can the reader take away from the characters' moral ambiguity?

It's very important to me because I think most of life exists in this gray area. None of us are perfect, and Sam and Margaret remind us that there are times when our hearts might be in the right place, but we still end up doing the wrong thing. What I love about both of these women is that, as flawed as they are, they do their best to learn from their mistakes and to make amends when they need to.

What is next for you?

I'm hard at work on a thriller that follows a mother dealing with postpartum depression, whose partner disappears mysteriously when their baby is only six weeks old. I think there is something so uniquely scary and precarious about this tender time, and I'm so excited to normalize the experience of PPD, as well as to explore all the questions that would arise if we felt like we could no longer trust the parent of our child.

DISCUSSION GUIDE

1. Discuss the different meanings behind the title of the novel. What do each of the main characters hope to escape from? How is escape both physical and psychological?

2. *The Perfect Escape* is narrated in alternating voices, primarily those of Sam and Margaret. What was it like to get both women's perspectives on events? How did having two narrators change the pacing of the read? Was there one narrator that you connected with more than the other? Why?

3. Why do you think that Diana, Sam and Margaret are able to form such a close bond so quickly? What do each of them see in one another, or provide for one another?

4. The characters' actions in *The Perfect Escape* are rarely presented in black and white – many decisions that the characters make are morally ambiguous, leaving the reader to decide what defines morality. Discuss scenes that contain this moral ambiguity, and if you think that different actions are justifiable – for example, Sam's decision to reunite with Harry, Margaret's financial secrets or Harry's return to Elizabeth.

5. Discuss the ways that Sam and Margaret's decisions to keep secrets from their friends and family impact the outcome of the novel. Why did they choose to keep these major secrets about their relationships and pasts? What were the consequences of doing so?

6. Female relationships – particularly those between sisters and between friends – are at the heart of *The Perfect Escape*. How did these relationships contrast with the women's relationships with men? Why do you think that the author chose to focus on these particular connections between women?

7. How does the Catskill setting impact the storyline and atmosphere of *The Perfect Escape*? Take a look at the ways that small-town life impacts the secrets each character keeps.

8. Compare and contrast the different ways that each of the main characters deals with their grief in the novel. How does it drive each of them? Do you think that Sam and Margaret are able to come to terms with their grief?

9. What did you make of Margaret's decision to rip up Conway's card in the final pages of the novel? Why do you believe that she did this? Would you have made the same choice?

10. What do you imagine happens to Margaret and Sam after the novel's end?

LEAH KONEN is the author of *All the Broken People* and of several young adult novels, including *Love and Other Train Wrecks* and *The Romantics*. She is a graduate of the University of North Carolina at Chapel Hill, where she studied journalism and English literature. She lives in Brooklyn and Saugerties, New York, with her husband; their daughter, Eleanor; and their dog, Farley.

VISIT LEAH KONEN ONLINE

leahkonen.com

🐦 @LeahKonen

📷 @LeahKonen

dead good reads

In partnership with Sainsbury's

Not heard of Dead Good?
Let us introduce ourselves. We're a community of crime fiction readers dedicated to discovering and sharing unmissable books, TV shows and films.

Whether you're on the hunt for an intriguing mystery, an action-packed thriller or a creepy psychological drama, we're here to keep you in the loop.

We've partnered with Sainsbury's to bring you the best new crime books at brilliantly low prices. From big bestsellers to fresh, new voices, you can count on our recommendations to help you find your future favourites.

And if you're looking for more gripping must-reads, head over to our website or follow us on social media for reviews, discounts and exclusive giveaways.

Sign up for our free newsletter:

www.deadgoodbooks.co.uk/sainsburys